LOVE'S MORE THAN A NUMBER

BARE RIDGE
BOOK 2

B.D. STOREY

INTRODUCTION

Welcome to the second book in the Bare Ridge series. While each book can be enjoyed as a stand-alone, they are best enjoyed in order of publication, as you'll see many of the same characters in each book and there may be spoilers if you jump ahead.

Bare Ridge is a fictional small town set in the foothills west of Monument, Colorado. Aside from the town itself, most of the specific surrounding locations you will read about are actual places.

Writing this book proved to be a challenge in that I wrote this purely from Kathi's point of view. Our society always treats age differences between couples differently when the man is older, something I always thought was unfair.

Kathi was an interesting character for me to write and she was constantly talking to me as I was writing the book one. More than once she forced me to stop what I was writing and focus on writing part of her story. She always had good things to tell me and she is a prime example of the character pushing the story. I hope you enjoy her story.

To stay up-to-date on the rest of the Bare Ridge series, and in the loop on everything else I'm working on, make sure to sign up for my newsletter at my website, as well as giving my Facebook, Goodreads, TikTok, and Instagram sites a follow!

Bob

Website:
   https://BDStorey.com

ACKNOWLEDGMENTS

This is where I get to thank all the great folks who helped me get this book out to you, the readers.

As always, the first to thank is my wife Pam. She pushes me to write and gives me that '*what were you thinking*' look when I run a plot or scene by her. She is always the first to read the draft, the first to help me flesh-out scenes and imagery, the first to tell me to "try again." Love ya, Pam.

Now on to the beta readers. This is the second book Robin Maguire has read for me and her feedback always makes me look hard at what I've written.

My favorite librarian, Tori Linville Hopper, has read all my works and gives me a younger, fresher perspective. She is also quick to point out my overuse of words and the occasional 4th-wall break.

Cindy Silver has proven to be frank in her advice, and doesn't hesitate to call me on phrases that make little sense to her.

Elizabeth Mackey developed the amazing cover. I couldn't be more pleased with what she created for my story. You can see more of her work at https://www.elizabethmackeygraphics.com/

I'd like to give a big shout out to all of you who have taken a chance on my work. I hope I've given you some entertainment value for your hard-earned dollar. I appreciate you!

Thanks,
    Bob

PROLOGUE

I sat in the car, listening to the muted sounds of the garage door opener as the chain moved the door down its tracks. The door closed with a satisfying clunk, shutting me off from the world yet again. I was home.

Taking a deep cleansing breath, in through my nose, out through my mouth, I let all the tension from the crappy date flow out. Grabbing my clutch, I slid out of my car and walked up into my house, the clicking of my high heels loud in the enclosed space.

As I passed through the front room, Simon rose from the back of the couch like a little guardian panther, yawned, stretched, then laid back down, head on paws. I stroked his black furry head as I passed by, his deep purr vibrating against my hand.

In my bedroom, I got undressed on autopilot, letting my clothes drop to the floor. I groaned in relief as I slipped out of my heels. I dearly loved how they made my calves look, but they were painful to wear for long periods of time.

If men only understood the pain we women went through to look nice.

One long, hot shower later and my outlook on life was better. I put on some comfy plaid flannel pajama pants and a softly worn oversize black t-shirt that I had saved from my late husband's wardrobe. Perfect lounging attire. I pulled my phone from my clutch and padded barefoot to the kitchen.

A quick raid of my freezer, and wine cooler, and I was soon settling down on the couch with a pint of mint chocolate chip and a glass of my favorite white wine.

I tucked my feet up beside me, grabbed the remote, and began scanning the channels. I stopped at one of the movie channels. One of my favorites, *Sleepless in Seattle,* was playing. I'd lost count of the number of nights I sat engrossed in the antics of Sam and Annie. It was the perfect post-screwed-up-date flick.

As I pulled the top off the ice cream, Simon uncoiled to a standing position from his blanket. He took a long, leisurely stretch before he over and softly head butted me before curling up in the hollow of my legs.

"Why are men such pigs, Simon? Present company excluded, of course."

Aside from blinking his large yellow eyes at me, Simon was silent on the topic. Then again, having been neutered early in his life, he was probably a bit jaded on the subject.

Tonight had been another failed date, the latest in a depressingly long series of them.

"I don't get it, Simon," I say, waving the spoon around and dripping ice cream on my pants. Simon stretched again and then licked at the fallen drips.

"I think I'm pretty. I like to dress nice, keep myself in shape. Some people say that I have a good sense of humor. So why do I seem to attract all the losers?"

I studied my cat as he made absolutely sure I had no more ice cream to clean from my pajamas. Simon was a superb listener, never rushing in to fix my problem or muttering nonsensical advice. More men needed to be like Simon.

My attention flicked back to the screen as a truck almost hit Meg Ryan. I took a big bite of ice cream, working and moving it as it melted in my mouth while I contemplated my lack of love life. Washing the ice cream down with some wine, my thoughts flew back to Jake's words from a few months ago.

"You are one of the smartest, most beautiful women I know. Any man should count themselves privileged to spend time with you. I think you need to find a different pool to swim in."

That had been a few months ago when he was going through a rough time. Being arrested, almost losing Sarah. But it all worked out for him; he and Julia were back together. I nodded as I let the wisdom of his words settle over me.

"Maybe Jake was right, Simon. Perhaps I need to find a different pool."

Simon settled into the gap of my lap, staring up at my ice cream, ever hopeful.

That made two of us.

ONE

S itting across from the CEO of Harrison Enterprises was not the way I had envisioned my Monday morning starting, but here I sat. That the CEO was also my former brother-in-law, and not particularly fond of me, was the cherry on the Monday sundae.

Samuel, my late husband's younger brother, had inherited control of the business when Jeremy had passed. Samuel and I had never been best of friends, but we had remained civil over the years. He had always chafed being second behind Jeremy when it came to the business.

Now that he was in charge, Samuel only wanted two things from me. He wanted me gone, but perhaps even more than that, he wanted my stock. He controlled 43% of the company's shares and hungered for my 8%. If he got it, he would have a majority interest in the company, meaning he could drive the company the way he wanted without regard for the board of directors.

Unfortunately for him, the only way he could get rid of me was to fire me and I had never given him cause. Samuel wasn't stupid. I was the Director of Community Engagement. He knew I had done an exemplary job keeping the company's image positive within the community. He also knew I was well-connected with the social elite within the Denver area, a group that he wanted to remain on good terms.

That's why he was taking the longer game. In truth, I wasn't overly concerned about the possibility of being ousted from the company. Between the investments Jeremy had set up and his life insurance, I was financially secure for the rest of my life. Most of my salary over the years had funneled into the investments and the rest allowed me to indulge myself in my hobbies, particularly my love of good horses and riding them.

Samuel's assistant delivered a coffee service and quietly left the room. Reaching for the coffeepot, I poured myself and Samuel a cup, added creamer to mine and then stirred before sitting back, cup in hand. He finished fixing his coffee, adding sugar but no creamer, before taking a sip, eyeing me over his cup. I said nothing, knowing he didn't like long pauses in conversation. However, I didn't mind them, so I was content to wait.

He broke the silence first. "Where are we with the dinner and gala?" he asked as he sat his cup down.

I quickly brought him up to speed on our plans. Abigail, my assistant, had updated me on both events before Samuel had called. He followed along, nodding as I recited the details of the preparations.

"Good, very good," he said once I had finished my update. "Have we received any RSVPs?"

"A few, but it's still early," I replied. He nodded, glancing at something off over my shoulder.

Shifting his eyes back to me, he spoke again. "I can only assume Regina Vaughn will be there?" he asked, not hiding his distaste at having to speak her name.

Regina Vaughn was old money in the city and one of our largest sponsors. Her donations each year to our charitable causes ensured we always met or exceeded our goals. Samuel hated her. Well, that was not accurate. He loved her connections and money. What he did *not* like was her lifestyle.

I placed my cup down, giving him a questioning look. "I'm sure she will be, Samuel. I still don't understand what your issue is with her. I have lunch with her fairly often and she's a very nice, pleasant woman. She gives generously to our causes."

Samuel gave a small sniff of disdain. He picked at an imaginary piece of lint on his suit sleeve, flicking it down towards the floor.

"That woman has no sense of propriety. She's a mature woman of good breeding and social standing. Yet, she continues to flaunt her… dalliances in public. It's quite embarrassing and immoral."

Samuel was as straight-laced as they came. Even in today's world of equality and inclusion, he was a firm believer that a woman's place was in the home, supporting the male breadwinner. He firmly believed that his wealth and family bloodlines should set him apart from the average person, which in turn meant the average person should acknowledge his superiority. Combined with his sexism, these qualities made him a most unlikable person, not to mention a flaming asshole at times.

At sixty-three, Regina was over twenty years my senior. Her husband of forty years had passed shortly before Jeremy, leaving the bulk of his wealth to her and their three adult children.

For a little over a year, Regina had mourned his loss. But life plodded on and her children resumed their lives, spending very little time with their mother outside of holidays. Regina became lonely and threw herself into her philanthropic and charity work.

Her wealth also attracted men like flies. Unfortunately for them, Regina showed no interest in the mature and wealthy men who sought to gain her attention, and indirectly, her money. What shocked the social circles was Regina's pursuit of a different type of man. A *younger* type.

Regina began dating several men, all under the age of 30. She also didn't care one iota of what anyone else thought and explained it to me at lunch one day.

"Kathi, darling, you must understand. Harold was my first and only lover and he was very… old fashioned. Sex was once a week,

regular as clockwork, and always missionary," she said, picking at her salad.

"I used to read all kinds of stories on the Internet and I wanted to try those things I was reading about. But I would never cheat on Harold. He was a good husband and a good father. Now that he's gone, I have mourned him, my kids and I have moved on, and I have all the time and money I need to live a more... fulfilling life."

She leaned closer, whispering so that others around us couldn't hear.

"And darling, nothing is more... filling than a well-endowed young stud who can rise to the occasion multiple times a night."

I must have blushed because she just laughed quietly and patted my hand. "As the saying goes, my dear, don't knock it until you've tried it."

"Have you given my offer any more thought?" he asked, snapping my attention back to him. I smiled kindly, shaking my head slightly.

"Samuel, while I appreciate your generosity, I have no desire to sell my company stock."

He leaned forward, arms on his desk, hands clasped as that small self-righteous smirk he enjoyed appeared.

"Kathi. Be reasonable. You never loved the company, and Jeremy only gave you the position to give you something to do."

I bristled inside at the insinuation, but kept my face neutral as I counted to ten. I wouldn't give the self-righteous prick the satisfaction of seeing me angry.

"I'm afraid the answer is still no, Samuel." I said, giving him a small smile. He harrumphed and sat back up straighter, turning to his keyboard.

"Very well. Keep me informed if there are any changes to our plans."

Knowing a dismissal when I heard one, I rose to leave. He called out before I had reached the door.

"And Kathi, I want these events to be flawless. I would view any mistakes as a... failure on your part. Understand?" he asked. His eyes were cold and unforgiving in their intensity.

I nodded and headed back to my office. His message was loud and clear.

———

Abby looked up, saw the look on my face, and followed me into my office.

"Are you fired?" she asked, settling into her chair across from me. Taking a deep breath, I closed my eyes and slowly let the breath out, willing the tension away. Popping my eyes back open, I gave her a small, half-hearted smile.

"No, not yet at least. Just another veiled threat and a push for me to sell my stock."

"Boss, why don't you just walk away from all this?" she asked, waving a hand around my office. "You're a great boss and it would suck to lose you, but still, why stay?"

I kept quiet, not really having an answer for her. How do I tell her what it felt like to work here with Jeremy for so long? The business and his obligations had been our life together. It may not have been exciting, but it was not unpleasant.

"Well," she said, rubbing her hands together before leaning onto my desk. "Let's talk about more important things, such as that date this weekend. How did it go? Did he stay for breakfast? Did you call out his name in passion as he gave you at least three super orgasms and numerous small ones? Did you suck him down like a banana?"

The one thing I dearly loved, and cringed over, was Abby's lack of a filter and her carefree attitude toward sex. Perhaps it was just the way of her generation. She was in her mid-twenties and a vibrant, carefree woman. She would always tell me, or anyone else, exactly what she was thinking. It was nothing for her to regale me with a detailed description of one of her hook-ups. *Explicit* detail.

Luckily for me, and her employment status, she managed to maintain a professional manner around those higher in the management structure than her and keep the orgasm counts to her discussions with me and a discrete few others.

Sighing, I shook my head.

"No, nothing like that. I ended up on the couch with a pint of ice cream, and a glass of wine, watching -"

"*Sleepless in Seattle*," she said, finishing my sentence for me as she rolled her eyes. "What was wrong with *this* guy?"

"All during dinner it was a constant stream of mansplaining all the world highlights. He was nothing like the guy I talked with at the gym. *That* guy would have been interesting. But when we sat down for dinner, he morphed into an asshole." I grimaced at the memory of him dominating the conversation the night before.

"I take it he didn't get any goodnight tongue?" she asked, waggling her eyebrows.

I huffed, shaking my head. "No, there was no tongue exchange, or any exchange, for that matter. Halfway through the main course, I excused myself to the restroom and kept on walking. I paid for the dinner before I left, though. I couldn't stand the thought of him trying anything at the end of the date. *Blegh*." I did a full-on body shiver just at the thought of how unpleasant that would have been.

"Maybe Jake was right," I muttered.

"What's that?" Abby asked.

I looked up at her and gave a small, disgruntled sigh. "I said 'maybe Jake was right.'"

Her eyes lit up at the mention of Jake's name. "Ohhh, that delicious cowboy you know? Why you never rode that stud is beyond me," she purred. *Filter. Lack of.*

I grinned and shook my head. "One, ew. Jake is like a son to me and two, down girl. He's happily married. Again."

She just tapped a single fingernail against my desk. I noted her polish was natural this week and not some new design or neon colors she liked to use.

"Hey, nothing stops a girl from appreciating a nice piece of Grade-A cowboy. You should invite him to lunch one day. I could give him a *personal* tour," she said, humming lightly.

I stabbed a finger at her. "I can fire you and replace you tomorrow, you know. And again, he's *married*."

She just gave me a smug grin in response. "No, you can't. I'm great and you can't live without me, or pull off half the things we do for the company."

I gave her my best glare, but she just looked nonplussed. She was right, and she knew it.

"Anyway," she said. "What was Mr. Delicious right about?"

"He said I needed to find a different pool of men."

"Ohhh, brains, too. Yum," she replied with another waggle of her eyebrows. "I've been telling you that for the last year. I still think you should have gone out with Mario."

I rolled my eyes and heaved a sigh before glaring at her. She had been harping on this for the last three months, doing her best to get me to go out with Mario, a young man who worked down in our mailroom.

"For the last time, Abby, Mario is *nineteen*, and he works in the mailroom. His age notwithstanding, the one hard and fast business rule to live by is to *never* 'shop' in the company store."

She waved off my objections. "Yeah, yeah. You stick with that rule, grandma. You're missing out. Word has it he has a huge—"

"ABBY!"

She broke out laughing as she got up and returned to her desk.

It was close to two when I realized I had been reading the same vendor proposal for the last twenty minutes. I tossed the papers onto my desk and made the executive decision that I had done enough for the day.

I let Abby know I was heading out for the day and was soon winding my way south. There was still a slight chill in the air, but I would warm up quickly once I was on my horse and riding.

The sun was shining in a clear blue sky and the air felt alive on my skin as I turned my car off the paved road and into the gravel driveway for Attwood Ranch.

A boarding facility, and sometimes rescue, Attwood Ranch was an oasis unto itself. I loved that place and had been boarding my horses here for years.

Nestled in the foothills west of Monument and on the outskirts of Bare Ridge, the ranch was a place of peace and tranquility. As soon as I set eyes on its buildings and pastures, the stresses of the world melt away.

About 100 feet off the road, the gravel path split. To the right, it curved in front of the owner's house before connecting back to the main road. If you went straight, it led towards a large gravel lot behind the house. Several horse trailers sat off to one side and a pathway led off to a large barn area with several small paddocks and a riding arena.

Mary Attwood, the owner, was as close to a sister as I had. I met her years ago while looking for a place to board my horses and we had been friends ever since. She and her son, Jake, ran the place.

Both Jake and Mary had had their fill of hard times these past years. First, it was Mary's husband passing away suddenly. That sent Mary into a deep depression. When Jake and his sister Nichole were floundering and unable to help her, I took it upon myself to move in and practice some tough love with her. In the end, my nagging her, and never leaving her alone helped her return to her family.

Not long after Mary's recovery, Julia, Jake's then wife of two years, left suddenly. He came home to an empty house. No note, no rings... nothing. The divorce almost killed him. It took Mary and me almost a year of talking to him, listening to his rants, holding him as he cried, and spending hours talking with him before we were able to pull him back to the land of the living. It had been Sarah, his two-year-old niece, that really helped him. Nichole made it a point to bring her by often and he just latched onto her.

That little girl was convinced her Uncle Jake was the greatest thing on Earth. He played with her, colored with her, held her while they watched cartoons. From the minute she walked into Mary's house, Sarah was glued to Jake's side. It was nothing for Mary or Nichole to find them both asleep, cuddled together on the couch in the mornings.

Whenever Jake started withdrawing or wallowing in his grief, a quick call to Nichole and Sarah was deposited with Jake for the day. That little girl was the best medicine there could have been for him.

A one-two punch of bad luck almost sent him back under. He had broken up with the girl he was dating and Nichole and her husband had died tragically, leaving Sarah under Jake's guardianship. Then, while he was still reeling from those life-altering changes, his ex-wife Julia showed up out of the blue, asking for his forgiveness and trying to explain why she had left him high and dry. It was a lot for him, and I could only offer a shoulder to lean on as he struggled with the hurt and love he still had for his ex.

Thankfully, even after a horrible custody battle with Sarah's paternal grandparents, as well as a huge misunderstanding over Julia and a former boyfriend, Jake and Julia worked things out, retained guardianship of his niece, and even remarried. Julia was now just over four months pregnant and Jake was back on top of the world.

As I pulled up and parked, Mary stepped out of the house wearing her usual attire of faded jeans, a T-shirt with a flannel shirt over it, and well-worn boots. She was almost twenty years older than me and I just prayed that I looked as good as she did when I reached her age.

She reached the car just as I got out. She enveloped me in a hug, giving me a good squeeze before stepping back.

I glanced around but didn't see Sarah screaming around the yard or on her swing set. If I could bottle and sell that girl's energy, I'd make a killing.

"Where's everybody?" I asked.

Mary gave a short laugh.

"Jake's in town. Julia and Sarah are taking a nap. Between the baby and Sarah, Julia's worn out. Jake and I are covering as much as we can, but her energy levels get zapped quickly."

Mary started towards the barn and I fell in step, boots crunching on the gravel.

"You playing hooky today, Kathi?" She glanced over at me as we walked.

"Sorta. I was bored and pissed at Samuel and the sun was shining so brightly through my window that I took it as a sign that I should come see Ringo."

"What did the asshole do now?" she asked. Mary hated Samuel, always had. I guess me never having anything good to say about him when she asked may have biased her thinking.

I shrugged. "Nothing he hasn't done before."

She elbowed me lightly. "When are you going to just chuck that place and come work here with me? You may act like a society diva up there, but I know better. You belong out here, eating dirt and wrangling horses."

I paused on the path, letting her words sink in. She'd pitched this idea at me several times over the years and I couldn't deny its appeal. But something always seemed to hold me back. I did enjoy attending the opera or symphony with my friends. However, I had to acknowledge that I never felt more relaxed or happier than when I was working or riding my horse and spending time here with Mary and her family.

I looked at my best friend and realized how even with all the crap that had landed on her these past few years, she was always smiling. She enjoyed her life, her family, and her ranch.

Mary patted her pockets before I could answer.

"Shoot, I left my gloves in the house. You go ahead. I think Jason brought Ringo back in earlier this morning," she said as she spun on her heel and headed back to the house. Jason was the farm's foreman and Jake's right-hand man. I would always be happy to have him taking care of Ringo when I couldn't be there.

I continued on to the barn, eager to saddle up my horse. It had been a couple of weeks since I'd been able to ride him and work with him, and I missed it.

I'd been giving serious thought to cutting back even more at work and helping Mary out or volunteering more, like she had been bugging me to do. I made a mental note to evaluate those possibilities again after the company's gala event was behind me.

The horses in the stalls to the front of the barn eyed me curiously as I headed for the tack room. As if he could sense that I had arrived, Ringo's grey head popped out of his stall at the far end of the barn and he nickered at me, ears pricked in my direction.

"Just a sec boy, gotta get my tack," I called out as I pulled open the wooden tack room door.

And then all hell broke loose.

The door slammed against the barn wall and a man screamed "GOTCHA!" as he leapt out at me. I shrieked as large arms enveloped me. The training I'd recently taken in a self-defense class took over. Without thinking, I grabbed a handful of his shirt and flung my knee straight up, right into his nuts.

TWO

My attacker gave a high-pitched keen, grabbed his crotch, and fell to the ground as I stumbled backwards until I hit the stall wall behind me. My heart raced, and I was pretty sure that I'd peed myself a little as I screamed at my attempted rapist.

Chest heaving, I glanced around the barn. A pitchfork was leaning against the tack room wall. Skirting the new eunuch as he continued to whimper and roll on the ground, I reached out and grabbed the fork. I stabbed the tines downward towards my attacker.

I growled, prodding the prone form in the back with my new weapon. "Stay right there, asshole!" My hands were trembling but if this guy tried to get off the ground, I intended to turn him into a pincushion.

"WHAT IN THE SAM HILL IS GOING ON?"

I glanced up at Mary standing in the barn doorway. Even from where I was standing, I saw her eyes widen. She hurried over to where I stood vigil over the injured predator. I nudged the groaning lump on the ground with my pitchfork turned raper-sticker, my heart still racing.

"This piece of shit jumped out of the tack room, yelled, and attacked me. Call the Sheriff. I'll stab him if he moves."

"Kathi, stop that." Mary tried to push the pitchfork away with her foot, but I resisted.

"Mary! He attacked me! He could have knocked me out and raped me!"

She huffed at me, moving to the other side of the body. "If he was going to rape you, why yell?" I cocked my head at her, considering her words. Why was she defending this obvious asshole?

Mary bent over to get a good look at the guy as he turned his head and groaned again. She then did the last thing I expected. She burst out laughing.

I stared at her, wondering what parallel universe I was in. She put her hands on her knees and kept laughing. I stared, perplexed, as she dropped to one knee next to my attacker. I moved to her other side, pitchfork ready.

"Mary, what are you *doing*? Have you lost your *mind*? Move away from him. He attacked me! Call the Sheriff!"

Then, to my utter amazement, she reached over to grab the guy's chin and turn his face up towards her. His eyes were screwed shut, and he was taking small, rapid breaths. If his jaw were clenched any tighter, I'm pretty convinced he would have shattered his teeth.

"You gonna live, Mark?" she asked, succumbing to a snort that led to more laughter.

"Shiiitttttt." That one agonized word hissed out from between his clenched teeth.

I inhaled sharply at the name. Wait. Mark. This was Mark? The *farrier* Mark? The guy who always trimmed my horse's hooves so well?

Mark had shown up last year to help his uncle, Mary's normal farrier. For various reasons, I had never been at the barn when he was taking care of Ringo. I had a general description of him from the others, but had never met him. I had his contact number, and we had exchanged texts if he needed to know anything, or if I had a concern about my horse's feet.

Right after Jake and Julia got back together, Mark left town again, apparently to go help some friends with something. I never got the full details. His uncle had picked back up doing the farrier work. But it appeared Mark had returned.

"I told you these pranks were going to end up backfiring on you," said Mary, shaking her head as she rubbed Mark's shoulder.

My racing heart finally slowed back to a normal rate and my breathing slowed back down. I leaned the pitchfork against the wall and stared down at the still-groaning farrier.

"Can someone *please* tell me why he was trying to kill me?"

Mary pushed off from the ground. She was still chuckling when Mark finally rolled over and struggled to his knees. He dry heaved, paused, and heaved again, staying bent over. Mary reached down to help him, but he waved her off.

Mark gingerly worked his way to his feet, still bent over at the waist. He straightened up, groaned, and bent back over. Mary lost it again.

"Mark, Mark, Mark. When are you going to learn, huh?" she asked between laughs. I just looked back and forth between them, confused.

Mark took a couple more deep breaths, hands on knees. He slowly straightened, pausing a few times until he was almost upright. His head swiveled towards me, and despite the pain that was etched on his face, he smiled. *Oh. What a smile...*

For the first time in a long time, I felt a tingle of excitement go through me.

He had sparkling brown eyes, deep and full of humor, even as his breath was still uneven from his ordeal. Brown, wavy hair topped a nicely angled face, which was covered by a decent scruff, giving him a rugged look. One might even call it sexy and something low in my stomach agreed with that assessment.

A black t-shirt stretched tightly across his chest, advertising the defined muscles that the shirt covered up. His biceps flexed, causing those sleeves to expand to their fullest, almost bursting at the seams, hinting at the power in those arms. Given what he did for a living, I knew those biceps were well-earned. For a fleeting moment, I wondered what it would be like to trace my fingers across that chest and up those arms.

I gave myself a mental shake. *Whoa girl, get a grip. This guy attacked you.*

"Sorry… Sorry Mrs. Harrison. I… thought you were Mary," he got out as he winced before bending back over slightly.

I glanced over at Mary and then back at Mark. "Would someone like to catch me up?"

Mary wiped the tears off her cheeks and jerked a thumb at the still somewhat pale-faced Mark.

"Dipshit here likes to pull pranks on me. Thinks it's just looooaads of fun," she quipped. "When his truck left, I let my guard down. By the way, Mark, where is your truck?"

Mark took a couple more deep breaths and straightened fully, that shirt stretching across his chest and abs. Lots of abs. Once again, that small zing shot through me, accompanied by an intense desire to rub my fingers across those abs and find out just how many there were.

Holy crap, what was wrong with me?

"I parked it down the road, just past the curve," he said, one thumb pointing back towards the road.

Mary patted Mark on the arm, grinning at him. "Well, then. The walk back to it should help loosen up those abused body parts. Don't let us keep you from leaving."

Mark did a small squat, wincing slightly before rising back to his full height. He turned away from me and trudged towards the front of the barn. I let my gaze follow him, noting that his jeans seemed to fit really well. He presented a delightful view as he left.

Holy buttons, girl. What are you doing?

Embarrassed, I turned my gaze away only to see Mary looking at me, smirking. I didn't need a mirror to know that my cheeks and neck were coloring up with being caught staring at Mark's ass.

"Nice view, huh?" asked Mary. A grin split her face as she wiggled her eyebrows at me.

"Mary!" I said. But despite that, I looked back over my shoulder. Mark was almost back at the house. He paused and glanced back over his shoulder. Seeing me watching, he smiled again. He flipped me a small two-finger salute as he turned and resumed his walking.

I shook my head at my foolishness as I finally stepped into the tack room to grab Ringo's gear. I was too old to be looking at that man, no matter how fine-looking he might be. It was time to forget the crazy start to my barn visit and move on to the male I was really here to see - Ringo.

Three hours later, I had Ringo all brushed and back in his stall. I loved my horse. No matter how shitty my day was, being with Ringo made it better. Whether spending time riding the trails surrounding the ranch or working him in the ring, it always cleared my mind and brought peace to my soul. Regardless of what life threw at me, Ringo was always there.

I slid the stall door shut and latched it. Ringo stuck his head out, rubbing up against my face and blowing softly. As I rubbed his nose, I pulled a peppermint ball from my pocket and peeled it out of its wrapper. I reached up and twitched his forelock straight as he happily munched on the sweet treat.

Gravel crunching alerted me to my visitor.

"You're gonna spoil that horse."

I turned to smile at Jake as he walked over. He wrapped me up in a hug and I squeezed him tight.

After a moment, I pushed off of him. "Hey," I said, sniffing with indignation. "It's my horse. I can spoil him if I want to," He chuckled, not buying it. After giving Ringo another pat, we both turned and headed to the barn door and out towards the house.

"So," he said, a mischievous grin on his face, "word has it you have a wicked knee."

I felt the heat rush up my neck as Jake broke out laughing. I smacked him with my gloves. He kept chuckling as he backed away, covering his crotch with his hands.

"I surrender, I surrender. Julia will kill you if you hurt her favorite toy," he said, grinning.

"She's pregnant. It will heal up by the time she needs it again," I said, stepping towards him. He laughed and skipped out of my reach.

"How did you hear about that?" I asked, catching up to him.

"I just came from Haskell's place. Mark stopped by while I was there. He looked pale and was still walking funny. Haskell and I busted a gut laughing after he told us what happened."

I bit my lip, trying to contain a laugh that wanted to bubble up. "I'm so embarrassed, but it was his fault."

"Oh, he readily admitted that. Did you really threaten to stab him with a pitchfork?" he asked, turning to stare at me.

I nodded. "It was the only thing handy."

He shook his head and then grinned at me. "Remind me never to never make you mad."

I gave him a mock glare, shaking a finger in his direction. "You would do well to remember that."

As we made it down the path and to the small parking area that supported the ranch, I popped my car trunk and pulled out the old pair of canvas deck shoes I kept there. It only took me a moment to slip out of my riding boots and deposit them into the plastic bin I had for just this reason. You never knew what you might step in being around horses, and I didn't want any surprises in my car.

I was slipping on my shoes when the back door to the house opened, and Julia stepped out. Spying me, she waved as she held the door open. Sarah came exploding out of the house, closely followed by Mary.

"Unka J!" Sarah screeched as she tore across the gravel as fast as her little feet would carry her. Jake turned towards her, laughing, his entire face beaming. She launched herself at him and he scooped her up, swinging her in the air before letting her settle down on his hip. She was squealing as he smothered her in kisses.

Julia stepped up and slid her arm around his other side. Her face glowed as she raised her chin expectantly. He dropped his lips to hers and at that moment, Sarah and I ceased to exist in their world.

I watched enviously as they kissed. When Jeremy and I had first married, we had been in love, or at least what we both thought was love. Over the years, as he became more involved with his business, and I devoted my time to my horses and charities, we settled into a comfortable companionship.

Although I'd never say so out loud, I was jealous of the level of love Jake and Julie shared. When the kiss finished, they lingered for several seconds, staring at each other. A blind man could have read the love in those eyes. With Sarah on his hip, the three of them were the perfect family.

Jeremy and I were never blessed with children. We'd been married for just over five years when we became frustrated at my inability to become pregnant and produce the next Harrison heir.

We talked with our doctors and found out, much to his embarrassment and our sadness, that Jeremy was sterile. It had hit us both hard. For Jeremy, it was a hit to his masculinity. He was seeing the end of his line. He could never pass the business down to his son. That would fall to his brother Samuel and his sons.

After the stunning revelation, Jeremy threw himself even more into his work and we settled into a peaceful coexistence. Divorce was never an option. We both had promised each other "for better or worse" and that was the way it would be.

Sarah pulled Jake over to the swing set and the two of them were soon laughing and giggling. She flew down her slide, ran around to the ladder and had Jake help her climb back up so she could slide down and repeat the process.

Julia leaned against my car, crossing her hands over her stomach. I stood on one side, Mary took the other.

"You tired of people asking how you're feeling?" I asked, nodding at the baby bump.

"Nah." Smiling, she ran her own hand across her stomach. "It doesn't bother me. What bothers me is the inability to last more than an hour without peeing, not to mention my aching boobs."

Mary chuckled, shaking her head at the memories.

"When I was pregnant with Jake, I think I threw up at least once a day until he was born. Nichole was an easy pregnancy, but Jake did his best to kill me before he arrived."

Julia looked over at me, grinning. "So, Kathi. Word has it you're a real ball buster."

Mary's snort of laughter explained how Julia knew about my earlier incident. I glared at Mary, who just raised an eyebrow at me. "Is there anyone you haven't told? Shit, it was just a few hours ago."

"Well, I only told Julia, but, like Jake said, Mark told Haskell, so I'm sure it's all over town by now."

"Great. Just great. So much for stopping at Scott's for dinner."

Julia and Mary cracked up as Jake walked up with Sarah perched on his hip.

"Hey, someone mention Scott's? Sarah has a hankering for some nuggets, so I thought we could all do dinner."

"Nuggets!" shouted Sarah, laughing and giving Jake a slobbery kiss on the cheek.

"Dinner I don't have to cook? Count me in," said Mary, rubbing her hands in glee.

I shook my head. "I'll pass guys. I need to get home and get cleaned up. Busy day tomorrow." They all protested, but I stuck firm to my decision. I desperately needed a shower.

They loaded up in the minivan while I got into my car. I followed them to Scott's, honking as I continued on past the diner.

Driving the winding roads to my house, I wondered what it would be like to come home to someone I could share my day with, cuddle up on the couch with, or even share a meal. I sighed. Given my dating history, my prospects were not promising. I needed to own up to that and move on with my life.

THREE

I t had been a hectic morning. The caterer called first thing with issues concerning the salads for the dinner. Right after I hung up with them, three of our largest sponsors called one right after another. Each wanted assurances that their name would display prominently in our media and programs for the night. I promised each that they would be the highlight of our advertising.

This was the part of the job that required all of my people skills. Some folks just needed the limelight, and it was my job to make sure they were happy with the lights we shone on them and their businesses.

At lunchtime, I worked out some of the morning's stress at a sweat-inducing spin class. One long hot shower later and I was back at my desk, nibbling at my Cobb salad. I'd barely chewed my first bite when Abby knocked and quickly stuck her head in my doorway.

"I can't believe you're keeping secrets from me," she said, glaring at me.

I looked at her, puzzled.

"What are you babbling about? Can it wait until after I enjoy this delicious plate of crispy water and cheese?" I asked.

"No, it *can't*." Pushing the door open the rest of the way, she stepped into my office and strolled towards my desk. My eyebrows shot up at what she carried.

A vase of yellow flowers. Yellow roses, in fact. Perfectly opened and laced with baby's breath throughout the bouquet. It was a stunning arrangement.

My mind scanned through all of my recent memories and came up empty. I couldn't think of a reason someone would send me flowers.

Abby smirked as she sat the vase down on my desk. I let my fork drop back down on my forgotten lunch. I pulled the vase closer, leaning my nose into the delicate petals and inhaling gently. The aroma was heavenly.

"Soooo," Abby drawled. "Who is 'M'?" She punctuated her question by flipping a small envelope onto my desk. An *opened* envelope.

"Hey, did you read my card?" I asked, glaring at her as I grabbed the envelope. "That might've been private!"

"As if," she said, not looking the least bit sorry. "Of *course* I read the card. How's a girl to stay in the know around here? Now, again, who is 'M'?"

I ignored my insolent assistant and slid the small card out of the envelope.

"Kathi, I'm sorry about yesterday. My balls hold no grudge against you and they should feel better in a few days. M."

I laughed at his choice of words. My mind flashed back to that black T-shirt and the muscle-enhancing tightness of it as I felt the flush filling my cheeks.

Abby began tapping one manicured nail against my wooden desk like a woodpecker hunting for bugs in a tree.

"Spill it, boss. Who's 'M'? Why are you blushing? More importantly, how do his *balls* play into this? *Please* tell me it involves sweaty, soiled sheets?"

I glanced back up at her, evil thoughts flowing through my brain. Payback was due.

"Oh, just someone I met yesterday at Mary's. You should have seen him in his tight, black T-shirt. Mmm. *Delicious*," I said, adding a small, contented sigh for effect.

Abby's eyes bugged out and I bit back a laugh. Her lips started melting into a slow grin as she leaned forward, folded her arms on my desk, and speared me with her gaze.

"And why, Mrs. Harrison, will his balls need a few days' rest? Hmmm?"

I just shrugged my shoulders and gave her a knowing little smile, admitting to nothing but implying everything. This was fun.

Her eyes widened, and her eyebrows shot up towards her bangs.

"You didn't?" she hissed.

"Well, he could barely walk when he left the barn. I have to tell you, it's a good thing I'm keeping up with my spin class and cardio, because, *phew*, my heart rate."

I made fanning motions with my hand, cooling myself off.

The look on Abby's face almost caused me to explode with laughter. Before she could take a breath to ask me for more details, my phone buzzed. She grimaced at the interruption. A glance at the display showed me it was Samuel. I picked up the receiver and touched one finger to my lips.

"Yes, Samuel?"

"*I'd like to see you in my office, please.*"

I straightened at the serious tone of his voice. "Of course. I'll be right there."

In typical Samuel fashion, he hung up, message delivered. I slipped the handset back on the cradle and stood up. I bent over to take one more sniff of my flowers and headed towards my door.

"Wait, what about 'M'? I need details!" she said, following me. I kept my pace up as I headed to the elevator.

"Sorry, Abby," I called back over my shoulder, giving her a small wave of my hand. "Work calls."

I laughed evilly to myself as I made my way to Samuel's suite.

———

Forty-five minutes later, my mind was reeling as I strolled back into my office. Abby looked up. I caught her attention, nodding towards my office. She grabbed her small notebook and followed me.

I slowly sat down in my seat, letting the leather adjust and comfort me as I leaned back. I let my head rest on the back of the chair and closed my eyes, collecting my thoughts. Abby wisely remained silent. She could read me better than most anyone else and knew that this wasn't a time for flippant chatter.

Taking a deep breath, I let my eyes slide open and sat up straighter in the chair, easing up to my desk. Abby had her notebook open, pen at the ready.

"Our *esteemed* boss," I stated, "seems to think that we are so outstanding at our job that we can pull miracles out of a hat. He has given us an opportunity to ensure that the name 'Harrison Enterprises' becomes a powerhouse name within the political circles of Denver."

"I'm almost scared to ask," Abby said, twirling her pen.

"Hold on to that feeling. Have you heard of Councilman Danvers and his charitable organization Kids Outside?"

She shook her head. "No, don't think I have."

"It's a non-profit geared to help under-privileged kids experience all that the great outdoors of Colorado has to offer."

Abby still looked confused. "And how does that provide us with a challenge?"

"Well, it seems the program had planned several weeks' worth of activities at one venue up near Cherry Creek. But a fire took out their two main buildings and heavily damaged their event hall."

I waited, giving her a chance to ponder the situation. When she blinked several times, I knew she had put it together.

"Please tell me he didn't?" she asked, shaking her head.

I chuckled and nodded.

"Yep. Samuel got wind of the situation. He contacted the councilman and told him we would come up with a way to give forty 13- to 15-year-olds a few weekends of outdoor fun. Our only saving grace is that it's still during the school year."

"Just how are we supposed to do that?" she asked, tapping the desk with her pen. "We do corporate events, business events, that sort of thing. I don't do *outdoors*," she said, shuddering. Given how she dressed, and her inordinate attention to her nails, I had no problem believing her.

"We have three weeks to work something out. The first weekend that the councilman is advertising will be the first weekend in April."

I had to laugh at Abby's horrified expression. I didn't give her a chance to expound on the looming deadline.

"That's why we're paid those huge salaries." I bent my head towards my computer. "Get me a list of the camp and outdoor facilities in the area. Once you have it, we'll start calling."

She started back towards her desk, grumbling under her breath. She stuck her head back in the door and pointed at me.

"Oh. And don't think I've forgotten about the mysterious 'M'. You still owe me the details," she said over her shoulder as she cleared the doorway.

After she had shut the door behind her, I grabbed the vase and pulled the beckoning blossoms closer. I breathed them in deeper this time, letting the soft scent fill me.

My thoughts raced. *I can't believe he sent me flowers. The last time I got flowers was my last birthday before Jeremy died.*

After giving the roses one more sniff, I pushed the vase back to the corner of the desk. Opening my lower desk drawer, I pulled my phone from my purse.

Scanning through my contacts, I found the entry marked "Farrier." I had updated it when Mary told me that Mark had taken over for his uncle. We had only texted a couple times before he had left. Most of those were him confirming that Ringo's hooves had been taken care of or me asking him to look at something the next time he worked on my horse.

I gave my flowers another appreciative glance before clicking on the message icon next to his contact.

> Kathi: Thank you for the flowers. They're very lovely. You didn't have to do that.

I sat my phone back on the desk and, grabbing my mouse, opened up a browser window on my computer. I wanted to do a quick survey of options out there while Abby compiled a full list. Before I could type in my query, my phone pinged with an incoming text.

> Mark: You're welcome. I felt it was the least I could do after scaring you. Again, I'm sorry.

> Kathi: I'm sorry I, well, hurt you. Are you okay?

> Mark: I will be. Guess that's what I get for not making sure of my target.

I laughed softly. I could only imagine what Mary would have done to him with that pitchfork if he had scared her. Regardless, it would have been painful. Very painful.

> Kathi: Well, I just wanted to thank you for the lovely flowers. Bye.

I laid the phone back on the desk and began looking at the booking schedule for a local kid's camp. Unfortunately, all the slots for the next three months were already booked. Sighing and mentally cursing Samuel, I went back to the search page to select the next place.

For the rest of the week and into the next, Abby and I scoured the city and surrounding area, looking for a place, any place, to meet our needs. We failed miserably. Trips to the zoo and a water park would not cut it for a councilman. Given the size of the area we had to work with, it shouldn't be this difficult to find a place.

After yet another morning of failures, we were sitting at my desk, munching the lunch we'd ordered from the deli around the corner. Printouts and brochures from the places we had called or visited littered my desk.

I spun in my chair and looked out over the Denver skyline. A haze hung over the mountains today, more than likely just smog from the cars and other traffic. Behind me, a salami-infused sigh escaped from Abby.

"Well, we've beat our heads against a wall for over a week now, and we're no closer to a solution. What are you going to tell Samuel?"

I spun my chair back around, leaning back, and shrugged. If I was being truthful, I had no idea what I was going to tell Samuel.

"In other news," said Abby, brightening, "it's your birthday Saturday. Doing anything, or, any*one*?"

I rolled my eyes to the ceiling and back to my overly sex-focused assistant.

"For your information, I plan to spend a quiet evening at home with some good food and drink, watching an outstanding piece of cinematic work."

"Right," she said. "That translates into a bottle of wine, Chinese takeout, and your favorite rom-com. Outstanding is debatable." She paused. "Hey, here's an idea," she said, pointing at the flowers. "Call up this 'M' and see if he's available for some sheet-wrestling or soapy shower sex."

I couldn't help it. My thoughts drifted to a shirtless Mark soaping up in my shower.

Abby cackled as the blush crept up my neck. "Ladies and gentleman, we have a winner. Just make sure to rinse off the soap before you gobble his—."

I sprung forward in my chair, eyes wide. "Abby!"

She batted her eyes and smiled sweetly, trying to look innocent and failing.

I leaned back in my chair, glancing over at the flowers. An image of Mark in the barn flashed through my brain. I sat upright in my chair again, realization bringing a grin to my features.

The barn. Mary's barn. A barn filled with horses. A barn on a ranch with training rings and miles of trails.

Abby clapped her hands and squealed, pointing at my face.

"I know that look! That's your 'I figured shit out' look. I love that look. Regale me, exalted one."

I swiveled my gaze to Abby and let the smile creep onto my face. I held up one finger and then picked up my phone. I punched number two on my speed dial list and waited. Abby was almost bouncing in her seat. Four rings and then the line connected.

"Hey, girl. You playing hooky from work again?"

"Hey, Mary. No, not at the moment. Listen, I'm in a bind, and I am hoping you can help me out. Are you available for lunch tomorrow?"

"Sorry, I'm going to be out-of-town tomorrow. I can do Friday. Where?"

"How about we just do Scott's? Noon work?"

"Sure. And since it's your birthday this weekend, I'll even buy."

"You don't have to do that, but I appreciate the offer. See you on Friday. Give Sarah a hug for me. Bye."

I hung up and looked over at Abby who was glaring at me. I smiled and pulled a rose out of my vase and sniffed it lightly. Sadly, they were a few days old now and losing their fragrance.

"A week. It took you a *week* to remember that you knew someone who runs a horse ranch?" Abby asked, shaking her head.

I shrugged. "Better late than never." I clapped my hands and rubbed them together a few times. "Okay, we have work to do. I need you to get our legal folks on the calendar for tomorrow. We need to discuss insurance and liabilities."

Abby began taking notes as I started outlining the rest of the tasks needed for our plan. I said a silent prayer, hoping that Mary wouldn't shoot down my idea, because I didn't have a backup plan.

FOUR

It was another beautiful Colorado morning as I passed through Monument on my way to Bare Ridge to meet Mary. Small puffs of clouds stood out in stark contrast to the bright blue sky as they danced in the wind. Fresh air rushed through my open windows, laden with the smell of trees and grass.

I loved this part of the country. The only way it could be better was if I were out on Ringo and had the wind whipping in my face as we rode and played.

Abby and I had crammed a ton of work into the last day and a half, fleshing out most of our plans. While I was meeting with Mary today, Abby would work on logistics. We would need transportation for the kids to and from Mary's place, assuming she was on board with the plan.

The only other outlier to deal with was food, but I had hopes that Scott, the owner of the diner where I was meeting Mary, would help with that task.

It was almost noon when I pulled into a parking spot at Scott's. The diner was a throwback to a time when Americans lived for the open highway. Its original owners had modeled it after one of those old

Airstream trailers, only much larger. The metal of the sides and surrounding space reflected the sunlight back so well that when you were standing near it, you could feel the heat coming off of it.

I stepped up the stairs and pushed through the double plate-glass doors. The inside of Scott's was about what you would expect for an older burger joint that was modeled after an even older diner setup. They had floor-bolted silver stools, their seats covered with worn and cracked red vinyl, sitting in front of an old weathered counter. Groups of salt and pepper shakers, ketchup bottles, and screw-top jars of sugar divided the counter into zones, each ready for customers.

The swinging door into the back kitchen was scarred-up stainless steel and hung at an odd angle. The back counter stored all the various things needed to support the waitresses. A small window in the back wall had an old ticket wheel hanging at a weird angle. The prerequisite battered bell sat on the ledge under the wheel.

A Muzak system wheezed through the tinny-sounding speakers, the tired music wafting over the buzz of conversation and the clink of plates and utensils. A few customers were at the bar, plates with the leftovers from lunch still in front of them as they chatted with their friends and finished up their drinks.

I looked to the left to see the five or six booths. Mary was in a booth near the back, talking with Jill, one of Scott's long-time servers.

Jill was a free spirit in tight jeans and today sporting a Broncos t-shirt. She told everyone that she was a child of the Sixties. She had never married and never wanted to be married. She once told Jake, much to his embarrassment, that she loved sex too much to settle down with just one guy.

And I have to give credit where credit was due. She didn't look sixty or even fifty. She was a few inches taller than me, with dishwater-blond hair that fell in small waves to the middle of her back. Jill was curvy, and she knew how to use the curves to her advantage. She filled out her shirt and jeans well. I could only hope I would look as good when I got to that stage of life.

"Hello ladies," I said, sliding into the booth across from Mary.

"Well, if it isn't the important city-girl come to hang out with us lowly country folk," Jill said, grinning at me.

"Well, one must do what one must," I said, putting some extra haughty in my tone and including a delicate sniff.

Jill and Mary looked at me with wide eyes for a few beats before we all cracked up laughing.

Jill flipped open her order pad. "What'll it be, Kathi?"

"Club sandwich with provolone, chips, and water with lemon, please."

Jill scratched at her pad and headed towards the kitchen as I turned my attention back to Mary, who was watching me curiously.

Mary and I took a few moments to catch up on the latest happenings and news around the Attwood place, which consisted mainly of her telling me all the cute things Sarah had been doing and the status of Julia's pregnancy. By the time we were done, Jill had returned with our food and drinks.

We busied ourselves with the first bite or two of our sandwiches. Mary took a drink, wiped her mouth and placed her hand on the tabletop.

"Alright, what was so important that you took time out of your day to drive down here from Denver just to have lunch?"

One thing I loved about Mary was her no-nonsense approach to life. She had never been one to beat around the bush.

"What?" I asked, my hand fluttering to my chest as if I was clutching pearls. "Can't a girl just want to have lunch with her best friend?"

She met my feigned innocence with a glare of granite. I crunched through a few chips and had a drink while she stared. Swallowing, I shook my head slightly.

"So distrusting," I said.

Ms. Granite kept up her boulder impression. She finally cracked a smile when I snorted, trying to keep my laughter in.

"Fine. Have you ever heard of an organization called 'Kids Outside'?" I asked.

Mary took a bite of her burger and chewed slowly, her eyes slightly unfocused as she thought. I pulled a piece of the bacon off my club sandwich and nibbled on it.

Mary swallowed, wiping a sliver of mustard off the corner of her mouth, and shook her head. "Nope, can't say as I have. One of your charities?"

"Not until a few days ago," I said. "It's apparently a pet project for one councilman in Denver. They try to get inner-city and under-privileged kids involved in outdoor activities. Camping, canoeing, things like that.

"Anyway, they had a multiple weekend program setup, but the venue fell through. They tried to find a replacement place, but everything was already booked. The councilman was lamenting at a lunch a few weeks ago and Samuel overheard him."

"Ah - here it comes," Mary said. I laughed and nodded.

"Yep. Samuel saw a chance to boost his standing with the Denver government and increase the image for Harrisons. So, he told the Councilman that Harrisons would be happy to pitch in and solve his problem."

I paused, taking another bite of my delicious sandwich. A glance at Mary had her giving me that knowing look. Mary was a sharp businesswoman and I suspect she was already seeing the path of this conversation. I swallowed, took a sip of water, and continued on with my pitch.

"Abby and I racked our brains for a week and came up with nothing. Then, as I was smelling the flowers that Mark sent me it—"

Mary threw a hand up, interrupting me. Her eyes narrowed and she leaned forward. "Wait. What? Flowers? Why would *Mark* be sending flowers to you?"

I was mentally kicking myself. Then, as if putting gas on the fire, Jill was stepping up to check on us and overheard our last exchange. Her eyes darted to me, a surprised look crossing her face.

She whistled. "Wait just a sec. You got flowers from Mark Danlock, that fine specimen of studliness? Girl, you've been holding out on us," she said, sliding into the booth next to Mary. She looked around, making sure no other customers were in earshot, before leaning in and lowering her voice slightly.

"So, spill. Is *all* of him as good looking as the rest of that hard body? Does he have a big dick? Please tell me you ate him up like a melting ice cream cone. Details, girl. Details." She spread her hands on the table and stared at me expectantly.

Mary choked on the drink she had taken. I stared at Jill, shock and heat washing over my face. The line of questioning made me wonder whether Abby and Jill were related.

"Calm your hormones!" I hissed at Jill, who had the audacity to still look unashamed.

I took a deep breath. "He sent them as an apology for what happened at the barn the other day."

Mary started laughing even harder. I felt my face flame even hotter as Mary caught Jill up. Jill was laughing so hard that Scott had to come out from the kitchen to find out what was going on. She waved at him as she wiped some tears from her cheek. She was wheezing and laughing so hard she could barely speak.

"Please... *please* tell me... tell me you offered... to kiss... kiss them all better?"

She and Mary broke up again, leaning against each other as they cackled. At that point, I didn't think my face could get any redder.

Mary started to snort and then waved her hand at me. She took a big gasping breath, trying to regain some control.

"I know what we need to do," Mary said, panting, trying to breathe, laugh, and speak all at the same time. "Her... her birthday is... is Saturday. We... we should have him... have him go to her house... and put a bow around it..." she sputtered, before descending into snorts, unable to finish.

Jill started wheezing again, and for a moment, I actually thought she was having a heart attack. I sat there, flame-faced, and ate my sandwich as the two juveniles sitting across from me reveled in their sophomoric hilarity.

Scott appeared at our table once again and gave Jill the stink-eye. He wiped his hands on a greasy rag and tossed it over his shoulder.

"Hate to break up your fun, Jill, but maybe you could do some of that *work* I'm paying you for?" he asked, arms crossed over his apron-covered belly.

Still chuckling, Jill slid out of the booth and ambled back towards the kitchen. She glanced over her shoulder at me and broke up laughing as she pushed through the door into the kitchen.

I grabbed Scott and asked him to sit. He slid in beside Mary and kicked back, stretching out the leg I knew was replaced years ago after a nasty accident. "What can I help you with?" he asked, curiosity lacing his words. I gave him an overview of what I had proposed to Mary. I asked if he would be interested in using his restaurant to help with the food for the event. He looked more and more interested as I spoke, leaning forward and nodding. When I finished my pitch, I glanced back and forth at them, waiting. He was the first to speak.

"If Mary is good with it, I can set up a grill. Hamburgers, hotdogs, bags of chips, bottles of water. Easy to fix, easy to clean up. I'll hire some of the local kids to give me general help. How many do you think you will have at a time?"

"Twenty, thirty at the most."

"Easy to do from my side. Just let me know the dates and numbers and I'll lay in extra supplies. We can work out the costs after."

I reached over and squeezed his arm, giving him a grateful smile. "Thank you so much, Scott. This will be a tremendous help to us and the kids."

"I'm always happy to help with something like this. It sounds like it's going to be good for those kids." He nodded towards us. "Now, if you ladies will excuse me, I need to get back to my kitchen." He slid out of the booth, nodded his head at us, and stumped back to his kitchen. He was yelling for Jill as he disappeared through the swinging door.

Mary sat back and cocked her head at me, giving me the once over. "Let me see if I understand," she said. "For four or five weekends, you want to turn my place into a daycare? You want to bring kids who've never seen or been around horses to my ranch and entertain them? That about the gist of it?"

I nodded. There was no beating around the bush. That *was* pretty much the extent of it.

"I would like to organize riding lessons, demonstrations, and a trail ride or two." I said. Now it was up to her. I tried to keep my anxiousness from showing. I didn't have a backup plan.

Mary was considering it. I could almost see the wheels turning as she worked it through her mind.

She sighed. "Kathi, I like the idea. I do. But I'm not sure Jake and I can handle all of that. You need dead-broke horses and Jake and I only have six that fill that bill. And the weekends are my busiest lesson times." She looked worriedly at me.

I exhaled. "I know it sounds like a lot. But I'll be there every step of the way. I could let you use Ringo and I'd bet that there are few of your other boarders would let us use theirs. If we split the kids into several groups, then that lessens the load. I'll also pay you $500 for every weekend that we are running. If that's not enough to cover your losses, let me know."

Mary stared out the window for a few moments before turning back to me. "Even with you there, we're gonna need more help. But that's not even the biggest kicker. I have some insurance, but not enough to cover an operation that size," she said, tapping her finger on the table. "All it would take is one kid to get hurt and a parent to sue us and I'm toast."

I nodded. I'd been expecting this argument.

"I've already talked with our legal team and our insurance underwriters. We will consider this a Harrison event and cover all the risks. We will sign a contract with you that releases you from any responsibility. Basically, we are hiring you to provide services. All the parents will sign a waiver acknowledging this, and I know you have plenty of signage making people aware of the Colorado Equine Activity Liability law. If you need more, let me know and I'll get them for you.

"Abby is calling all the fire stations in Monument, Colorado Springs, and a few other smaller areas to find EMTs to ensure we have medical staff on hand. We will buy helmets for everyone, and you can give them your standard safety briefing."

Mary sat back, watching me as she worried at her lower lip. She sat there for a few seconds before sitting up straighter.

"Okay. I still need to talk to Jake, but I'm on board. What demonstrations were you thinking?"

"Nothing fancy. Whatever you can come up with."

A slow grin crossed her face. I felt the short hairs on my neck stand up as she studied me.

"I think they would just love a demonstration of jumping. And it just so happens I know someone who is an excellent jumper." She inclined her head to me.

I blanched. "Me? I... I can't. I mean, I've not done that in a long time, Mary."

She stared at me, waiting. *Shit.* Well, I *was* asking her for a big favor. The least I could do was help out however she needed.

"Fine," I sighed. She nodded, but that grin didn't go away.

"I also think they would benefit from a demo from Mark on how to trim and shoe a horse's foot."

I felt my face betraying me at the mention of Mark's name. *Get a grip, Kathi.* Ignoring my reddening cheeks, I bobbed my head in agreement. "Sure, I think that would work. I'll let you work that out with Mark," I said. I was hoping that this conversation would die there, but given these two, I really should have known better.

She grinned and shook her head. "Nope, I'm going to be busy talking to horse owners and getting other things ready. I think *you* should contact Mark."

My damn traitor cheeks flamed. I was sure they were brighter than the sunlight reflecting off the outside walls of this restaurant.

"I don't like you," I grumbled.

"Wounded, I am," she spat back. Clearly, she showed no signs of being wounded one bit.

I just laughed at her, taking a long drink of water and hoping that my red face calmed down soon. Thankfully, she moved on and didn't pursue that line any further. We went over a few more items as we finished lunch. Before we could slide out of the booth, Jill came back over.

"So, Kathi." She placed a hand on her hip, giving it a sassy cock out to the side. "Is it really your birthday Saturday?"

Crap. I'd really hoped she'd missed that slip of Mary's earlier. Sighing, I smiled up at her.

"Yes, but it's no big deal. Just another day. If you will excuse me, I'll be on my way," I said, pushing out to the edge of the booth. But Jill stayed where she was, trapping me.

She turned and smiled sweetly at Mary. "It would be a shame to let that day go uncelebrated. What do you think, Mary?"

I glanced at Mary and Jill and saw something pass between them.

Mary smiled just as sweetly as her partner in crime. "Why, Jill, I think you are correct. And, since this is such a special birthday, we should go all out."

"Special, you say?"

Mary nodded, that sick smile stuck on her face. "Yep, a milestone birthday."

"Oh, even better," cooed Jill. "What milestone?"

"Mary, don't you dare!" I hissed.

Ignoring me, Mary held up her hands, four fingers raised on one, a fist on the other. Jill gasped and covered her mouth with one hand.

"Oh! Well, that settles it. Friday," she crowed, rubbing her hands together. "Kathi, we will pick you up at six. Wear something sexy and sinful 'cuz we're gonna party! And if we're really lucky, we can find someone to take you home and celebrate the night with."

I cringed as Jill emphasized the word 'celebrate' by winking.

I glared at Mary. She didn't even try to look apologetic. I thought about telling Jill I had plans, which would have been a lie. Just like it was a lie when I told Abby the same thing when she'd asked me last week. But I paused. I hadn't been out on a date in almost three weeks. What was the worst that could happen?

I knew I was going to regret this, but perhaps it wouldn't be completely terrible. I took a deep breath and looked back at Jill, plastering a smile on my face.

"Sure. Sounds fun."

"Great! I know the *perfect* place. You two are going to love it!"

With that, she dropped the check on the table and headed back behind the counter.

I looked over at Mary, who quickly wiped the smirk off her face. It wasn't even Saturday, and I was already wondering if I had made a mistake by agreeing to this.

FIVE

I was finishing up my makeup when the doorbell rang. Mary was one of the few people in my life who had the gate code to just come over any time she wanted, and, true to form, she was right on time for our girls' night out. I opened the door and a smiling Jill marched in, followed closely behind by a laughing Mary.

Jill was wearing a cherry red mini-dress. It was so tight that one glance told me she wasn't wearing underwear. The front was cut low enough that any bra would have been visible, and the bottom was short enough that if she bent over, everyone would know all her secrets. Her hair was a high mess of curls, with a few loose tendrils falling around her face. Around her neck was a small leather choker with three diamond studs embedded in the front. The five-inch stiletto heels she wore were as red as her dress. I shook my head in amazement, and possibly a little awe. She could definitely carry the look off.

"Happy Birthday! It's time to party!" whooped Jill, hugging me, then grabbing Mary & pulling her into a group hug. I closed the door behind them as they moved into the front room. As I followed them, Jill gave me the once over, then shook her head.

"Is that what you're wearing?" she asked, her voice filled with clothing-choice disgust.

I looked down at the jeans and the nice blouse I was wearing, then back up at her, raising my eyebrows. "What's wrong with what I'm wearing? Mary is wearing almost the same thing." I waved my hand at her. "Aren't *you* a tad bit overdressed?"

Jill flipped her hand at Mary. "If I thought I could get her to wear a dress, I would. Besides, she's the driver. There's no fun for her tonight." She started pushing me towards the hall, heels clicking on the hardwood floor.

"Bedroom, now," she demanded. Her finger poking me between the shoulder blades felt like a police baton.

"But" was all I got out before she smacked me on the ass.

"No 'buts'. Move it. We don't wanna be late." Almost laughing at the determination in her voice, I hastened my steps to avoid another threatened butt smack.

Once we were in my room, she descended on my closet like a swarm of locusts. She started tossing hangers to the side, muttering to herself, pausing occasionally to glance at the item she held.

I turned to look at Mary, who was leaning against the doorway and trying not to laugh.

A skirt came flying my way, smacking me in the face. I pulled it off and held it out, recognizing it as one I hadn't seen in years.

I shook my head, protesting her choice. "Jill, this skirt is too small."

"That makes it *perfect*," she said, darting over to my dresser, holding onto a white shirt she had dug out of the deep recesses of my closet. A pair of my nice, lacy, red panties flew at me, followed by the matching push-up bra.

Ignoring the look of uncertainty that I'm sure covered my face, Jill grabbed the skirt from my hands and dumped everything on the bed. She began tugging at my shirt.

I snarled, pushing her hands off of me. "I can dress myself, thank you very much."

She waved her hands towards me. "Well then, girl, get a move on. There's booze to drink and asses to squeeze." She tossed the words over her shoulder as she stalked back into my closet.

I glanced at Mary, who grinned and shrugged. When she wanted to be, Jill was the proverbial immovable object. I stripped down and began redressing, mumbling to myself about crazy geriatrics.

I managed to tug the skirt on, but it was a challenge. It was a mini pencil skirt that I bought on a whim a few years back and had never worn. It was snug, but not uncomfortable. Luckily, the panties Jill had picked out were cheekies. I didn't feel any panty lines as I ran my hands down the sides and across my ass.

The shirt Jill had tossed me was something I purchased for an intimate dinner with Jeremy. An in-home dinner. It was sheer to the point of being virtually see-through and had driven him wild that night because I hadn't worn a bra. While I was preparing dinner, his eyes stayed locked on my boobs. I don't think he managed three bites before he was all over me.

The shirt fell about two inches above my skirt and exposed my belly. The sleeves were long and cuffed. In the mirror, the red bra shone through the sheer material like a star. The reflection of my tight stomach made me also glad I had kept up on the crunches.

"Jill, I can't wear this out in public. Find something else," I whined, still looking at myself in the mirror. I also couldn't help thinking that my legs looked damn good in the skirt, but I wasn't telling her that.

She stepped back out of the closet with a pair of black heels. At four inches, they were the tallest heels I owned. She paused in front of me, giving me the once over, having me twirl.

"Perfect. Now you're ready to party," she cooed.

"Jill, I look like a college girl getting ready to prowl frat row on a Saturday night," I said, slipping on the heels she held out to me and wrapping the ties around my ankle.

She rubbed her hands together in glee as she laughed. "Close. There will probably be frat boys where we are going." She grabbed me and began pulling me towards the front door as I stumbled along behind her. Five minutes later, we were in Mary's purple hell-wagon and roaring north towards Denver, AC/DC blaring through the speakers. That drive was the last clear memory I had of the night ahead.

My eyes blinked open, and I quickly shut them. The inside of my head pounded like a horse thundering down a track. I tried to swallow but my throat felt like someone lined it with sandpaper. It hurt to breathe. Hell, it hurt to *think*.

Groaning, I dragged my legs up and over the edge of the bed. As I struggled to sit up, the world spun like a carousel. My feet hit the cold hardwood floor, sending a shock through me to match the pounding in my head. It took a few deep breaths to fight down the urge to decorate the floor with whatever foulness was in my gut. I struggled for control of my stomach and head, considering it a win that I hadn't collapsed to the floor in a heap.

Vague memories flashed behind my eyes. Jill. Mary. A dance club. Guys. Young guys. Tequila. A *lot* of tequila. I made a mental promise to myself to *never* drink tequila again. As my head thumped again, I changed that promise to just never to drink any alcohol again.

Before I could contemplate how to stop the horse that was galloping through my head, the door opened up and Mary came into the room.

"Morning Sunshine. Happy Birthday! It's past noon and time for all the good little campers to rise and shine!" she said, all chipper and non-hangover-y. I immediately wanted her dead.

"I hate you," I whimpered, holding my head. I mentally begged the head horse to please stop running.

"And that's the thanks I get for bringing water and ibuprofen," she said in a sing-song voice.

"Fine. I love you again. Gimme," I groaned, holding my hand up and flipping my fingers. Shit, even that hurt.

Mary put the life-saving pills in my hand. I sat them on my tongue and held out my hand and a bottle of water got placed in it. I moaned when the cold goodness washed through my mouth. I swear it was all soaked up by my tongue and nothing went down my throat. The bottle was empty before I knew it.

Mary took the empty container from my hands. "I put one of Jake's t-shirts and a pair of Julia's sweatpants on the end of the bed. Fresh towels are in the bathroom. I even took pity on you and left a tooth-brush and toothpaste. Take a shower, and when you're ready, find the kitchen. I'll have coffee ready, Party Girl. Oh, and I had Jake go get your car and bring it here. Didn't know what time you'd be crawling out of bed and I've got lessons soon."

I groaned, putting my head between my hands and resting my elbows on my knees.

"Please. *Please* tell me I didn't do anything too wild."

The bitch just laughed as she left the room. At that moment, I hated her so much. And then it hit my pain-riddled brain. She didn't answer me.

Shit. What had I done last night?

As I shuffled to the bathroom, I tried to remember what had gone on that night. One thing was definitely sure. I was definitely too old to be acting like a twenty-year-old college girl prowling the clubs. How did I ever let Jill talk me into last night?

Thirty minutes later, after a steaming hot shower, I felt more human. Mary had left a small plastic bag on the end of the bed. I picked up the skirt and shirt from the floor. The state odor of spilled tequila wafted up, making my already unhappy stomach roil. Holding my breath, I shoved the soiled skirt, shirt, and panties into the bag. I had no intention of letting any of those items touch me until at least two washings. I glanced around for my bra but didn't see it. Never mind. I'd have Mary find it later. I gathered the rest of my stuff from the dresser and shoved it into the bag before leaving the bedroom.

I stumbled slowly down the hall, the horse in my head down to a slow trot, thanks to the painkillers and the shower. I sniffed and caught a whiff of coffee. Like a bloodhound on a hunt, I latched onto that heavenly aroma and followed it into the kitchen.

Julia was sitting at the table munching on what appeared to be apple wedges. She also had a bowl of grapes. The mere sight of that piece of fruit had my stomach debating leaving the party early. I gulped hard, begging my stomach's contents to please stay home.

I eased down into a chair, a light groan escaping my clenched lips.

A cup of coffee appeared in front of me, along with a small plate containing two pieces of toast. I took a long sip of the life-giving nectar. A snort pulled my attention over to the fruit chomper.

Julia picked up a grape, but paused before she popped it into her mouth. "You look like you had a great night. Remember any of it?" Her shot fired, she popped the grape into her mouth and began chewing.

Mary slid into the seat next to me. She was also smiling at me, amusement dancing in her eyes. Alarm bells and red flashing lights went off in my foggy brain.

"What?" I croaked.

Mary took a sip of her coffee and then gave me that same sickeningly sweet smile again.

"Oh, nothing. Nothing at all," she replied, exuding innocence.

I looked from Julia to Mary and got a sinking feeling in the pit of my already churning stomach. I closed my eyes and laid my head on my arms as both of them burst out laughing.

"You're an excellent dancer," said Julia.

I turned my head on my arms to take in Mary, who wasn't even trying to hide her guilt. I tried to still my head and heart as I whispered to her.

"Please tell me you didn't take pictures?"

Her answer was to shove her phone into my face. Even blurry-eyed, I could make out the photo of a couple of women and several guys on the dance floor. I wasn't positive, but that appeared to be Jill and me surrounded by a sea of guys.

Raising my head back up, I took a deep breath and reached for a piece of toast, taking a big crunchy bite. As I chewed, I looked at my supposed friend, who wiped a suspicious grin off her face and tried to paste on a sympathetic smile instead. I wasn't buying it. I nodded slowly towards the photo.

"Okay. I can live with that. I was just dancing and no one I know would be there, or know anyone there. That's good," I said, sighing with relief.

I looked at Julia just as she flicked her eyes to Mary and back at me. I glanced at Mary and that feeling of dread did a two-and-a-half double-gainer into the acid pool that was my stomach.

"Mary? It was just *dancing*, right?"

"Well…"

"Don't you 'well' me Mary Attwood. What else?" I said, loudly and instantly regretting it. The horse, who had calmed down, hooked up a wagon and began running around my brain. I could feel my heartbeat behind my eyeballs.

I held up my hand. "Wait. Before I forget, I didn't find my bra. If you find it, I'll get it later."

"About that," Mary said. Her jaw muscle was twitching with her effort to not laugh. I just knew in my heart that I wasn't going to like the answer to my next question.

Closing my eyes, I asked again, quietly. "Mary, where's my bra?"

Mary actually grinned before she swiped at her phone and showed me another picture. It appeared to be of some light fixture or something. Given my troubled vision, it was hard to make out.

"Mary?" I fixed her with a look. "What is that? Where. Is. My. Bra?"

"You threw your bra up into the lights over the dance floor," she said, barely containing her laughter, almost snorting. "And it was impressive how you stripped out of it and never even stopped your groove."

Julia was no help. She giggled around her bite of fruit. "Damn, Kathi. Once I have this kid, we have *got* to have a girls' night out."

I glared at her and then tried to take a deep breath. It didn't work very well.

"I'll not be going back there, and its just a bra. Yes. Yes, if that's all I did, I can live with it." I breathed a sigh of relief.

Bing.

All three of us looked at my purse. *Was that my text sound?*

After watching me fumble with the simple snap on my clutch, Mary took pity and reached over to open it for me. I pulled out my phone and glanced at it. Sure enough, there was a text alert. I processed the name. Blinked, wiped my eyes, and gave the name another look.

Mark.

Why would Mark be texting me? And why, suddenly, was I filled with a sense of dread? Maybe it was nothing. Maybe he was coming to trim Ringo today and just wanted to check in. Yeah, that was it. Reluctantly, I clicked on the message icon.

> Mark: Good morning. I hope you doing?
> Head hurting?

My heart dropped. Nope. Ringo wasn't involved in this text. Shit. How did he know? I glanced up at Mary and then over at Julia, who took that moment to shove some grapes in her mouth. Even hungover, I could see her eyes sparkling as she tried not to laugh. I turned my attention back to Mary, my supposed, possibly soon-to-be-dead, friend.

I looked at her, seriousness, or at least as much seriousness as I was able to muster in my hungover state, radiating from my eyes. "Mary, did you tell Mark about last night?"

Mary looked shocked, one hand coming up to clutch at her chest.

"Absolutely not! I would never rat out a girlfriend like that. I'm hurt that you even asked," she replied. The mirth dancing in her eyes combined with the haughty sniff at the end of her declaration of innocence just made my head hurt.

Julia snickered and used the apple in her hand to point at the phone. "You gonna answer him?" she asked.

"I hate you both so much right now," I said. I blinked my eyes several times, trying to clear them as I thought about a response. Denial makes a good first line of defense. I began tapping at the keys.

> Kathi: I'm not sure what you are talking
> about, but I am fine. But thank you for asking.
> Bye.

I hit send, hoping that would be the end of it. My phone pinged almost immediately with a response. I started reading and, knew it was not the end. Not even close.

Mark: Well, when you called and woke me up at two this morning, you certainly sounded like you were having a good time, which, based on the conversation, I assume involved a lot of alcohol. :)

I closed my eyes and began shaking my head ever so slightly. Acid began burbling in my stomach.

Eyes still closed, I set the cell phone down on the table. "Mary. Please tell me I didn't 'drunk dial' Mark from the club?"

"Nope, you did not," she said. I breathed a sigh of relief, thoughts spinning through my head. *But then what is he talking about? Did he just dream that I called him? Oh. Is he dreaming about me? What? And why does that make me feel all squiggly in my belly?*

Then Mary broke through my thoughts. "You did it on the drive home."

Oh. Dear. God. I dropped my chin down to my chest.

I moaned as I opened one eye to peer at Mary. Shit, she was still grinning. "If you still love me as a friend, you'll tell me you grabbed the phone from me before I said something stupid."

"Well," she said. "I *tried* to take the phone, but you held it away from me and told me to, and I *quote*, 'Leave me alone so I can talk to the stud.'"

I let my head drop slowly to the table, thumping my forehead lightly against my arms. Death was looking good. Please, let me die right now.

Bing.

With a sense of dread, I read the new message.

Mark: And just so you know, I would find a saddle very uncomfortable.

"Saddle?" I croaked. How could this get worse?

Mary's face lit up in recollection. "Yep. You told him you wanted to throw a saddle on him and ride him all night."

Julia snorted. "Oh, I *have* to use that one with Jake."

I groaned into the table top. "Please God, take me now. I'll have to

find a new farrier. I don't think this could get any more embarrassing."
Then the universe showed me just how I was oh-so-wrong.

Bing.

I looked at the phone and then up at the two of them. They both
had expectant grins on their faces. Hussies.

I reluctantly glanced at the message.

> Mark: And for the record, I don't send those
> kinds of pictures to ladies. That information
> should only be provided in person.

I felt the blush start at my cheeks and rise along all the way to my
hair. I looked over at Mary. A crowbar wouldn't remove the shit-eating
grin tattooed on her face.

"Pictures?"

Mary flushed red. Oh God. I knew it was going to be bad when *she*
blushed.

She stammered out words I really hadn't wanted to hear. "You, um,
wanted to know how, you know, how *big* he was and if would send you
a… well… a picture."

Yet again I fought down the urge to throw up. Julia lost it, howling
in laughter. While she celebrated my pain, I put my head back on my
arms, swearing to myself that I was never drinking again or going
anywhere with Jill. In fact, killing Jill would solve the problem nicely.
They would throw me in jail and I'd never see these people again. Yep.
Plan made.

"Oh my God, you asked him for a *dick pic*?" Julia asked once she
got her breath. "Go Kathi!" she said, raising her hand for a high five,
which I ignored.

"Right," I said, dragging myself up out of my chair. Before the
offending instrument delivered yet another embarrassing message, I
powered the phone off and shoved it into my clutch. I downed the cup
of coffee, praying the caffeine would jump start my recovery.

"If you two former friends will excuse me, I am going to go home,
curl up into a ball, and die."

I picked up my bag of dirty clothes and my clutch and held my head as high as I could. I looked over at Mary, nodding at her.

"Thank you for driving last night. For the record, I will never go out with you and Jill again. *Ever*."

"Awww," she said, grinning. "Jill will be so disappointed. She wanted to fix you up with one of the guys. He really liked your bra-removal moves."

I glared at her, willing her head to explode, but alas, nothing happened. To her credit, she did walk me to the door and gave me a hug. She might have been chuckling while she did it, but she at least won a few friendship points back for seeing me out.

"Are you sure you don't want me to drive you home?" she asked.

I shook my head. "No, thank you. I'll be fine. The painkillers are somewhat working and I'll keep the windows down. I'm right as rain."

As I turned the doorknob, Julia got in a parting shot. "Hey, if he changes his mind and sends you a pic, how about sharing with us? Curious minds and all."

I turned to her and slowly flipped her off. She laughed and went back to eating her fruit.

Stepping out into the bright light caused my eyes to water even as I threw a hand up to block the sun. As I moved off the bottom concrete step onto the sidewalk, I looked up and towards the driveway, searching for my car.

As if the universe had not smacked me enough, there stood Mark, leaning against his truck. I watched as he shoved his phone back into his pocket. He grinned and gave me a small finger wave.

Well, fuck a duck.

I may have been hungover and embarrassed, but the unfogged part of my brain still checked him out from head to toe. All of my lady parts convened a quick meeting. They agreed he checked all their boxes and wanted a closer examination. I promptly told them to calm the fuck down.

A light orange t-shirt stretched taut across his chest and shoulders, and with his arms crossed, his biceps threatened to rip his sleeves. A faded baseball hat sat on his head, holding back those shiny brown locks.

And dear Lord, the dimple that appeared when he grinned. God, if he was only ten years older.

Oh great. You asked him for a dick pic, and now you're checking him out. You need therapy, girl, and lots of it. But this isn't your first walk of shame, so pull it together.

I squared my shoulders, pulling myself taller as I stepped onto the gravel and gingerly walked towards him and my car. Barefoot on gravel was not the best way to be moving in a hungover state, but I wasn't going to give him the satisfaction of watching me fumble with putting on high heels. I also didn't need to look behind me to know that my two ex-friends were at the window watching like spectators at a football game.

The handsome hunk stood there watching me, that self-righteous grin on his face, as I picked my way over the sharp rocks. When I got close to him, he touched his fingers to the brim of his hat. I didn't look him in the eye. As I stepped around the front corner of my car, my heel came down on a piece of pointed gravel sticking up, causing me to yelp and jerk my foot up. I dropped my purse and flailed my arms out, trying to catch the fender of my car.

Mark stepped forward to help, but I threw up a hand, stopping him in place. The bastard grinned and stepped back as I bent down to pick up my belongings. Keeping up on my toes to save my abused heel, I limp-stepped to my car door. I heard Mark moving behind me, but I kept my eyes focused on my door as I thumbed the unlock button.

The unwritten rule of a shame walk was to never acknowledge the lesser beings around you. Own the shame, wear it like a cape. Be a shame superhero.

I opened my car door and tossed my belongings to the passenger seat before sliding into the car. Again keeping my focus straight ahead, I fumbled with my seat belt twice before it clicked into place. That seemingly impossible task completed, I started the car. I reached up to the visor and pulled down my sunglasses. I was sliding them on when Mr. Gorgeous Smugness imposed himself into my sight. He tapped lightly on my window. Taking a deep breath and composing my face into an emotionless mask, I hit the button on the armrest and the protective barrier slid down.

"Yes?" I asked, my tone filled with as much non-polite politeness as I could muster.

"You dropped these," he said, his voice low and rumbly. I tried very hard to ignore that rumbly vibration as it moved over me, but despite my best efforts, a few of my areas purred in response.

I glanced down at his hand. The heat started at my neck and shot to the top of my head. Dangling from his index finger was a pair of lacy red panties. The very ones Jill had insisted I wear.

It must have been the last hurrah of the tequila coming from the depths of my veins, combined with the shiver his rumbling voice was giving me, because I didn't immediately snatch them from his hand. Oh no. Instead, I had a sudden rush of bravery and without really thinking things through, responded. Not knowing where the hell this was coming from and really not caring at the moment, I used one finger to pull my sunglasses down my nose so that I could stare over them. I looked him in the eye as I gave him my best smirk.

"What, don't want to keep them as a trophy? Isn't that what you *young* guys do?"

His grin slipped for a moment, and I could have sworn an intense look of disappointment flitted across his face. But it was only momentary, and in a blink, the grin was back. With a flick of his wrist, he tossed my errant underwear through the window and into the back seat. One arm resting on the top of my car, he leaned down closer to my open window, laying his other arm on the door frame.

"Kathi?" he said, lowering the volume of the rumble, but not its intensity. Only the tequila knew why I leaned forward to hear him better.

"Yes?"

His eyes searched mine. "I don't take what I don't earn. But you know what?"

Don't answer, it's a trap.

"What?" *Stupid tequila.*

"I would *love* to earn them. Be safe driving home."

My mouth hung open, my face flushed deeper red, and I swear the temperature in the car shot up thirty degrees. *What the hell?*

He nodded to me, pushed off the car, and turned back to his truck.

I sat there a moment, trying to catch my breath. His rumbling voice still echoed in my ears and caused a warmth to spread throughout my body as I put the car in reverse and backed out of the driveway. I was ashamed of the drunk call and letting myself get sucked into the last exchange. Mostly, though, I was ashamed that I scoped out his ass as he walked away. However, I wasn't so ashamed as to admit that I would *really* like to see that view again.

It was going to be a long ride home.

SIX

"So, all you need to do is sign these copies where the yellow stickers are and we will be set," I said to Scott and Mary, who sat across from me in the booth at Scott's diner. I had agreed to meet them here for lunch and to discuss the event. The remnants of said lunch had been pushed to the side as we finished up some paperwork.

Abby and I had finished all the logistics and insurance two days ago. We had a bus company setup to handle transportation and enough EMTs for each day to satisfy our insurance company. Samuel had given his blessings on the cost, and the councilman was thrilled. Once Mary and Scott signed the contracts, we were good to go.

Scott signed the indicated places and pushed up out of the booth before looking back down at us.

"Just let me know how many you will have for that first weekend and we can go from there. I can use what I have on hand and then lay in extra for the rest of the weekends," he said, wiping at his apron and nodding at us. "Looking forward to it, Kathi. Take it easy, Mary."

As he stumped back to the kitchen, Jill wandered over, dish towel over one shoulder and a couple of dirty glasses in her hand. I scowled up at her, my hangover memories still strong.

"What?" she said, looking down at me. She tried to look innocent, but I saw the twitch of her lips and the laughter dancing in her eyes.

"Don't you 'what' me. I'm never going out with you ever again." She tipped her head back and laughed as I glowered at her.

"Girl," she crowed, "you don't know the meaning of the word 'party.' It took five shots of tequila to get you loose enough to start having some fun."

I glanced around to make sure none of the other customers could overhear us. That would be just perfect if one of the gossipy townspeople heard me talking about losing my bra due to a tequila-filled night. Not to mention, Samuel would literally have a cow.

"Fun? I can't ever show my face there again. Not to mention my bra is probably still hanging in that light," I hissed.

"Okay, that *was* pretty funny," she said, setting the glasses down on the table. "You had every guy's attention after that. Hell, once your boobs started bouncing for everyone to see, I was pretty much ignored."

That all-too-familiar heat exploded up my neck. Jill started laughing harder. A snort from across the table yanked my eyes in Mary's direction. I glared at her as she fought to keep her laughter inside. Before I started on her, the bell over the door jingled as someone came in. Jill's face lit up at the newcomer.

"Mark! Hey stud, you are a sight for sore eyes, darling," she crooned at him.

Oh shit. I took a calming, deep breath. *Why'd he have to come in here right now? Right when Jill was reminding me of that night? Shoot me now.*

I glanced up as Mark stopped beside Jill and wrapped her up in a side hug. Out of nowhere, an odd flare of annoyance blossomed as I watched him cuddle up to Jill.

What the hell was that all about?

Mark nodded to us, his eyes landing on mine before he spoke. "Kathi, how ya feeling today? Head doing okay?" he asked, not even bothering to hide his grin.

Oh, here we go. Own it, just own it.

I smiled sweetly up at him. "I'm fine, thank you. Nothing for you to worry about."

He let Jill go from the side hug and crossed his arms over his chest, one hand reaching up to swipe at his nose as he sniffed. I couldn't help myself. My eyes traveled to his arms, noting the way the muscles flexed and pulled at the sleeve of the faded green t-shirt he wore today. Or how tanned his arms looked. As an image of those bare arms picking me up started forming in my head, a sharp pain in my shin jerked me out of fantasyland.

I glanced over at Mary with wide eyes and a 'what the hell' look. She nodded slightly towards Mark and raised one eyebrow. My daydream about his arms must've still been fogging my thought processes, because I was clueless as to what she was trying to tell me. She rolled her eyes at my obvious idiocy before looking up at Mark and taking things into her own hands.

"Mark, got any big plans for the next few weekends?" she asked.

He reached up and pulled his ball cap off his head and scuffed his hair before reseating the cap. My fingers twitch as I imagined what that hair would feel like as it filtered through my fingers. I gave myself a quick mental shake. *Jesus girl, get a grip. This isn't high school. This guy is barely in his twenties and about fifteen years younger than you.*

He shook his head before setting his cap back in place. "No, nothing out of the ordinary. Need help with something?"

Mary nodded her head towards me. "Nope, but Kathi does." She looked back at me, smiling, trying to appear innocent. I wasn't buying it. Once we were alone, I was going to claw her eyes out.

Mark slid his gaze over to me, the grin on his face causing one corner of his mouth to lift higher. It felt like his eyes were burning through me as my cheeks heated. There was something in that gaze, something giving me the impression that his idea of doing something for me differed from mine. As if betraying my mind, several other parts of me whipped out pad and paper and began making a list of what *they* wanted him to do to me. I took a quick sip of my drink, stalling for time.

"Yes," I tried to say, but my throat sounded like a frog had taken up residence in there. I smiled up at him. Trying to be the professional I knew I could be while keeping my obviously insane hormones under control, I took a few moments to catch him up on the outreach plan and what would happen at Mary's place.

When I finished, he nodded enthusiastically. "That's a great thing to do," he said. "I think that's outstanding for your company to step in and help. I know the kids will be thrilled. What can I do for you?"

He flashed me that grin again, and the lists that my parts were making went into extra pages.

I gave him my best non-hormonal salesperson look. "Well, I hoped you would volunteer to do demonstrations of trimming and shoeing. I know you probably do a bunch of work on weekends, so we'd compensate you for any lost wages or other expenses."

He studied me for a few moments quietly, pursing his lips. It was a simple request, but he was taking an awful long time thinking about it. Just as I thought I would need to plead my case, he nodded, and I felt relief wash over me. And maybe, if I was honest with myself, I also felt a bit of excitement knowing that he was going to be there, working with me.

"Sure. Love to do it. You let me know when, and I'll be there," he said.

Mary tapped the table twice with one finger, dragging my attention from Mark's handsome face. "See, told you he would help you if you asked."

I glance back up at Mark and smile. "Thank you, Mark. We really appreciate it. Let me know how much we need to compensate you for any missed work."

He waved a hand at me, dismissing my words. "No worries. Not going to cost you a cent," he said.

"Aw, told ya he was a good one," said Jill, reaching up to pat Mark's cheek as he turned toward her. Another stab of annoyance at Jill raised its head.

What on earth was going on with me?

I had no idea why I was feeling so annoyed at seeing Mark grinning at Jill.

I looked up at him and smiled. "That's very gracious of you, Mark," I said. "Thank you. We are still finishing up some details but the first weekend will be April second through the fourth, and then every weekend after that for the next month. I can give you a better schedule once we have it all nailed down." He nodded again. Thinking we were done, I turned my attention back to Mary.

"But," said Mark, pulling all our eyes back to him, it *will* cost you in another way."

"Excuse me?" I asked, puzzled. "You just said—" Mark raised his hand up, stopping my response.

"I said it wouldn't cost you a *cent*. I didn't say my time was free," he replied, a mischievous glint lighting up his eyes.

I glanced over at Mary, who shrugged her shoulders.

Turning back to Mark, I asked, "Um, okay, Mark. If you don't want money, what do you want?"

"Dinner."

"Oh." I raised my eyebrows, thinking. "Well, okay. I guess we can arrange a gift certificate or something. What restaurant were you thinking of?"

He chuckled and shook his head. Then he gave me a look that was hard to read. He was smiling, but his eyes said something else that I couldn't figure out. I refused to let myself get draw in by the dimple that smile created and its effect on my pulse rate.

"No, you don't understand. I want dinner with *you*. A date. You. Me. Dinner," he said, as he crossed his arms and stared at me.

For several seconds, there was no sound at the table. Mary was staring up at him with her mouth open. Jill turned her head to face him, eyes wide.

I was speechless, my mind failing to fully process the words he had spoken. It sounded like he had just asked me to have dinner.

Mary suddenly broke out laughing and clapping her hands slowly.

"Damn Mark, good one. Not as funny as tying those old horseshoes to my bumper, but still. Good one."

My nervous laugh sounded as strained and I hoped the others didn't pick up on it. Of course. It was just another one of his pranks. Jill snorted and hugged Mark again.

Stop touching him, Jill. I quieted that inner voice as quickly as it shouted its protest.

Mary wiped her eyes and sighed. She looked up at Mark again and chuckled lightly. Her laughter died on her lips as she squinted at him. She looked at me, then back at Mark. I watched her as she bounced back and forth between us, confused. Suddenly, her eyes widened and her jaw dropped.

"Holy shit," Mary whispered. "You're not joking, are you? You seriously just asked Kathi out on a date, didn't you?"

My eyes widened as I stared up at Mark. He held my gaze, allowing a small wisp of a smile to grace his lips. My heart started beating so loud I was sure everyone there could hear it. *Had he really just done that?*

"I did," he confirmed, never breaking eye contact with me. "Kathi?"

Jill and Mary both looked at me as I tried to get my mouth to work. I knew I looked like a deer caught in the headlights of a car. Mary kicking me under the table brought me back to reality. Once again, as seemed to happen any time I was around this man, heat crept up my neck.

"Oh. I… that is, I…" I grabbed my glass and took another drink, my mind refusing to put coherent sentences together. I sat the glass back down and gave Mark what I thought was a gracious and heartfelt smile.

"I'm flattered Mark, really. You're a nice guy, but I think, given our age difference, that wouldn't be appropriate. Can't we come up with something else?"

Come up with something else. Please come up with something else. Please don't come up with something else…wait…what?

Mark put one finger to his chin and stared off into the distance, seeming to consider. I held my breath. Decision apparently reached, he turned that dimpled grin back to me.

"Nope. That's my price. One dinner. With you."

I couldn't help the small groan that escaped. I really needed Mark to help us out to round out the schedule. Between Mary and me, we'd come up with quite a few activities, but not enough to fill the weekend. I'd even volunteered to give demonstrations on jumping.

"I'm sorry, Mark—"

"Mark, how bout we check back with you tomorrow?" Mary piped up, cutting me off.

Mark glanced at her, then back at me. He nodded slowly.

"Sure, take your time. You both have my number. Call and let me know. Or you know… a text." He gave Jill a quick hug, touched his fingers to his hat at us, and headed towards the door. We all stared at his retreating form. It didn't escape my attention how nicely his worn jeans hugged his rear as he left the building.

"That boy's as good going as he is coming," purred Jill. I was tempted to growl at her.

Where was all of this coming from?

Jill turned to look at me. Her hand struck like a snake, popping me lightly on the head.

I reared back in the booth. "HEY! What was that for?" I asked, rubbing at the painful spot.

Jill crossed her arms and just shook her head. "Have you *lost your mind*?" she asked. "How can you seriously turn down a date with that stud? I'd climb that boy like a monkey in a tree."

"*Boy*," I spouted back at her. "He's way too young for me. I could almost be his *mother*. We have nothing in common. What would we talk about or do?" My body, betraying me once again, listed a few things it wanted to do with him. Or *to* him.

I was prepared for Jill to argue back. Instead, she started laughing. I glanced at Mary, but she shrugged her shoulders. We both looked back at Jill.

"Wow," she said, her breath coming in pants. She took a deep breath but managed another weak laugh before grinning at me.

"Girl, I haven't had a laugh that good in months."

Jill glanced back over her shoulder before sliding into the seat next to Mary. She leaned forward, keeping her voice low.

"Question for you. Did you have fun the other night?"

I glared at her. "We will *not* speak of the other night."

"Yeah, yeah, grandma. Answer the question. Forget the aftermath. Did you have fun?"

I sat back, crossed my arms, and stared at her. Neither of the two had the decency to look ashamed about 'The Night', or, as I had been thinking of it, 'Tequila Trouble.'

It had taken me most of the next day to recover. But, if I was being honest, I had to admit that I'd had a good time. It'd felt good to have cut loose, dance, and hang with Jill and Mary. It had been a long time since I'd let myself have that much fun, despite Abby making it her life mission to get me laid. She'd been ecstatic when I mentioned my birthday plans. After that night, she'd also read me the riot act for not snagging some bedtime companionship and sweating my way into forty.

I rolled my eyes and muttered under my breath.

"What was that? Didn't quite hear ya?" Jill said, cupping a hand around one ear.

"Fine. I had fun. There. Happy?" I asked. My scowling at her didn't appear to bother her one darn bit.

"Oh, I will be in a moment. Second question. Did you have anything in common with those guys you were dancing and rubbing up against?"

"Keep your voice down!" I hissed, glancing around the diner. Luckily, no one was close enough to overhear her.

Jill just sat there staring at me, one eyebrow cocked up.

I gave my head a small shake. "No, I didn't know them. So, nothing in common. Is the third degree over?"

"Last question," she said. The look in her eyes told me I was going to dread this last question.

"How old were those guys you were having fun with?"

"That was the *tequila*, not *me*."

Mary snorted and then tried quickly to cover her mouth. Her innocently blinking eyes did not fool me.

"Well," said Jill, "that may be true for later in the evening. Answer the question."

"No idea."

Jill leaned forward. "Let me give you a clue. That place is one of my favorite bars because it has, shall we say, a very selective entry policy. Remember getting carded?"

I nodded. I thought it unusual at the time, but figured it was some weird law I was not aware of.

"Before Friday night, *you* would have never been allowed through the door," Jill said. "They only allowed you in because your birthday was the next day and *I* knew the bouncers."

I gave her my most clueless look, since I had no idea what my birthday had to do with it.

Mary just laughed and shook her head. "You're gonna have to spell it out for her. Use small words." I glared at Mary as Jill shook her head.

"Kathi," Jill said. "That was a cougar bar. You know what that is, right?"

I couldn't speak, my brain stuck trying to grasp her words correctly. It didn't slow her down.

"Their policy for admittance is very strict. They don't allow women under forty inside. Guys have to be between twenty-one and thirty-two," she replied. Jill leaned a bit closer, grinning before continuing. "So, Miss Prim and Proper, you spent the night partying, dancing, and getting up close and personal with a bunch of guys Mark's age. Well, some younger, some older, to be honest."

And the hits just kept coming. I looked at Mary, who was doing all she could to not laugh and failing miserably. When I looked back at Jill, her grin was both evil and smug, all at the same time.

"But, you... that is, you didn't go home with us. So, you actually..." I let my voice trail off as Jill nodded her head slowly as her lips rose in a wicked grin.

"Yep, I found me a nice boy-toy and played with him all night long. Oh, the stamina of youth. It was a shame to ruin him for girls his age." She sighed, a small smile on her face as she stared off into the distance.

God, she was as bad as Regina.

"Well," I said, trying to hold on to my dignity, "that was then. Now, if you are through harassing me, I will head back to my normal, boring world."

I slid out of the booth and stood up. Jill was out of her side of the booth and standing next to me in a flash. Her hand on my shoulder stopped me, keeping me looking at her.

"Look," she said, her voice low but with a serious tone, "I used to think the same as you and because of it, I spent a lot of years alone. I went through something that changed my thinking, something I won't go into." She paused, giving my shoulder a light squeeze before continuing.

"Age is just a number, honey. An indicator of time passing. Love's more than a number. It doesn't care about age or gender. Accept it when it comes and be happy. Life's too short to not be happy."

The words and the way she said them struck me, and I experience a pull deep down in my chest as she searched my eyes for a few more moments, then squeezed my shoulder again. Turning, she nodded at Mary, picked up her glasses and headed over to the counter to check on her other customers. I gave Mary a hug when she stood up and promised to call her later. After making my way to my car, I pulled out onto the road. As I turned for home, Jill's words played over and over again in my mind.

Later that night, as I sat on my bed in my PJs, I stared at my phone, all of my thoughts bouncing around like bingo balls in a cage. Even after coming home and going through my nighttime routine, I still couldn't get my mind to stop thinking about Mark and Jill's parting words.

Memories flitted through my mind of lunch with my friends and with Regina. Listening to her talk about her latest young lover. And how, once she left, we ridiculed her.

And then there was Samuel's view on things, not to mention my own thoughts about the age difference. All of these things weighed heavy on my mind, Jill's words running over the top of all of it.

Simon broke me out of my thoughts when he leapt up on the bed and began head butting my arm. I reached up to rub his black furred head, as he purred and rubbed my arm, begging for more attention.

I stared at the tuxedo cat in front of me. "What should I do, Simon? He's so much younger than me. What would people say?"

Simon took that moment to plop down, hike up his back leg, and bend over to clean himself. I had to admit, I admired his flexibility.

"You have no shame, do you?" I asked. I carried on speaking, since he obviously wasn't going to answer me, ignoring the extremely limber cat and his grooming habits.

"He's younger than me, Simon. I mean, he *is* good looking. Okay, he's a stud, just like Jill said. Those arms, and that chest." I gave myself a small shake, stopping that train of thought before it got too far out of the station.

Oblivious to my issues, Simon finished cleaning himself, head-butted my arm again, and proceeded to curl up in a ball next to me.

I eyed him, jealous of the few worries he had at the moment. "So sorry my problems bore you." His tail flipped once, acknowledging that he heard me speak, before wrapping back around his curled form.

After rolling my eyes at the little unhelpful black and white furry circle, I stared at my phone and tried to make sense of my thoughts.

Dinner. He wanted dinner. Was I overthinking this? Possibly. He didn't ask me to marry him or spend a night with him. Just dinner. I could do dinner. Friends do dinner all the time. Dinner. Nice, safe dinner. What could go wrong?

Nodding to myself, decision made, I scrolled through my contacts until I came to Mark's entry and selected the message option.

I stared at the small cursor blinking in the empty message box. I typed out a message, erased it, typed it again, erased it again. The right words didn't seem to want to come out.

I berated myself for acting like a teenager with a crush. I typed my message and hit send before I could overthink it. Panic bloomed like gas on a fire. Teenage drama, indeed.

> Kathi: Hey, are you still up?

I waited for what seemed like hours, but was in reality only a minute or two, before my phone chirped and the response popped in.

> Mark: Nope, sound asleep.

I grinned. He was just as much a smartass as Jake.

> Kathi: Wake up then.

> Mark: <yawn> Okay, I'm awake. And I still don't send those kinds of pictures.

As my cheeks flushed, I reminded myself that I was never drinking again.

> Kathi: That is not why I am texting.

> Mark: Glad we cleared that up. Soooo why did you text me?

This was the moment of truth. I took another deep breath and pressed the keys before I could change my mind.

> Kathi: Are you sure about this dinner thing?

His response was almost immediate.

> Mark: Yes.

> Kathi: Okay. I'll have dinner with you.

> Mark: Excellent. This Friday night work for you?

Lord, that was in four days. Just four days. I bit my lip as I responded.

> Kathi: I guess that'll work. What time?

> Mark: How about 5? Oh, and I hope you like airplane food.

I cocked my head to the side as I reread his message. Airplane food? Why would he be asking me about that? No. He couldn't mean, that is, he couldn't be planning to fly us somewhere for dinner? Best to nip that in the bud right away.

> Kathi: Mark, that's way too expensive for a simple dinner with a friend.

> Mark: Trust me, you're gonna love it. Dress casual.

I sighed. Seems he didn't want me to argue with him.

> Kathi: Okay. I'll trust you.

I sent him my address and the code to the gate and he wished me goodnight. I put my phone back on the nightstand and then stretched out on my bed. I stared up at the ceiling as Simon crawled up on my stomach and assumed his catatonic sleeping position.

"Simon, what have I done?" I asked softly. I smoothed my hand over his head, praying that the reticent feline would answer me with some divine wisdom. Alas, it was not to come, unless his wisdom was that I should think about things and figure it out on my own. As it was, I drifted off to sleep, waiting for a response as Simon snored gently on my chest.

SEVEN

It had been four long days since I'd agreed to dinner with Mark. Abby knew something was up, but I refused to divulge any information. She'd been like a dog with a bone, peppering me with questions, digging at me constantly. I seriously believed she missed her calling in life. I'm sure she would have been the CIA's best interrogator without breaking a sweat.

When I called Mary to tell her we could count on Mark, she laughed and asked me when she should expect the wedding invite. She also told me I had a curfew, and that she would not wait up. I'd told her exactly where to put her invitation *and* her curfew.

Now it was Friday night, and Mark would be here soon. I stepped back to admire myself in the full-length mirror next to my dresser, and I had to admit that I looked pretty good. The woman staring back at me could easily pass for someone much younger than my forty years.

When I began getting more serious about my jumping and riding, I found out quickly that my physical conditioning and overall fitness was sorely lacking. I began working out most every day of the week in some form. I joined a gym near work and hired a trainer to help me set up a workout and fitness routine.

After Jeremy's death, I threw myself into my work. I cut way back on the jumping, only doing it occasionally to keep myself and Ringo in practice. However, I kept up the workout routine because I realized I had more energy and felt better overall. It also didn't hurt my vanity that I got more than my share of admiring looks around the gym.

I turned sideways, checking the fit of my jeans as I smoothed one hand down the side of my blouse. I glanced at the dresser where Simon sat, peering at me occasionally as he groomed himself.

"Simon, have I lost my mind?"

The cat paused mid-lick of his raised paw, gave me a two-second stare, before swiping his face with the now saliva-loaded appendage. He repeated the cleaning process several times, once again not bothering to answer my question.

"I mean, come on. What was I thinking saying yes to Mark? Does he think this is an actual date, or just friends having dinner? And let's not forget the age difference. People are going to think I'm his mother. God, I'm as bad as Regina. I know it's for the kids, but this is a bad idea, right?" I asked, never giving thought to how babbling to a cat said little for my sanity.

Simon's yawn stretched his mouth open, displaying all of his teeth. As he closed his mouth, he gave me a look that I swore was his way of saying I was indeed crazy. He twitched one ear, hopped down from the dresser, and strolled out of my bedroom, tail held high.

"I'm feeding you the cheap cat food for dinner!" I yelled. With a last glance at the mirror, I followed the stuck-up cat.

The small clock on the oven read 4:45. Mark was going to be here soon. It was too late to call and cancel. I looked down at the cat, who was now munching his food.

"This is a bad idea, Simon. He's taking me to the airport and there's no telling where we will end up. How does a farrier even have that kind of money?"

I closed my eyes and took a deep breath. I needed to relax. If Mark was a sleaze or an asshole, Jake and Mary wouldn't trust him around their family and ranch. He and Jake were friends, and Jake was pretty picky about who he let get close. My mind flashed back to Jake's words from that day before court.

Find a different pool to swim in. Guarantee you, there is someone out there for you. He won't care about your age.

I paused, considering those words. Had Jake known that Mark was interested in me? Being friends, it seemed he could have had some inkling. It made me wonder just how long had this set up been in the planning phases?

I glanced down at my unsupportive companion. "I think me and my adopted nephew need to have a talk, Simon."

The gate buzzer went off, sparing Simone from answering. My time to reconsider this date was up. I glanced at the monitor mounted on the wall near the refrigerator. A black car was at the gate, one that I didn't recognize. It wasn't Mark's truck that I had seen at the farm so many times. Well, maybe it wasn't Mark after all. Who was this? As I moved my finger to activate the intercom, an arm came out, and the hand began stabbing at the keypad. The man's face was now clearly visible. It was Mark. What car was he in?

As the gate was lumbering open, the butterflies in my stomach began stretching and limbering up. Moments later, when the doorbell rang, they all lined up for takeoff. With a final deep breath, I stepped up and opened the door.

My breath caught in my throat and all I could think was... w*ow!*

He looked... good. Real good. A small zing zipped through me as my eyes roamed over him. He had trimmed up his scruff, but not shaved it off. It gave him a slightly bad-boy look and I really, *really* liked it. His shirt was a nice crisp white button down and I appreciated the way it fit, just tight enough to outline his chest and broad shoulders. His dark jeans looked new, and he was wearing a nice pair of loafers, instead of the cowboy boots I expected.

"Kathi?"

His voice brought me out of my thoughts. I had no idea how long he had been talking to me. I gave myself a mental shake.

Get a grip, woman. He's young enough to be your son. This is not a date-date.

I bit my lip. "Sorry, hi. Would you like to come in?"

He shook his head. "Actually, I think we should go ahead and leave." His eyes traced over me before he continued, his voice deepening slightly. "But, wow, Kathi, you look fantastic! Here, this is for you," he said as he brought his hand from around his back, holding something out to me.

A rose. A single white rose.

Mark had been the first man to send me flowers in a long time when he'd sent that bouquet to my office a few weeks ago. Now he'd now done it again, and in a much more intimate way. The zing that was still buzzing inside of me ramped up to a light, all-over tingle.

I took the flower from his hand, giving it an appreciative sniff. "Thank you, Mark. It's lovely."

"It pales compared to you, Kathi," he said, giving me a softer smile. I couldn't help the eye roll and the small snort.

He looked surprised at my response. "What?" he asked, stiffening slightly. *Did he always look that innocent?*

Now I felt a little like a jerk. Here he was, being nice to me, and I was laughing at him. I smirked at him, trying to lighten the moment. "How often does that line work for you?"

It worked. He grinned at me again as the zings began moving around like pinballs hitting bumpers. A warmth grew inside me, like someone had stoked the bank embers of a fire back to life. What was going on here? This was dinner with a friend. Not a date. Certainly not a date-date. But what was it about his dimpled smile that made me feel like this?

"First time I've ever used it, so I'll let you know at the end of the night. Shall we go?"

I placed the flower on the small table in the hallway and stepped out onto the porch, closing the door behind me. I followed him down the brick steps to the driveway and paused to admire the sleek, waiting car. Given he was a young guy working with horses and around farms, I'd expected him to arrive in his truck. What I hadn't expected was to see him drive up in an all-black Cadillac. I was even more surprised when he opened my door for me and waited expectantly.

"Thank you," I said before pivoting to sit down and into the car. As

I did, his cologne breezed past me and I found it a pleasing combination of warm leather and a smoky fire.

The smooth black leather seats were comfortable and the entire interior was clean and shiny. Once my feet were in, Mark closed the door and moved around to the driver's side. A short minute later and we were turning out of the driveway. Soft classical music whispered from the speakers.

I glanced over at Mark and couldn't help the thoughts running through my head. He was an enigma. To see him at work and around the farm, he was a typical working ranch hand. Dusty jeans, worn t-shirt, boots. Absolutely nothing about him would scream at any level of sophistication.

But tonight he was completely different. I couldn't think of any other term, just... perfect. Nice clothes, manners, very nice car, classical music. I was having a hard time reconciling this Mark with the one I had kneed in the gonads.

His voice brought me out of my musing. "You're thinking way too hard over there. Should I be worried?"

"No," I replied, bring my thoughts back to the moment.

"So, what's got you all quiet?" he asked. Before I could answer, we were at the interstate junction. However, instead of heading towards Denver, he turned south towards Colorado Springs.

"We're flying out of the Springs?" I asked, again trying to figure out what he was planning. He glanced at me, smiling, before turning back to the road.

"Our plane is in the Springs," he said. Once he was on the interstate, the car's acceleration was so smooth that I couldn't even tell we sped up.

I ran my hand over the black leather dashboard. "Nice car."

He glanced at me again before looking back at the road.

"Thanks. You sound surprised?" he asked. His curiosity appeared genuine.

"I figured that you'd pick me up in the truck," I replied, not wanting to insult him. Instead of being offended, he laughed. I relaxed my shoulders in relief.

"Well, sorry to disappoint you. If you want, we can turn around and I can change vehicles?"

Stop being a jerk!

I fumbled for words to reassure him. "No, please. It's okay. I just assumed..." I let my words trail off, not wanting to finish the sentence and make even more of a fool of myself.

"Ahh," he said. "You assumed since I was a '*young kid*'," he said, using air quote for emphasis, "I'd only have a beat-up old truck. Right?"

The accuracy of his statement was frightening. Since he'd arrived at my gate, Mark was proving to be nothing like I expected, and I didn't enjoy making a fool of myself.

I looked over at him. "Look Mark, I'm sorry if I offended you. You're... well, you're not what I expected tonight."

His laughter surprised me and made me feel even more embarrassed.

"You think that's funny?" I asked, a small touch of unease and anger in my tone. He immediately stopped laughing and a slight grin quirked up a corner of his mouth.

"Yes, I do. I'm *glad* I'm not what you expected. That means there's a lot for you to learn about me as I learn about you. I think that's a good thing." He paused, giving me an opening, but I stayed silent. As I considered his words, my anger at his laughter eased.

"And for the record," he continued, "I have several vehicles. The work truck you've already seen. I have a Jeep that I usually drive when I'm not working. And of course, I have this car that I like to take out whenever the situation warrants."

His words piqued my curiosity. "And why did tonight warrant?"

He gave me a longer look. His eyes captured mine, and they were full of heat and promise and something else I couldn't really identify.

"Because I wanted to impress a beautiful, intelligent woman," he stated quietly.

The squadrons of butterflies that had been lying in wait throughout our conversation launched themselves in my stomach at the same time that a subtle warm wave flushed through me. I knew right then that tonight would not be like any other date.

No, this wasn't a date, and I needed to make sure he knew that.

I sighed. "Mark, I want to make sure you understand that this is just dinner with a friend. Not a date, okay?"

He gave me a side glance and looked back at the road.

"Whatever you say, Kathi." But by his tone, I could tell that he didn't completely believe me. And if I were completely honest, I wasn't sure I did, either.

For the rest of the trip to Colorado Springs, we kept the conversation to familiar topics, mostly about Mary and Jake, the ranch, and his work as a farrier. It seemed like no time passed, but it was actually close to 5:30 p.m. when he began making his way through the city towards the airport.

I spied the control tower and the tops of a few hangers, which caused me to once again wonder where we were flying. When he slowed and turned into a parking lot, my confusion reached new levels. This wasn't an airport, just some undefined building. There were several cars around us and the sidewalks led to some stairs, which led up to a set of double doors, which a family was exiting.

On a second glance at the building, I noticed what appeared to be a large airplane sitting off to one side of the building. It was huge and silvery; old looking. The tail seemed to stretch up to the sky for miles. When I looked closer, it appeared as if the plane and the building were merged. I looked over towards Mark only to see a smile spreading across his face. He shut the car off and popped the locks.

"Ready to eat?" he asked, still grinning.

I was confused and I'm sure it showed. "You said we were flying somewhere, but this isn't part of the airport. What is this place?" I asked, waving my hand towards the building.

The corner of his mouth twitched upwards slightly. "Kathi, I *never* said we were flying anywhere. I asked if you like airplane food. This place is where we are eating. It's called the Airplane Restaurant."

"Huh?" I asked, still lost. *Brilliant response, Kathi.*

"Come on, you'll see," he said, opening his door. As he stood up, I reached for my door handle, but he ducked his head back in and fixed a stare on me before I could grab it.

"Please don't," he said. I paused my hand where it was, waiting as he came around to my side of the car. After opening my door, he held out his hand.

As I placed my hand in his, a light shock ran up my arm. It was like touching a piece of metal after walking across a carpet. As he helped me to stand, I heard his sharp intake of breath and knew that he'd felt it, too.

I willed the fluttering in my stomach to be calm. "Mark, I *am* capable of getting out of a car."

Still holding my hand, he cocked his head at me. "Without a doubt. But, my grandmother, if she were still alive, would lecture me to death on the proper manners to exhibit when escorting a lady. A switch *might* have been used to emphasize her point." Then he got a lopsided grin on his face and leaned in a little closer.

"Besides," he whispered, his lips next to my ear and his breath causing a delicious shiver to trail down my neck, "this way I get to hold your hand."

I groaned and rolled my eyes as he started laughing. He placed my hand in the crook of his arm and led me towards the restaurant.

When we entered the building, the size and decor was a pleasant surprise. It was older, but cozy and classy at the same time. The interior held a dining area on one side and a small bar area nearby. Part of what appeared to be the plane's wing and engines was visible, with the wing serving as a roof to the larger dining area.

Pictures of aircraft, along with other flying memorabilia, lined the walls. Several couples and a few families occupied some tables, and a few others were at the bar. Several enticing aromas tickled my nose and I couldn't help but turn my head towards what must be the kitchen, based on the clatter of plates and pans.

Mark led us over to a young woman standing near a small podium. She smiled at our approach and welcomed us.

"Good evening! Welcome to the Airplane Restaurant. Just two?" she asked.

He smiled and nodded at her. "Yes, and we'd like to sit inside the plane, if possible."

"Absolutely, sir. Right this way," she said. Picking up some silverware bundles and a couple of menus, she led us off towards a small set of stairs.

We followed her up the stairs and I was surprised when we were actually inside what appeared to be the airplane I saw from outside. To our immediate left was the cockpit, plexiglass across the doorway allowing for a view inside while keeping everyone out. A narrow aisle ran down the center of the plane. At the end of the aisle, there appeared to be another plexiglass-covered opening.

On either side of the aisle were cozy two-person booths. The interior was what you would expect from an older plane. Small booths butted up against the rounded fuselage walls. Track lighting ran along the peak of the ceiling over each row of booths.

The waitress led us to the farthest booth from the stairs. Mark held my hand again as I lowered myself and slid across the brown and spongy cushion. Mark waited till I was seated, then slid into the other side. The booth was just big enough for the two of us without being cramped.

Once we were settled, the hostess handed us our menus. "Your server will be right with you. Enjoy your meal." With that, she disappeared back down to her post to help the next waiting customers.

Glancing around the intimate space, I shook my head and focused back on Mark, who had an amused expression on his face.

He sat back, watching me. "Not what you were expecting?"

"To be honest, no. You had me thinking we were flying somewhere, so I was trying to figure out how a farrier afforded that. Then you pulled up in that nice car and…" I let those last words trail off as I realized I was babbling, and again voicing the terrible assumptions I had made.

He chuckled as the waitress came up to take our drink order.

"Trust me?" he asked. I nodded. He asked for two glasses of some beer I did not recognize. The waitress smiled and left.

"It's a local brew from a brewhouse I discovered last month. It's really good and I think you'll like it."

"Okay."

I turned my attention to the menu, trying to buy some time to recover from the constant surprises and my mistaken assumptions. I had to laugh at the names assigned to some of the dishes.

"'Reuben von Crashed?' Seriously?" I asked.

He shrugged and chuckled. "No worse than 'Air Tower Nachos.'"

When the waitress came back with our drinks, we both ordered the cheeseburger with onion rings. After she left, Mark took a sip of his beer and set the glass back carefully on the table. When he looked up, his eyes locked with mine. I suppressed a shiver at the intensity of that gaze as a warmth began spreading within me. He blinked and just as quickly, the intensity dialed down and he grinned at me.

I took a sip of the beer and glanced at the glass, pleasantly surprised. It was very good, with a hint of citrus complimenting its light flavor.

"You like it?"

I took another slow sip, letting the liquid sit on my tongue as I enjoyed the flavor. I swallowed as I set the glass down. I smiled at him even as I let my tongue take a final swipe at the inside of my mouth.

"It's actually very good. I love the bit of citrus. Lime?"

My praise caused him to grin and nod. "Yes. The guys who brew it really like to try new things. I've got several of their beers at the house and I always pick up the new flavors when they come out.

"As I said earlier, this place," he stated, waving his hand around at the inside of the plane, "is not what you were expecting, is it?"

"No, it's not. I am curious about why this place?"

"So you wouldn't be worried about your society friends seeing you with me. Hopefully, you would relax and have a good time."

Sitting back against the booth, I stared at him, not sure if I should be upset or ashamed at his unfortunately accurate assessment. When I didn't speak up, he continued.

"Look. You're already nervous about the age difference between us. I get it. Really, I do. I also know you're big in the social circles of Denver. Our society applies a double standard regarding couples who have an age difference. Older men get congratulated and patted on the back if they date or marry someone much younger. However, society gives women a hard time and frowns upon them if they do the same. Is that a fair assessment?"

I nodded, using the moment to take a healthy drink of my beer, loving the flavor more and more. He nodded as well and continued.

"So, I brought you here. We're an hour or more away from Denver. I like this place. It's different. The food is good, and I bet that no one from your social circles would ever enter this place voluntarily. Correct?"

I nodded again, because knowing my friends, he wasn't wrong.

"Great. That means that you can relax, eat a great burger, drink an excellent beer, and we can get to know each other better."

As if on cue, our food arrived. We took a few moments to get everything situated. As I took my first bite, Mark watched expectantly. The burger melted in my mouth and the seasonings exploded with flavor. Something in my expression must have betrayed me, because Mark chuckled.

He bounced his eyebrows and grinned. "Good, huh?"

I chewed the bite slowly, savoring the heavenly sensations playing across my taste buds. Swallowing, I dabbed at my mouth with my napkin before looking back at him.

"I think this has to be the best burger I've ever eaten."

He nodded before taking a healthy bite of his own. I found myself observing his jaw and how it worked as he chewed. All the preconceived notions I had about both tonight and Mark rattled through my head, embarrassing me. It was dawning on me at how unfair I had been to Mark. All of that and more swept through my mind as I realized he was gazing at me intently. He swallowed and took another drink.

"You're still thinking too hard over there. Talk to me, Kathi."

I took another bite of my burger, stalling for time. Mark didn't fill in the time with idle conversation. He waited, giving me his complete and undivided attention. Somehow, I knew Mark wouldn't be checking his phone or glancing around at the other diners, or trying to mansplain the workings of the federal banking system. Instead, I would have his undivided attention.

And I found that thought incredibly appealing.

Finishing my bite, I took a deep breath and confessed.

"Mark, I owe you another apology. It seems like all I'm doing tonight is apologizing to you."

He started to respond, but stopped. Maybe something in the tone of my voice registered, or he saw something in my eyes. He waited a few seconds before responding.

"For what?" he asked as he leaned forward, focusing on me.

"For making some horrible assumptions about you. It was wrong and I feel bad about it. So, I'm sorry." I searched his face, looking for any hint of his reaction.

He continued to gaze at me. The quiet stretched for what seemed hours, but was really only seconds. He glanced down at his burger, then back up at me.

"Kathi, you have nothing to be sorry about. I told you in the car that it was a good thing that your expectations were wrong. Hell, you know virtually nothing about me, so all you could do was make assumptions."

"That still doesn't make what I did any less terrible, or make me any less ashamed."

He cocked his head at me, and I could see the wheels turning. I was beginning to understand that he liked to consider his words before speaking. I wonder how frustrated that made some people. He nodded his head and in an instant, that small grin was back.

"Apology accepted. What say we fix your assumptions? I know the perfect way to do that, if you're game."

I chuckled. He made things easy. "Sure. I can't make things any worse. What do we need to do?"

He grinned even bigger as he leaned forward, crooking one finger at me. I leaned in towards him, inhaling in his woodsy, leathery scent.

"We should go on a *date*. You ask questions and get to know me."
He wiggled his eyebrows at me and my jaw may have dropped.

I felt the flush at my neck at the realization I'd played right into his
trap. Very well. If that was how he wanted to do it... then *game on.*

EIGHT

I glared at him, and he grinned back. Frustrated, I had to concede that he had suckered me into admitting this was a date. I grabbed an onion ring, chewing to give myself time to recover.

Sitting back, he took a sip of his beer. Setting it back down on the table, he gave me his full attention once more.

"I'll start. Do you have a middle name?"

Nodding, I finished chewing and swallowing. When I didn't respond, he cocked an eyebrow.

"Leanne," I replied. I threw in a heavy sigh for dramatic effect, hoping for some sympathy. He seemed unsympathetic.

"Kathi Leanne Harrison. Is Kathi short for Katherine?"

"Nope, just Kathi."

He nodded before picking up his burger and taking a bite. He glanced at me, eyebrows going up in a query. His message was fairly clear. Fine. I could play this game.

"Do *you* have a middle name?"

He nodded as he finished his bite and swallowed. "Mark."

I cocked my head, not sure I had heard correctly. "I thought that was your first name?"

"Nope."

I waited for an explanation, but he just smiled. I hated having my own tactics used against me.

"Fine. What's your first name?"

"William."

"So William Mark Danlock. Why go by Mark and not Willie or Bill?"

"My dad's name is William and my mom calls him Bill. So being called Mark made it easier and less confusing for her. Then he looked at me, one eyebrow raised, and grinned. 'Willie'? *Really*?"

I suppressed a laugh. "Not Junior?"

He shook his head. "Nope, different middle names. Dad was named after his father and always hated being called 'Junior'. He didn't want me saddled with that."

Before I could ask my next question, the hostess entered with a couple holding a small toddler. She walked them past and seated them somewhere behind us. Mark followed them with his eyes, exposing the right side of his face. A thin white scar ran almost the length of his jawline.

"How'd you get that scar? Horse kick you?"

He turned back to me, his eyes focusing on me as his hand idly rubbed the scar.

"No, crab pot."

"Um, how could a pot do that?"

He took a drink of beer. "Well, I wasn't paying attention when my crewmates were moving a pot over to the launcher. Luckily, it only brushed me. If it had hit my head straight on, it would have probably killed me. Hazards of working on a slippery deck in the middle of a pitching sea."

What was he talking about? "I'm still not following?" I said, confused.

"Do you remember when I disappeared late last year and didn't show back up until a month or so ago?" I nodded. His uncle had helped with the horses while he was gone.

"A buddy of mine called me and asked me to come up and help him out. He's a deck boss on a crab boat. One of his deckhands got sick and couldn't sail with them, so they needed a replacement. I talked with my uncle and headed up to Alaska to try my hand at crab fishing. I'd seen it on TV and decided I wanted to give it a try."

Realization came quickly. "I've seen the commercials for that show. I even watched a couple of episodes. Those guys are crazy! You actually did *that*? And those pots are *huge*."

He rubbed his jaw again before giving a short laugh.

"Yeah, those guys are a different breed. Anyway, I was the new guy on the boat, what they call the 'greenhorn', if you remember that term from the show?" he asked. I nodded, and he continued.

"My job was to bait the pots. One day, we were working to get the pots into the water and beat some weather that was coming in. I'd grabbed a bait bundle and, instead of waiting like I was supposed to, I made a mistake and rushed in too soon. The empty pot was swinging towards the launcher and I got too close. At the last second, I heard the guys yelling at me and saw the shadow of the pot heading towards me. I tried to stop but skidded on the wet deck. I barely got my head turned enough to avoid getting it crushed. One of the wire strands of the pot nicked me as it swung by, opening my jaw as neat as a knife through butter." He rubbed at the scar again.

I gasped at the thought of his jaw being torn open and resisted the urge to reach out and touch the scar myself. "What did they do? Take you to the hospital? That must have taken a long time."

He shook his head and took another drink.

"No hospital when you're a couple hundred miles away from land. Captains put extra money towards first aid supplies. In my case, the cut was bloody, but not deep. One of the crew had some medical training, so he cleaned it up, put in a line of surgical glue, then closed it with a bunch of butterflies. Taped gauze over that and made me wear a water-proof hood to keep as much of the water out as possible. Lucky for me, I'd got a nasty cut last year which required stitches and a tetanus shot. Bandaged up, I was back out on the deck in an hour and working like nothing had happened." He shrugged.

I stared at him, wide-eyed. This man was full of surprises. "What if it had been serious?"

"They'd have contacted the Coast Guard and started back towards port. It depends on the seriousness. But life out there is tough. The crew deals with most of the injuries as best they can. Set a finger, stitch a wound, bandage you up, and get back to work."

I shook my head at the 'indestructible' mindsets of most guys. Didn't matter the age, they were all the same. Get up, rub some dirt in it, and keep going. Mark's next question pulled me back to the present.

"What do you do at Harrisons?" he asked, dragging a crunchy onion ring through ketchup and plopping it into his mouth. A small bloop of ketchup stayed at the corner of his mouth. The tip of his tongue flicked out to lap it up, and I found myself unusually focused on his mouth after that. So focused that I forgot to answer him.

"Where'd you go, Kathi?"

His question broke me from my trance, and my gaze shot back to his eyes. *Stop looking at his mouth, Kathi.*

"Sorry. I'm the Vice President of Community Outreach. It's my job to make sure we present the company in a good light to the community. I work with our CEO and board members to set up charity events and public relations events that help the community and put Harrisons in a positive light."

"Like sponsoring this event for the kids?" he asked. I nodded, taking a moment to munch on my sandwich.

He took a sip of his drink, peering at me over the glass. Setting it back on the table, he gave me another one of those intense glances.

"You like helping folks, don't you?" he asked.

"I do," I replied, wiping at the corner of my mouth and dropping my napkin back to my lap. "I think Jeremy created the job just to give me something to do. However, once I got my teeth in it, I found I had a knack for it. That, and I liked the way it made me feel. I've been fortunate and I like helping others who might not be as lucky."

"That's a good philosophy to live by," he said. "So, you've worked there a long time?"

I nodded, mentally tallying up the years. "Almost half my life has been tied up with Harrisons in one form or another. Jeremy and I married right out of college, and he started working there almost immediately. Then, I started there and the years sort of passed by."

The waitress returned to gather our plates and empty glasses. Once she left, Mark leaned forward on his elbows, looking at me with a serious expression on his face. I waited, unsure of what was about to happen.

"Okay, time for the third degree. What's your favorite food?"

I couldn't help but laugh. "Seriously? Third degree? When do the rubber hoses come out?"

His finger waggled in the air before my face. "Quit avoiding the question. Chop chop."

"Hmph. Fine. Pizza with pepperoni and Italian Sausage."

"Favorite movie?"

"Easy. *Sleepless in Seattle*," I said.

He leaned back in his chair and looked at me like I'd lost my mind and juggled kittens to boot.

"Please, tell me it's not so? *You've Got Mail* was a *much* better movie." He crossed his arms over his chest and gave me a hurt look. I wasn't buying it. "I'm not even sure we can be friends now."

"You can't be serious. He was *lying* to her. He should have told her as soon as he knew it was her." I crossed my own arms, daring him to contradict me.

He rolled his eyes before answering. "But if Annie had dropped all that sign nonsense and realized she was playing it safe with Walter, she could have gotten with Sam sooner." His finger tapping on the table emphasized each of his points.

I glared at him for a moment until the reality of the conversation caught up to me. I held up my hands as I spoke, amazement in my voice.

"Wait, wait, wait. *You* like rom-coms? We are seriously arguing over which was the better rom-com?"

Mark shrugged and gave me a slight wave of one hand. "Sure, what's not to like? Love, hope, happy ending. Isn't that what we all want?" He leaned forward and cocked his head, giving me a strange look.

"Let me guess. You 'assumed'," he said, flashing me air quotes, "that since I'm a guy, all I cared about was movies with lots of explosions and gunfire, and a bunch of chase scenes?"

He took my silence and downward glance as an answer to his question. His smirk was icing on the cake.

"Fine. Yes, that's what I thought. You were right. Happy?" I threw my hands up in the air.

He laughed lightly and shook his head. "Oh, let me see, a woman tells a man he was right. I think this has to be recorded somewhere. Other men will never believe this."

I smirked, trying not to laugh. "Laugh it up, fuzzball."

His eyebrows shot up slightly. "Did you just hit me with a *Star Wars* reference? *You* like *Star Wars*? You know Han shot first, right? It's a toss-up between *Star Wars* and *Lord of the Rings* as to which is my favorite series of movies!"

I gave him my most superior look. "Like hell he did. *Star Wars*, and all of its explosions, laser fire and ships chasing each other. Guess I wasn't too far off with my assumption," I said as I crossed my arms and mock-glared at him.

Chuckling, he nodded at me and touched his chest. "Touche."

"I will say, Mark, I'd never have taken you for a Tolkien fan."

He leaned forward, elbows back on the table.

"Love Tolkien. In my senior year of high school, our English teacher assigned us *The Hobbit* to read for the first semester. Hell, most of us thought *he* was a halfling, as short and hairy as he was. And lord, that man loved his food and drink."

The affection in his voice made me smile. "Sounds like you really liked him."

He nodded, his eyes brightening as he spoke. "I did. He really made stories come alive. He had us looking at the story from each of the character's perspectives. I can remember him asking us why Bilbo would do this or Aragorn would act a certain way. It was just how he taught."

He laughed softly and by the twinkle in his eyes and the up ticked corner of his mouth, I imagined he was recalling something amusing.

I had to know. "What?"

"When he signed my yearbook, he wrote 'Mark, may the hair on your toes never fall out.'"

"Oh, cool. He sounds like an outstanding teacher," I said, smiling at his obvious fondness for his old teacher.

I picked up my glass to take a drink and realized that Mark was looking past me. He crossed his eyes and made duck lips. He kept his face that way for a second or so and then let it morph into a grin. I glanced back over my shoulder to find an angelic little face grinning back at me.

Looking back at Mark, he was rolling his eyes and twitching his nose. The little girl giggled behind me.

Mark caught me staring at him. The smile that popped out made him seem like a little boy with his hand caught in a cookie jar.

"Sorry," he said.

I shook my head. "No need to say sorry. You like kids?" He nodded, eyes flicking back over my shoulder and then back to me.

"Always have. They're fun, innocent, full of life, and the simplest things make them happy."

He looked at the little girl one more time before focusing back on me.

"Did you and Jeremy not want kids?"

My face sobered as the innocent question stirred up old feelings, old wounds that, while time had dulled, still had an occasional ache.

"We tried for years but didn't find out until later that Jeremy couldn't..." I trailed off.

"Ah." Mark nodded, giving me an understanding look. "Mom and Dad always wanted more, but I ended up being the only child. I never asked why I had no siblings. Besides, Dad acted like a big kid most of the time, so Mom didn't need any others to keep track of."

His eyes brightened and his face softened as he spoke about them. It was easy to see he loved them dearly. "Where are your parents now?"

"Last time I talked to Mom, they were in Costa Rica."

I cocked my head, impressed. "Oh, wow. I've always wanted to go there. What do they do?"

He shrugged. "Just travel and enjoy life. Dad was into computers and programming in a big way when I was growing up. In my junior year, he created a program that did a better-than-average job at analyzing stocks and bonds. It was good enough that several Wall Street firms and a few software companies were after him to sell. My senior year, he sold the rights, patent, the entire package, for more money than he and Mom could spend in two lifetimes. They knew I wasn't going to college, so when I graduated, they set me up with a fairly decent size trust and gave me a graduation gift of about $25,000.

"I moved around, trying different jobs, just living day to day. I finally settled down in this area and now I live off a small stipend from the trust and what I make at my job."

The surprises just kept on coming with him. "Financially secure at your age. A blessing. Why didn't you go to college?"

"Wasn't for me," he said, toying with his glass. "I knew halfway through high school I didn't want to do any more school. I enjoy working with my hands and I'd gotten bitten by the bug to see the world." He shrugged slightly. "So, I did."

"And then your parents left to do the same thing?"

"Dad said he didn't like the way the wind was blowing with some of the political stuff going on in the States. When he sold the software, he set up an off-shore account. About a month after I had graduated, they sat me down at dinner and told me their plans. He and Mom moved to Norway, got citizenships there, and renounced their US citizenship. Now they spend their time exploring the world."

"Do you ever get to see them?"

He nodded as the waitress left our check on the table next to Mark. Once she was out of earshot, Mark picked up where he left off.

"Yeah, a couple times a year they fly in to visit with my uncle. I met them in New York two Christmases ago. We keep in touch with emails, texts, and calls. They're both happy, so I'm happy for them."

I shook my head, imagining the life of jet setting around the world. I know others found it appealing, but, for me, I was happy just being here. Visits to places are always nice, but it was nice to come back home.

"Do you think you'll ever do like they did? Take off and explore the world and never look back?" I asked, feeling anxious, and a bit scared at what he might answer with.

He harrumphed and shook his head. "No, I did a bunch of exploring over the last eight years. There are still a few places I wouldn't mind visiting. But," he said, pausing to lock eyes with me across the table, sending flutters throughout my chest. "I like it here. I see myself staying in the area, finding a beautiful, intelligent woman, and seeing what the future brings. Maybe she will want to go sightseeing with me."

We stayed that way, just quietly looking at each other for several moments, until the waitress came back up to check on the family. And then whatever moment we were having melted away. In my head, I recited my mantra for the night, just to remind myself. *This is not a date, Kathi, just dinner. Quit acting like its something it's not. He's too young.*

Breaking out of my head, I smiled at him.

"This has been a lovely evening, Mark. I think it's time I got back home."

I reached for the check, but he snatched it away, looking almost insulted.

"At least let me pay my part," I said.

He flagged the server over, handing her the check and his card. She excused herself and he turned back to me, smiling.

He raised his hand, stopping my objection. "I got this one. I asked you out, therefore that makes it my treat."

I snorted lightly. "You didn't ask me out. You took advantage of the situation."

"Potato, potahto, why argue over semantics? Besides, *you* agreed."

I cocked my head at him, a small smile tickling at my lips. "You can be quite infuriating, you know that?"

He gave me that dimple-ladened smile again and this time I felt it to my toes, and all the parts in between. A brief image of me kissing that dimple flitted through my head. The surge of desire that thought sent through me surprised me.

The waitress returned with the receipt. He signed it and returned his card to his wallet. He scooted out across the seats and stood in the aisle, holding his hand out to me. As I took it, the zing flashed up my arm again as I eased out of the booth. Mark placed his hand on the small of my back and guided me all the way out of the restaurant. At his car, he again opened the door and helped me into my seat.

When we got to my house, Mark shut the car off and was reaching for his door handle when I stopped him.

"Mark, no."

He paused, hand hovering, giving me a confused look, one eyebrow raised.

"Look, I think we should say goodnight here," I said.

He shook his head. "I should walk you to your door. My grandmother would insist."

I smiled despite myself, thinking of his grandmother lecturing a young Mark on manners.

"Mark, I don't want there to be any confusion. Tonight wasn't a date. It was two friends having dinner. Please don't read anything else into it."

"Okay, so the *next* time can be a date. You can choose where we go."

I glanced out into the night through the windshield, not enjoying being in this situation. I looked back at Mark and I had to admit; he was a strikingly handsome young man. That smile and those eyes had sent more than a few flashes of warmth through me tonight. Unfortunately, nothing changed the fact of the age difference, and that wasn't going to magically disappear.

"Look," I said quietly. "I enjoyed dinner and getting to know you. I really did. But Mark, it can't be anything more. If you were older, or I was younger…" I let my words fade away. I could see his jaw working via the lights from the dashboard. The silence stretched on for what seemed like forever before I saw his shoulders relax and he nodded.

"Okay, Kathi. We'll play it your way."

"Thank you, Mark."

I opened the car door, the interior lights flashing on and illuminating us both more clearly.

"Good night, Mark."

I swung my legs out of the car. Before I could slide out, Mark laid his hand on my arm. I felt the electric tingle from his touch run up to my jaw and turned to look at him. His gaze was almost unsettling, overwhelming in its intensity. As quickly as the intensity appeared, it faded, replaced by that devilish grin.

"I hear what you're saying, and I can understand. We had a good time tonight, and I think we connected. But I have to be honest with you. I would like to be *more* than friends. I'll play this by your rules, but all I ask is that you give it a thought."

As he finished speaking, his very warm hand slid lightly down my arm, his calloused fingers igniting and leaving small trails of heat and goosebumps in their wake. They paused at my hand, squeezing it lightly.

I could only stare as his hand finished its path and dropped to the console between us. I glanced up at him and my stomach flipped again. Mark's gaze was full of surety, of confidence, and a heaping dose of desire. In all my years with him, Jeremy had never looked at me in that way.

And in that moment, I realized it was a look I wanted to see again, and that thought both scared me and excited me from my head to my toes.

I slid out of the car, quickly shutting the door behind me before I did or said something foolish. I stood at my front door and followed Mark's car as it circled the drive and then out the gate, taillights disappearing into the night.

Why did it seem like letting him drive away was a huge mistake?

NINE

I stared out my office windows, taking in the jagged mountain peaks that formed the backdrop for the Denver skyline, lost in my thoughts. Thoughts that centered on Mark and the unease that swirled through me like a fog. I had done the right thing ending the evening the way I did, but I couldn't help but wonder what it would have been like if it had ended differently.

Even as I had tried to go to sleep that Friday night, all of my arguments chased each other around my head. Besides the potential social consequences associated with dating a younger man, I had no problems imagining what Samuel would say or do. If he ever found out, my time with Harrison Enterprises would be over.

I'd been alone for several years now and if I was truly honest with myself, I missed the comfort of a man being around, of having someone envelop me in the warm embrace of a hug. I missed the simple pleasure of having someone to sit on the couch and cuddle up in the dark with while a movie played. I missed the intimacy.

It was probably those thoughts that had led to my dream the night before. A highly erotic dream.

Over and over, that glorious tongue teased, probed, and licked at my wet heat. I clutched the sheets, urging my mysterious lover on until my stomach clenched and my toes curled, the release smashing me down like the surf pounding onto a beach.

As I fell back against the sheets, gasping for air, my lover moved over me, pushing my hips wide with his, not giving me a chance to recover before he drove his magnificent cock into me. It was big, oh so big, and it pushed the air out of my lungs in an explosive grunt. I moaned as he pulled back and then repeated the thrust, causing me to grunt again.

He settled into a rhythm over me. I tried to see his face, but it remained obscured. He pistoned into me, the slap of his skin meeting mine echoing in the room. I moaned in ecstasy, shoving my hips up to meet each of his savage thrusts. I urged him on as I gasped for air, willing him deeper. Begging him for harder.

Suddenly, he slammed forward, arching his back up as I felt him pulse liquid heat inside me. His head snapped up and I could see his face. Mark's eyes bore into me as he groaned and jerked against me. I screamed his name and exploded, fireworks going off behind my eyes.

I'd woken up at that point, my muscles clenching as I fisted the sheets and my stomach muscles spasmed from my orgasm. I'd never had a dream so vivid and so real that it caused me to wake up cumming.

A wadded up ball of paper smacked me in the head, pulling me out of my thoughts. I felt flushed from the relived experience. Combined with the tingling and warmth between my legs, I was going to need to change my underwear, and soon.

"HEY!" I yelped, spinning back around at my desk and glaring at Abby.

"Did you even hear a word I said?" she asked, pointing her pen at me like a conductor's baton. "You've been somewhere else all morning. What's up? And why are you all red?"

I cleared my throat, buying myself some time. "Sorry, some stuff's going on. Has the band signed on?"

Abby stared at me, smirking. "If you'd been listening, I answered that question about three minutes ago, right about the time you checked out on me. Girl, we need to get you on a date or laid or something. You need some *serious* relaxation."

I flashed back to the images of Mark when I answered the door and of his sweat-covered face as he drove into me in my dream. I smiled at the memories before glancing back up at Abby, who was sporting a know-it-all smirk.

"What?"

"Who is he?" she purred.

I shuffled the papers on my desk, refusing to look directly at her.

"I'm sure I don't know *what* you are talking about," I said, giving the page in front of me my undivided attention.

Abby reached over and turned the page I was so seriously studying so that it was no longer upside down. Caught, I looked back up at her.

"Spill it," she said, leaning forward to rest her elbows on my desk and plop her chin in her hands, looking like a cat eyeing a juicy mouse. "Agoddate? Maybe a goooood date? Hmmmmmm?"

"It wasn't a date, per se," I said.

"Then what was it, *'per se'*? You know me, I'll eventually get it out of you. I can break you like a wet paper bag."

I glared at her, refusing to acknowledge the truth of her statement. Then, realizing she was right, and I was just delaying the inevitable, I sighed and sagged back in my chair.

"Fine. If you must know, I had dinner with a friend Friday night."

"And was this friend a guy?" she asked.

"Yes."

"I see. A good-*looking* guy?"

"I guess so," I said, looking casually towards the ceiling, trying to be nonchalant. I failed because Abby began smiling ever so slowly.

"You're not fooling me with that lameness. Given that little smile, I'm betting he was delicious. What does he do? Where did you meet him? More importantly, did he stay for breakfast and did he snore?"

I gave her my best glare. "Why is my love life so important to you?"

She started tapping her fingernail on my desk. "It's my life's goal to get you laid again before your 60s. Now quit stalling. Deets."

God, she was infuriating. But I did love her so. Besides Mary, she really was one of my very few good friends who wasn't a society member.

"No, he did not stay for breakfast. There was no goodnight kiss. I told you. Friends."

"Friends can have sex. It's called 'friends with benefits.' Who is this friend, and do I know him?"

I shook my head. "No, you don't. Look, it was dinner. Nothing more, nothing less."

She paused, cocked her head at me, watching me for a second or two before she continued.

"Okay, what time did he pick you up?"

"Around 5."

"And where did he take you?"

"A place called the Airplane Restaurant. Heard of it?"

She nodded. "Cutesy little place down in the Springs. Not high end, but not trash either. An interesting choice. What time did you get home?"

I rolled my eyes at her. "Look, it was just dinner. Do we really—"

She quickly cut me off. "What time, Kathi?" I muttered something under my breath. She gave me an exasperated look. "Louder for the rest of the kids."

I spoke again, softly.

"Girl, I know where you live. I also have the gate code and a spare key. Why are you being so difficult? For all your other dates, you couldn't wait to complain. What gives?"

Terrier with a bone.

"Around 10:30."

The look of shock that flew across her features almost had me laughing. That shock slowly morphed into a cat-who-drank-the-cream look.

"Since you started dating again, you've not had a date last over two hours, and that includes dinner with those society ladies you hang out with. *Now* you tell me you had dinner with a male 'friend' for almost four plus hours," she said, air-quoting the word friend.

She leaned her elbows on my desk and rested her chin in her hands, her eyes alight with expectation.

I gave her my best glare. "You *do* remember I'm your boss, right?"

Her look never changed, nor did she acknowledge my inherent boss superiority. I shook my head slightly, smiled at her, and gave in.

"Do you remember when I met with Mary and Scott last week?"

"Mhhmm."

"Someone volunteered to help us out for free, to be there for all the sessions and help us with anything we needed."

"That's great, Kathi. I know we have a few gaps each day," she said. I glanced down at my desk.

"Um, not good?" she asked, puzzled.

"He wouldn't take money for his time, or to help offset his loss. He only wanted..." I let my words trail away. I hoped to gain pity from her, but I should have known better.

"Pray tell, what did he want?" she asked.

I let out a deep sigh, closing my eyes before answering her.

"Dinner. With me."

I watched Abby's eyebrows shoot up. Then she looked at me, head cocked slightly. I knew that look. She was recalling things in that file cabinet she called a brain.

"Wait. Who is this guy and what's he doing for the camp?"

"He's... well, he's the farrier."

"What's a farrier?"

"Someone who takes care of horses' hooves. Trims them, puts on horseshoes, things like that."

"What's his name?"

I was trying to avoid this, because Abby's brain forgets nothing.

"Mark."

I waited, knowing that it might take a few moments. In actuality, it didn't take her more than four seconds.

"Mark. Mark. Hmmmm. Oh, wait," she said, her face lighting up. "Would this be the infamous 'M' who sent you those flowers?"

Shit.

I straightened the papers in front of me. "Yes, that would be him."

The smile on her face was wide enough that it had to be painful. "*Soooo*, how much of what you told me the other day was bullshit?"

Abby stared steadily at me, refusing to let me slide. I slumped in my chair, knowing I couldn't fool her. Unfortunately, I'd never been able to lie to her about much of anything.

"Well, technically, it was all true. I just didn't tell you quite *all* the things."

I paused, praying she would let me slide. She twiddled her fingers at me, asking me to go on with my story. I told her everything that had happened that day. When I finished, I sat and waited for the inevitable. She didn't disappoint me.

She squinted at me for a few seconds, then her face slowly morphed. Her smile got bigger, her eyes brightened, and then her shoulders started shaking. I started counting and made it to six when she burst out laughing.

I calmly perused the papers in front of me, waiting for Miss Giggles to finish up. She rose to her feet, wheezing and waving her hand in front of her face and at me. She struggled to breathe, leaning on my desk. Finally, after several deep breaths, she calmed herself enough to speak.

"You know," she said, struggling to hold in her laughter as she walked to the door. "They have a song about this," she stated, eyes shining with glee.

Don't ask. Don't ask. Don't ask.

"Song?" I asked. *Stupid.*

She turned and stepped through the door, but glanced back one last time, a sickeningly sweet curl to her lips.

"Kathi and Maaarrrrk, sitting in a tree, kay eye ess ess eye-" was all she got out before I hurled the pad of paper at her. She launched into another laughing fit as she ducked into her area, my papyrus missile sailing past her in a flutter of sheets.

Now, not only did I have that stupid song in my head, but I found my thoughts drifting to what it would be like to kiss Mark under a tree. *Crap on a cracker.*

I handed my keys to the valet and took the offered ticket. As he drove away with my car, I stepped into the Brown Palace. I took a few steps in and paused, taking in the sheer beauty and opulence of this magnificent hotel. When Harrisons needed to impress a new client, the Brown Palace was our go-to destination.

I also enjoyed meeting my friends here occasionally for the infamous Afternoon Tea. As I strolled through the lobby, making my way to where the Tea was being served, I couldn't help but flashback to some of those happy memories. I entered the seating area, glanced around, and spotted my friends at a table near the back.

Martha Wallace had grown up with Jeremy and they had even dated in high school before she had met her husband, John, in college. John ran a very successful investment firm. Jeremy had used John's firm for all our investments. The Wallaces, prominent among the philanthropic scene in Denver, took part in any charity or fundraising effort happening in the city.

Rebecca Darmond, a former model, was always the epitome of fashion and appearance. Even at forty-five, she turned heads wherever she went. Her Scandinavian heritage had blessed her with blond hair, blue eyes, and that viking princess figure. She'd been in high demand during her career, but had parlayed that success into her own highly acclaimed modeling agency. She and I had met in college when I had pledged our sorority. Rebecca was a senior and took me under her wing, educating me in the ways of college and its internal student politics and social structures. She was married to her career, and I didn't see that changing anytime soon.

Olivia Foster was another sorority sister, but was ten years older than us. Her husband, Melvin, was a senior partner in one of the more prestigious Denver law firms. They had met in college and married the summer before he started law school. Melvin's career path had been mapped out since high school, thanks to his father's influence and money. Olivia had raised their two children and supported her husband in all ways possible. Rumor had it he was being prepped for a run at the state Senate in the next election.

I slid into my chair to a chorus of greetings. The table, with its crisp white linen tablecloth and lace doilies, contained a full tea service and a plate of assorted pastries. Mouth watering, I helped myself to a buttery blueberry scone.

Predictably, Marsha was the first to speak. "How is the planning going for the dinners? John and I do so look forward to attending this year. I was in San Francisco last weekend and I picked up the most divine new dress. Can't wait to show you."

I sipped my tea, washing down a small bite of scone. "I can't wait to see it. Planning is going well and I think this will be one of our better events."

"Is Aremjeo doing the catering?" asked Olivia. Of course she would ask about the catering. Olivia was a bit of a food snob, always had been. I laughed lightly, reaching out to touch her arm. "Of course. We have them on contract for the next few years."

"His chicken marsala is to *die* for. Please tell me that's on the menu this year?"

I nodded. "I made sure it was on the menu just for you, Olivia."

For the next few minutes, we caught up with the minor goings on within our group. The waiters came by to clear away the dirty dishes, replace with clean ones and ensure our tea carafe was full.

Rebecca tapped her spoon against her teacup, drawing our eyes to her. She had a smirk that just oozed smugness. That practiced look meant she had dirt and was ready to dish it.

"You will never guess what happened at the symphony last week?"

Olivia and Martha immediately gave Rebecca their full attention. Dirt or juicy gossip was like catnip to these two. They were staring like moths looking at a flame. Rebecca was eating up the attention. I just sat there, amused at these three.

"What?" asked Olivia.

"Well, we were waiting in the lobby before the start when Regina Vaughn waltzes in, pretty as you please."

"Oh, tell me she didn't..." started Martha but Rebecca started nodding.

"She paraded another one of her boys in. I swear this one couldn't have been more than twenty-three or twenty-four. It was pathetic. She was fawning *all* over him."

My mind flew back to having dinner with Mark. There had been no fawning. But there had been conversation, laughter, fun even.

"Kathi?"

I blinked, and everything came back to focus. My friends stared at me, concerned.

"I'm sorry. What were you saying?"

Rebecca hesitated for a moment, then continued. "I was saying that someone should speak to Regina."

"About what?"

"About acting more acceptable. A woman of her advanced years and social responsibilities should be more dignified."

I reflected on the last time we had discussed Regina and how I had been just as vocal as the others. This time, for some reason, I couldn't find it in me to be dismissive.

I glanced around the table at my three friends, my sorority sisters. In a few moments, memories and events from our past flashed before my eyes, and as I stared at them, I had a sudden wave of shame wash over me. How shallow we were and how intolerant.

I shook my head slightly and settled my gaze on Rebecca, the instigator of today's session of rebuke. "Rebecca, who was she hurting?"

Rebecca started to speak, but paused. Puzzlement flashed through her features.

"I'm sorry?" she asked, glancing back at Martha.

I continued, my voice firm, belying the nervous shake in my hands. "Who was she hurting? Regina. At the symphony. Who was she hurting?"

Rebecca glanced at the other two, her face flashing from nervous to uncertain before looking back at me.

"Um. No one, I guess. But everyone was embarrassed—"

"If she was hurting no one, then what is wrong with what she is doing?" I asked. "And before you continue, I've already talked with Regina. Do you have any idea *why* she does what she does?"

Three blank faces stared back at me. I tapped one fingernail on the table in front of me.

"For so many years, she was *required* to act a certain way, *behave* a certain way, *conform* to certain standards. Why? Because it was *expected* of her. She had to act that way to support her husband. Much like you do for your husband.

"Now, with her husband gone and her kids living their own lives scattered across the country, she's lonely and just wants to enjoy what's left of her time."

I stared at my friends, wondering if any of this was sinking in. Seeing no response or reaction, I pressed on. In for a penny, in for a pound, they say.

"She doesn't care what any of us think. These young men bring her joy and excitement. Something she has missed so much. She cares about having fun, exploring new things, and trying to enjoy her life regardless of what is *expected* of her by her friends and peers."

I took a deep breath, bringing myself back from the brink. Why was I reacting this way? Even as I asked myself that, I knew the answer and what I needed to do. I dabbed my mouth with my napkin and laid the linen on the table. I stood, giving one last glance at the three women I called friends, feeling a bit saddened for them, and for myself.

"Maybe, just maybe, we would all be better off if we thought less about what others think of us and focused more on what we think about ourselves. I may not agree with how she is going about it, but I can only help but be slightly jealous of her freedom and new outlook. Now, if you will excuse me, I must get back to work. Until next month, ladies."

For the first time, the thought of there not being a next month with these three flitted through my head.

I turned on my heel and quickly walked away, my emotions

dancing and swirling in my head as I left my speechless friends wondering what had just happened. As I stepped through the lobby doors and handed my ticket to the valet, I couldn't fully understand why Mark was centered in my thoughts.

TEN

The first weekend of the kids' camp was here before I knew it.

I leaned on the rustic four plank wooden fence, watching Mary give her speech to the kids. I'd opted not to speak, preferring to stay in the background so that the kids only saw one adult in charge.

The councilman and his entourage had come and gone, thanking Mary and Jake for their support. Of course, Samuel had been with him, introducing Mary and Jake like they were old friends, even though today was the first time he had ever spoken with them. He was always a good schmoozer, though, so it didn't surprise me when he acted this way. After several photos were taken and the interviews completed by the TV station crew we'd arranged, our dignitaries wrapped up their speeches and headed back to Denver.

The one souring moment was Samuel again pulling me aside and threatening me yet again on the value of my job should this event not be a success. I breathed a sigh of relief when his car pulled away.

I was thankful that today was a beautiful day. The sky was a brilliant blue, only a smattering of fluffy white clouds dotting the sky. A nice warm breeze gusted occasionally, but other than that, nothing moved the leaves in the trees.

Mary and Jake had really spruced up the area. They'd put down a fresh layer of gravel on the path from the main road to the barn. Everything had been leveled and raked. Jake even took the time to spray down the gravel and all around the barn to help keep the dust from becoming overwhelming.

The kids and their chaperones gathered around the round pens, sitting at the picnic tables surrounding the steel fence panels. The area buzzed with excited murmurs from the kids as Mary spoke, telling them about what all they would experience here at the ranch.

Jake had rented several large UTVs for use by the EMTs and for any other emergency that popped up. The beds on them were big enough to hold a stretcher, in the event an accident happened out on the trails. Jake had also set-up a small base-station and given out walkie-talkies to the volunteers. The setup allowed him to handle requests and direct the day's activities and give us all a sense of what was going on. I had mine clipped to the side pocket of my jeans, turned down so that I could monitor it but also hear what was going on around me.

Mary finished her speech and began forming the kids into lines behind their group leaders. She then introduced the chaperones, who would roam the facility, lending hands where needed.

Once the groups formed up, the leaders led their kids over to the equipment table, where the staff fitted each rider with a helmet. Properly geared up, the groups headed off to the round pens to get their first introduction to horses.

I watched the eager faces as the kids hung on the words of their guides. The kids' excitement was catchy and had me thinking back to my own first horse and the thrill of riding. Daq had been a beautiful black Tennessee Walking Horse mare with a heart of gold. The multitude of stupid and crazy things I did while riding her should've gotten me killed many times over. Through it all, Daq kept me safe, giving me confidence and letting me learn to love the joy and freedom of riding.

A voice rumbling close to my ear interrupted my memories. "Penny for your thoughts."

I jerked as my heartbeat went from normal to moon launch in less than a second. I snapped my head around to see a smirking Mark rocking back on his heels, exuding innocence. I lunged at him, hand in motion.

"Shit," I shrieked, smacking him on the arm before he moved out of range. He laughed as he backed away, his hands quickly reaching down to cover up his groin.

An old ball cap set back on his head, pulled down just enough that a slightly wavy tuft of his hair peeked out from under the brim. His gray t-shirt fit him like a second skin. I refused to acknowledge that a portion of my racing heart rate may have been a reaction to the slide of that t-shirt across his muscles. And I absolutely would not comment on the desire to see if his ass looked good in his well-faded and worn, but comfortably tight, jeans. Combined with the scuffed work boots, he presented an impressive picture of, as Abby would say if she were here, *yumminess*.

Even as I enjoyed my perusal of the man in front of me, I lectured myself for even dwelling on the way Mark looked, much less actually thinking that he was *yummy*. But there was still that small part of me that really found the sight of Mark attractive. Very attractive. And if I were being *really* truthful with myself, after our dinner, the small part of me that found him attractive was growing larger.

Despite this, I was ready to give him another smack for startling me. He laughed again and back-peddled, holding his hands up in surrender.

"Sorry, sorry," he said, chuckling but staying out of range.

"No, you're not. Not even a little," I growled, willing my heart to slow down as he continued to dance away from me.

At that moment, Mary arrived, interrupting my stalking before I corralled Mark. She looked at him and her gaze hardened.

"What did you do now?" she asked, giving him that impressive mom-face.

"Scared the shit out of me," I said, glaring at him. "Again."

Mary flipped her gloves in his direction. "If you've got nothing better to do, make yourself useful and go help Jake."

"Sure," he agreed, scooting out around us both, careful to stay out of hand-smacking range while tossing me a grin. Mary came to stand next to me as Mark turned toward the barn. But before taking a step, he looked back over his shoulder at me.

"Loved dinner the other night, Kathi. Can't wait to do it again. Ladies," he said, touching two fingers to the tip of his cap before turning and strolling up to the barn.

Unashamedly, I admired the stretch and pull of his jeans across what had to be a steel-tight set of buns as he walked up the path towards the barn. I had to give credit where credit was due. He had a really nice ass.

"Here," said Mary, thrusting something against my arm. I looked down to see a small bandana dangling in her hand. I looked up at her, curious.

She smirked at me. "So you can wipe the drool off."

I jerked my gaze from hers, my neck and face flushing at having been caught staring. She chuckled as she shoved the bandana back into her pocket.

She studied me. "I'm gonna assume that since he 'loved dinner the other night' and he's here today, that you went out with him."

"It wasn't a date," I huffed, crossing my arms like some petulant child. She wasn't so easily fooled.

"Then what was it?"

"Dinner. That's all."

"Did you play tonsil-hockey when he took you home?" she asked. I looked at her, shocked, and rolled my eyes.

"What are we, high-schoolers?" I asked. Some of the irritation I was feeling must have crept into my tone. Mary laid her hand on my arm, tugging at me. She dragged me over to the small bench near Sarah's play set, pulling me down and sitting beside her. She waited until I pulled my eyes off the ground to look at her.

"Was it that bad?" she asked, concerned.

I sighed deeply, letting my shoulders sag. "No, and *that's* the problem. It was actually a good time. We ate, we talked, and we got to know each other," I replied, then looked back at her. "Did you know he's been crab fishing up in Alaska?"

She shrugged. "Jake may have mentioned something about it a

while back. So, you had a good dinner with Mark." She cocked her head at me. "I'm sorry, but I don't see the problem."

I gnawed on my lower lip, debating. My sorority sisters were nice and I'm sure they would always be there for me, but Mary was my best friend. Perhaps she could help. I turned on the bench, pulling one leg up and over so I faced her more directly.

"The problem is, it was probably one of the best da... I mean, *dinners*, I've been on since Jeremy died."

Her eyebrows rose. "Seriously?" she asked.

I nodded. "Mary, it was so nice. He listened to me and engaged with me, pushing me on some things, agreeing with me on others. And he wasn't just humoring me. He was actually interested in what I had to say. I can't lie and tell you I didn't find that attractive as hell." I closed my eyes, letting the memory of that night flow through me.

I opened my eyes as she spoke. "Then I'm confused. What was the... oh," she said, her eyes softening with sudden realization. *Understanding.* "He's only 25."

I groaned as I pressed a hand to my forehead. "God, it's worse hearing it out loud. I'm old enough to be his *mother!*"

She studied my face, taking in my obvious discomfort. "So. I'm gonna guess there was no kiss goodnight."

I shook my head. "No, I made sure he was clear at the start that it was just dinner with a friend. That he was too young to date."

She chuckled. "And how did he take that?"

"Not well. Oh, he covered it up and told me he'd do things by my rules, but he made no secret about what he wanted the night to be."

"So, why the confusion? You were just friends having dinner," she stated. Then her head cocked to the side, and she narrowed her gaze.

"Wait. You're thinking about doing it, aren't you?" she asked.

I dropped my face into my hands, groaning. Taking several deep breaths, I sat back up.

"It doesn't matter if I am. I can't date him, Mary. He's too young. Doesn't matter how good looking he is, or how nice he acts, or how interesting he finds me. I *can't* date him."

She sat back. "Why?"

I threw my hands up, staring at her. I would have a better chance explaining the secrets of the universe than answering that one word query.

"Samuel would have a cow. I can hear him now telling me how this would affect the company's standings in the community and how he would be publicly impacted. Not to mention he would use it as a violation of our morals clause to have me ousted from my job."

She gave me an unbelieving look. "Seriously? He's *that* close-minded?"

"His picture is next to close-minded in the dictionary."

Mary looked off to the barn, her face virtually blank. I could tell by the slight movements of her eyes that she was running options in her mind, working out the best way to present her thoughts to me.

"These friends of yours in Denver that you're worried about. How often do you do things with them?"

"Mostly lunches during the week. Occasional weekend dinner. Symphonies, plays, that sort of thing."

"What did you do last Sunday?"

I was confused. She knew exactly what I did last Sunday.

"I had lunch and dinner with you, Jake, Julia and Sarah. We played games and hung out."

She nodded. "You spent the day with us, playing, riding, laughing, and having *fun.*" She paused for a second and then asked, "Do you have fun doing that stuff with your friends in Denver?"

I nodded. "I enjoy it. I like the symphony." *I wonder what she's getting at?*

"But was it *fun*?" she asked, pushing back. When I didn't answer right away, she nodded. Mary leaned forward, touching my knee with a finger.

"Did you have fun with Mark at dinner?"

"Yes." The answer was out of my mouth before she finished the question. She nodded again and tapped my knee.

"You had fun with him. And based on the way you were just staring at his ass, you *obviously* find him attractive."

My face flamed up like the sun. Mary laughed and then gave me another tap on my knee.

"Life's short. You and me, we've both been bitch-slapped by it. So, you go on a date with Mark and find out there is zero chemistry between the two of you. Or you find out you have a chance at something more than friendship." She shrugged as she looked me straight in the eyes, her face serious. "It's up to you, but I know what I would advise you to do."

I let her words rumble through my brain as I looked over at the barn where Mark and Jake were talking to the chaperones.

She spoke again. "Something else. Why are you so worried about being fired? I know Jeremy left you well off, and I'm sure finding another job would be easy if you wanted to work. Hell, I've tried to get you to work more with me here. So what's keeping you there?"

Her question stirred up all of my late night feelings and thoughts about my job. I liked what I was doing, but I wasn't in love with it. It was just what I did. I'd done it for years before Jeremy's death and I went back afterwards because it was comfortable. Solid, easy, non-changing.

I looked at her in the eyes. "You know, I'm wondering that myself sometimes. But that's a story for another day, I think."

At that, Mary stood up and dusted off her rear end. I took her offered hand and leveraged myself up off the bench. She threw her arm around my shoulder and pointed us towards the barn.

"Come on. You and I need to go ride some horses and stare at Mark's butt. You know, go have some *fun*."

"I hate you," I said, trudging with her up to the barn, my heart tripping along as I considered her wise words, visions of Mark's butt flitting through my head.

———

I buckled up Ringo's girth and waited. He liked to hold his breath to keep me from tightening his girth snugly, and even after all these years, was always trying to fake me out. I waited until he exhaled the big breath he'd taken and tightened the girth up one more time.

It was the last event of the day before we hustled the kids back off to the city and home. One of the overall goals of the event was to show the kids all the various types and aspects of riding. Dressage, barrel racing, and jumping, among others. Since I was the barn's resident jumper, Mary asked me to do a small demonstration.

Normally, I'd have thrown on some worn jodhpurs and my old Ariats and called it a day. Mary complained, whined and begged, and finally convinced me to go all out. I'd changed into the full show outfit. Luckily, my time in the gym ensured the form fitting breeches and my nice shirt still fit, along with my show jacket. I'd even brushed and polished my boots.

I finished fiddling with my saddle and checked the rest of my tack one more time. Satisfied, I pulled my helmet on, happy once again I kept my hair short enough to tuck it up into the helmet without putting it up in a bun. Grabbing Ringo's reins, I walked him out towards the riding arena.

Mary had created a great riding arena, one of the things I loved most about the farm. Roughly 80 feet wide and just over 150 feet long, it was big enough to set up a small jump course and have some fun riding around in. One side bordered a line of trees that kept some of the afternoon sun off the course. She had put in good layers for the footing, including a top layer of crushed limestone and sand mixed. It was several inches thick and gave a nice soft purchase. It covered a thicker base of larger rocks, which provided a solid support for the horses and easily drained water.

Jake had rented bleachers, setting them up along one side of the arena. Mary's back was to me, so I assumed she was explaining to the assembled kids what was going to happen.

I had helped her design the arena back when I was competing and we had used it to train a few others who were interested in trying their hands at jumping. For today, we'd pared the jumps down to seven, and I had worked up a small circuit. To give them a little thrill, I'd set the highest jump, a four footer, along the bleacher side, right in front of the kids. This would give them a good view of Ringo and me as we worked the jump.

I looked up as Ringo and I arrived at the arena gate, surprised to see Mark standing there. He gazed at me intently as I walked towards him, and I could feel him taking me in from my boots and up to my face. His eyes flashed with a heat that made my throat tighten and butterflies flit around my stomach.

"You clean up nice, Mrs. Harrison," his voice rumbled as I came to a stop next to him. I said nothing, but inside I felt warmed by the praise.

He opened the gate, and I walked Ringo a few steps inside the arena. I flipped his reins up and over his neck and he tossed his head, snorting and blowing. He knew what we were about to do, and I could feel his eagerness as I smoothed one hand down his shoulder.

Mark moved up to stand in front of me and dropped his hands down, cupping them.

"Thanks," I said. While I could easily mount from the ground, having a leg-up always made life easier. I set my left foot in his hands and lightly bounced twice on my right toes, pushing off on the third bounce. Mark easily gripped my left heel and calf and propelled me up in the air. I swung my leg over the saddle and seated myself without fuss. An easy, practiced flip of each foot set my toes into my stirrups quickly and I gathered up the reins. I could feel Ringo's excitement vibrating underneath me.

Mark's hand landed on my knee, and it felt like a hot iron. I glanced down at him, locking eyes. Concern and something else, something I couldn't quite place, stared back up at me.

"Be careful out there," he said. I could only nod, afraid I'd croak if I tried to speak. He squeezed my knee and slid his hand down my shin. Nodding, he moved back through the gate, closing it behind him as he went. My knee was tingly and warm from his touch, and my stomach was doing flip-flops. Whether from Mark's touch or nerves from the upcoming performance, was a toss-up.

I moved Ringo out to the outer edge of the arena and started him into a trot. As we both settled into the gait, my tensions eased. Mark faded into the background as my thoughts and mind slipped into performance mode and Ringo and I began to sync up.

I took us around the perimeter once, making sure both of us were loose and warmed up. I planned to work my way up through the middle of the arena, starting with the smallest jump, and finishing with the big one in front of the bleachers.

Ringo tossed his head as we settled into the run up to the first obstacle. I moved him into a smooth canter. Technically, it was a jump, even if it was only two-foot in height. Clearing it, I looked back down the arena at the next jump, plotting my lane and correcting Ringo's line with a twitch of my knee.

We worked smoothly through the jumps, and I was in the zone. I knew the the kids were clapping as I went cantering past them, but I didn't register any sound. My total focus was on the course, calculating strides and launch points. Ringo and I were moving as one and I'd never felt more free.

I cleared jump five and made my turn towards the treeline side of the arena and jump six. It was a square oxer, with a three-foot clearance, and a three-foot width between poles. This setup created a jump was a three-foot wall that was almost four-foot deep. I tapped my heels and Ringo picked up speed.

As we neared take-off, Ringo's muscles bunched, and I began leaning forward, anticipating the leap. It was the lean that was my undoing. Well, that and the stupid rabbit.

The hare-brained rodent broke from the treeline and made a mad-hatter dash right under Ringo's nose. All Ringo saw was a dragon coming to get him. My steadfast steed went from full speed, ready-to-jump to dead-stop, dropping his head and performing a perfect sliding stop that would have made a champion reining horse envious. Unfortunately for me, I wasn't in the right saddle for this particular move.

I left the saddle like a launched missile, flying towards the jump, providing the onlookers a textbook example of Newton's First Law of

Motion. I barely had time to think 'this is gonna hurt' as my ass finished its loop over my head and my entire back hit the arena floor with my butt slightly in the lead. I actually heard the air whoosh from my lungs as the impact forced all the air out of them. That whoosh was the last thing I heard as the darkness slammed down on me.

ELEVEN

My eyes snapped open, and the world was blurry and out of focus. I blinked several times, trying to get my eyes to work properly. It took a few seconds, but finally a fuzzy-looking Mark swam into focus, staring down at me. His lips were moving, but I couldn't hear what he was saying. Or any sound, for that matter.

Awareness came back in a tumble. The dragon-rabbit, the jump, my impromptu physics lesson.

Like a knob turning on a radio, the sound faded back in.

"Talk to me, Kathi," Mark's voice was calming, but tight, as was the skin around his eyes.

"Shit, that *hurt*." I closed my eyes, then popped them back open. My horse. "How's Ringo? Is he okay?"

I tried to push up, wanting off the ground to check on my horse, but Mark's powerful hands gripped my shoulders. He squeezed them gently, keeping where I was.

"Jake has him. Ringo is just fine. Please stay still until help gets here."

A UTV roared to a stop near us, stalling any further argument. A young lady dropped next to me. I recognized her as one of the EMTs we had hired. Brenda, I think her name was, but that was fuzzy, like my vision.

Mark held my head steady as she unsnapped my helmet, then worked it off my head and onto the ground behind me. She pulled a small tube from some spot on her shirtsleeve. There was a clicking noise and a bright light suddenly flicked into my eye and just as quickly flicked away, only to appear in the other eye.

"Do you know what happened?" she asked, looking back down at me.

"I tried out for the circus." She snorted before shaking her head. She held the pen light up in front of me.

"Use your eyes and follow the light, please," she said. She began flipping the small light from left to right, then up and down on my left eye, before repeating the process for my right. Finished, she nodded and stowed the light back into the small pen pocket on her sleeve. She reached across my stomach, taking both of my hands in hers.

"Squeeze my hands and wiggle each finger." I did as instructed for a few seconds before she stopped me. She scooted down and gripped the toes of my boots.

"Now the toes." It was difficult with the tight boots, but I wiggled them enough that she nodded again and let go and moved back up next to me.

"Whose the President?"

"Obama, but I didn't vote for him," I croaked.

She nodded. "Fine by me. Gonna check for breaks. Besides your back, does it hurt anywhere else?"

"You mean besides my ass? No, not really. Can I get up now?" I needed to check on Ringo.

Mark squeezed my shoulder again. "Let her finish," he said. I heard the worry in his voice and it made me feel like I had somehow disappointed him. Not liking that, I stayed put, relaxing as much as I could despite my anxiety over Ringo.

The young EMT ran her hands lightly across my legs and arms. A shadow fell over my face. Mary was grinning down at me, but it didn't quite reach her eyes. I stuck my tongue out at her and she harrumphed quietly.

"Nice hang time," she said. "You cleared the rails by about three feet, but your landing sucked. I'd give it a 5."

I laughed, which caused my back to spasm, sending a sharp wave of agony through me, forcing a groan out between my clenched teeth.

"Shit, don't make me laugh."

Mary knelt down and placed her mouth right by my ear.

"Mark cleared that fence from a standing jump and was halfway across the arena before you even hit the ground. I've never seen someone move that fast."

I glanced up at Mark, giving him a weak smile. It was like watching ice cream melt as the tension slowly disappear from his face, his shoulders dropped, and his whole body relaxed.

"Mary's being harsh," he said, nodding at where she still hovered over my head. "I'd give you at least a 7. Your legs came together and your toes pointed as you flipped."

"I hate you both right now." If they were digging at me, I was going to be okay.

"Well," said my young attending EMT. "Let's give standing up a shot, shall we?"

Mark and Brenda slid their hands behind my shoulders, and Mary supported my head as they slowly rotated me up to a sitting position. I took a few breaths and rolled my shoulders, wincing slightly as my back twinged. Mark's hands tightened, ready to hold me up. I smiled, slightly shaking my head at him.

I rolled my shoulders again, working out the tension in them and around my neck. The tightness there told me that tomorrow was going to suck. Easing my knees up stretched my sore butt. I winced and paused for a second, letting the throb stop before I finished standing up.

The world swayed for a moment, but Mark slid a hand around my waist. Gripping his arm for support, I took several slow, deep breaths to steady myself. I patted his hand, looking up at him.

"Thanks, I'm fine."

Mark apparently didn't believe me since he didn't let go as we walked towards the bleacher side of the arena. Jake was standing there, holding Ringo and watching us. I nodded at him and he returned it.

"Everything checks out okay, but I think it would be a good idea to head to the hospital," said Brenda. "Let them run some better tests and rule everything out."

As I turned to answer, I got my first good look at the kids. The raised eyebrows, the wide-open eyes, and the muttered whispering told me exactly what they were thinking.

If a skilled person like me got hurt, what would those horses do to them?

That thought stopped me dead in my tracks.

Mark halted with me, still holding my waist. He cocked one eyebrow in a silent query. I thrust my chin slightly towards the kids. He looked over at them and I saw their fear register with him. He looked back at me, that eyebrow raised again. I nodded.

He stared at me, and the tightness and twitching of his jaw told me what he thought about my plan. Unhappy he might be, but he nodded. He removed his arms slowly, ready to grab me if I collapsed. I patted his arm to assure him I was okay. Satisfied, he walked towards Jake and Ringo.

With just a few facial movements, Mark and I had communicated several questions and answers, and came to an understanding. I didnt' have the time at the moment to ponder the significance of that act.

"That's a good idea," said Mary, standing next to Brenda. "Let me get take care of the kids and I'll drive you in."

She turned towards the fence and stopped as Mark brought Ringo back over to me. He flipped the reins over Ringo's neck and took up a spot next to my saddle. I walked slowly to Ringo's side and reached my hand up to grab his mane.

Mary stepped over and grabbed my hand, alarmed at what I was doing. "What in the blazes do you think you're doing? Flying, ground, impact, hospital. Remember?"

I locked eyes with her, keeping my hand on Ringo's mane.

"Look over my shoulder at those kids' faces." Her eyes flicked over my shoulder for a moment and then flicked back to mine.

"If I walk out of this arena, those kids are done. You might get one or two of them back on a horse, but not the others. All they will think about is that if I can get hurt, what chance do they have of being safe or having fun?"

Mary's lips compressed for a second until she remembered the kids were watching her. Relaxing, she smiled at me, her words anything but humorous.

"We'll deal with it. I will not have you drop dead because something breaks loose later from that fall."

"I understand, I do. But I'm fine. Well, mostly fine. My butt and back will ache for a day or so, but I'm fine, Mary. Not the first time I've had a horse dump me, nor will it be the last."

"Kathi, it's not worth it," she growled. How she did that through clenched teeth as she smiled was actually rather impressive.

Brenda added her voice to the mix. "I agree with Mary. While I can't force you to go, I sure wish you would."

I looked at Mark again. Without a word, he handed me my helmet. When I finished snapping it on, he bent over and cupped his hands. With a quick lift, I was sitting back on Ringo. I gritted my teeth at the spasm of pain that rippled up my back when my butt hit the saddle.

I shifted around, getting comfortable, then nodded down at Mark. He gave me one more concern-filled glance as he rubbed his hand along Ringo's neck. I gave him a smile and a nod. Mark held my gaze for a moment longer before moving back to the fence. He didn't climb it. Apparently, he was staying closer this time. I could live with that.

Mary tugged Brenda towards the fence, shaking her head. I chose to ignore the words Mary muttered.

I touched my heels to Ringo and laid the reins across his neck, swinging him back out into the arena. We took three full laps, starting at a walk and working up to an easy posting trot. My butt pounded in pain at each impact, but I ignored it, locking it inside a box and storing it away until later. I ended my third lap and turned towards the first jump, moving Ringo back into a canter.

A few moments later, I was again approaching the ill-fated jump spot. Ringo's shoulders twitched, but he listened to me as I quietly reassured him. He never hesitated, surging forward with a burst of speed at the right moment. We made a textbook jump, easily clearing the fence and landing cleanly.

The impact was excruciating on my back, but I gritted through it. I started the last half lap that led me to the big jump. Accepting that the movement would hurt, I didn't hesitate. I urged Ringo forward, and we headed towards the poles. I had just enough time to glance at Mark, standing like a statue near the fence, before we were sailing over the jump.

We landed and I took as much of the impact with my legs and knees as possible. I steered Ringo in a small loop and brought him back towards the kids. They were all clapping and cheering. At that moment, I knew I had done the right thing. I might pay for it tomorrow, but those kids needed to know that I wasn't badly hurt.

They crowded around the arena edge and I moved Ringo close so that they could pet his nose and neck. I noted, with pleasure, that their eyes held excitement and happiness, not the fear from earlier.

After a few moments of allowing the kids to interact with Ringo and barrage me with excited questions, Mary took charge. In no time, she and the chaperones were herding everyone to the bus and getting them loaded up for the trip home.

All I wanted to do was get home and spend a long time soaking in my hot tub.

Mark walked beside me as I slowly rode a sweaty Ringo out of the arena and over to the barn. Reaching the small hitching post, I swung my leg over to dismount. I almost yelped when Mark's hands grasped my waist, lifting me up and away from my horse.

I wanted to tell him I could have dismounted on my own, but the look in his eyes told me not to argue with him. He lowered me slowly and set me gently on the ground, my hands sliding down his chest as I settled to my feet.

"Thank you," I said, patting his arm. His strong, muscular arm.

Strong arms that had held me like I was a precious flower that needed protecting. I didn't find the unpleasant in the least.

I removed my helmet as I walked towards Ringo's head. Without my asking, Mark started loosening the girth. I said nothing, recognizing he was doing it as much for him as me.

I moved around, slipping off the bridle and reins, putting Ringo's halter back on, and tying him to the hitching post. We worked silently together, removing the rest of the tack and hauling it to the tack room. While I was putting everything up, Mark went back out into the barn and led Ringo over to his stall.

I stepped out of the tack room in time to find Mark brushing Ringo. Finished, he hung the brush back on its hook by the stall door before leading my horse into his stall. A few seconds later, Mark emerged from the stall and shut the door, affixing the chain to the lock. Ringo stuck his head over the open dutch door, shoving Mark in the shoulder. Laughing softly, Mark rubbed his nose before turning back to me.

I stood there as he came up close to me. He stared down at me for several moments, letting the silence hang between us.

"You sure you're okay?" he finally asked, his voice still graveled with concern and worry. Something about it, combined with the look he was giving me, ignited a small furnace in my stomach and a warmth feeling began spreading through me. I smiled and reached out to squeeze his arm.

"I'm fine, Mark. Really. Nothing some ibuprofen and a long soak in my hot tub won't fix."

He looked skeptical, but finally nodded.

"You looked good out there, even when you did your trapeze act," he said, finally cracking a grin.

I tried glaring at him, but he stood there, grinning. He may have been smiling at me, but his eyes gave him away. I knew he was still worried about me. He popped his hat off and scrubbed his fingers through his hair. Those messy locks distracted me as I imagined my fingers running through them. Snapping fingers in my face broke me out of my thoughts.

He was leaning down, looking me in the eye. "Maybe I should drive you to the hospital. You're zoning out on me."

Mark looked up as someone entered the barn, boots scuffing in the dirt and gravel. I turned to see Mary heading our way. Her eyes were laser-focused on us, a small smirk adorning her face as she gave us that 'I knew it' look.

Great, just what I needed right now. Mary thinking Mark and I were making out in the barn.

"Sounds like a good idea," she said, looking from one to the other of us. "Maybe you *should* let Mark drive you to the ER. He can bring you back to your car after you're done getting poked and prodded."

I needed to exit before things got out of hand. The last thing I wanted to do was spend the next three hours sitting next to Mark in a crowded ER. That might lead to conversations I didn't want to have at the moment.

I waved my hand at them. "Trust me, I'm fine. I'm going to go home, take some Advil and soak in my hot tub. I've been hurt and sore from riding before," I said, glancing between the two of them. Neither looked convinced. Given the look on Mark's face, he was seriously considering throwing me over his shoulder and hauling me to the hospital despite my protests.

I backed away from them slowly, never turning my back. 'Never show fear' they say. Once I was far enough away, I turned and threw a quick "See you tomorrow" over my shoulder and made a beeline for my car. I kept waiting for the crunch of gravel from the impending capture, but neither followed. Moments later, I was in my car, smiling at them and waving even though my ass and back felt like someone had pummeled me with a rolling pin. I sighed, knowing this was just the beginning of my aches and pains.

"Maybe going to the hospital isn't the worst idea after all," I thought. Turning onto the road, I drove home, knowing I'd never admit that to either Mark or Mary.

TWELVE

I sank back against the plush cushions of my couch with a heavy sigh, letting the faint aroma of tea tree oil and eucalyptus fill my lungs, before letting my breath leak out in a slow, steady stream. Those bath bombs I had bought for sore muscles were indeed the bomb.

Two Advil and a long soak had done the trick. The aches were now a very mellow memory, and I felt more human. Wearing my favorite pair of flannel pajama pants, an old Foreigner concert t-shirt, and, more importantly, sporting bra-free boobs, I was prepared to relax after the tumultuous day.

Simon dropped off from the top of the couch and landed on the old throw pillow I kept there for him. I scratched the top of his head and he butted my hand, eyes closed, his face a mask of feline contentment. His paws pressed on my side and he began making biscuits, almost as if he were trying to help me with my remaining aches by giving me a massage.

I picked up the remote from the couch arm and hit the power button. The room exploded in sound, startling Simon, who did his best Halloween-cat impression. I quickly stabbed the volume button until the noise settled into something less than a jet engine. I glared down at Simon, who was slowly settling back on his pillow.

"If you would walk *around* the remote, instead of across it, this wouldn't happen. Serves you right." He licked his paw and wiped at his face, his disdain for my observation loud and clear.

I was perusing the movie channels when my stomach rumbled. Considering I hadn't eaten since lunch, which was hours ago, I could understand my stomach thinking I'd forgotten it.

I eased up off the couch with only a slight grimace, plodding into the kitchen, bare feet slapping quietly on the wood before I hit the cool tile of the kitchen floor. Simon followed me, assuming that since I was in the kitchen, then it was time to feed him. I swear the cat was just four legs carrying around a stomach that meowed occasionally.

I pulled open the refrigerator door and began searching the shelves. Sadly, there wasn't much to find. Milk, bacon, a cucumber that looked like it belonged inside a sarcophagus. Takeout Chinese containers with fried rice and orange chicken sat next to a bowl of mac and cheese from a week ago. A bowl of something that I did not recognize, and appeared to be on its way to sentience, occupied the back corner of the shelf.

"Should probably throw that mystery bowl out before it starts talking to me," I muttered to myself, glancing down at Simon, who responded by licking his lips. He seemed in favor of the idea as long as he got the food.

Nothing from the fridge seemed appealing. Guess I was going to have to order something. I closed the door and scanned the takeout menus magnetized to the front.

The ring of the doorbell startled me, sending my heart rate sparking. How did anyone get to my door? The gate should have kept them out. For that matter, why hadn't I heard the gate buzzer go off? Maybe they had climbed the fence? No, that would have created a different alarm.

About a year before Jeremy died, we'd had a series of break-ins in our area. The burglars had even beaten one older couple during one invasion. Jeremy had wasted no time in constructing a fence around our property with a coded gate at the front entrance.

After its construction, Jeremy had hired a security and monitoring company to come in and wire up the fence and all the windows in the house. He didn't want the doors wired because he didn't want the hassle of trying to deactivate a system when he came in and out. This way, the system never needed deactivation.

Several of our neighbors thought we were being overzealous. They thought that right up until someone attempted to get into the house two weeks after the system installation. Luckily, we had been out to dinner, so we weren't home when the police apprehended the individual, after being alerted by the monitoring company. It was actually funny to see both the fencing and security companies very active in our area after that night.

I fumbled to my right before finding the power button of the under-cabinet monitor for the security system. When the view finally cleared and sharpened, I tapped the small picture for the front door, enlarging it to full size.

In the security system, the porch light tied into the front doorbell and would pop on when someone rang the bell, giving me clear sight of whomever was standing at the door.

The monitors showed a man in a ball cap, holding what appeared to be two boxes of pizza and a bag. The ball cap kept me from seeing his face. I moved my finger to the alarm button under the monitor, prepared to summon the police. And I knew the gate had closed after me when I came home earlier.

Before I could decide between hitting the alarm button or just calling 911, the man turned enough that his face was clearly visible.

Mark.

What the hell was he doing here at this hour? How did he get past the gate? Oh yeah, I'd given him the gate code for dinner the other night. I racked my brain for reasons as to why he was here as I slowly headed to the front door.

I flipped the deadbolt, but left the chain connected. I cracked the door open enough to glance out. Mark grinned as he held the boxes and the bag towards me.

"I come bearing pizza." A quick sniff confirmed that there was indeed pizza in the boxes. I looked from the boxes up to his innocent grin. I had to admit, his grin was pretty cute.

I glared at him while trying my best not to smile, I asked, "Do you have any idea what time it is?" I kept the door firmly in place.

"Yep," he responded, popping that last letter of his answer. "It's pizza time. Can I come in? Pizzas are getting cold."

I considered him for a few more seconds before closing the door to slip the chain off. I opened the door again and stepped back, silently inviting him in. He bobbed his head, strode past me, and made a beeline for the kitchen. I closed and relocked the door before following my uninvited, but not overly unwelcome, food deliverer.

He sat the boxes down on the island and turned to me, hands already up in surrender mode as he spoke. "Before you get upset, Mary figured you'd come straight home, soak until you turned into a wrinkled prune, and totally forget about eating. I offered to bring you pizza, and she was all for it. Heck, she even wanted to pay for it. I refused."

Before I could answer, he turned to my cabinets and began opening them like he was a long-time resident. "Plates?" he asked, looking back over his shoulder. I hesitated, then pointed to his left. He nodded and opened the indicated cabinet, pulling out two plates and setting them on the island. While he started opening and closing drawers, looking for who knows what, I grabbed my phone and stepped around the corner and into the hallway. Once out of sight of the kitchen, I opened the message app and began smashing keys.

> Kathi: What were you thinking, sending Mark here at this time of night?

She must have been waiting because her response was almost immediate.

> Mary: He was very concerned about you. I thought it was so sweet that he wanted to check up on you and feed you. It made my old heart flutter.

I wasn't buying it, stabbing even harder at the keys.

Kathi: Don't feed me that crap.

Mary: I'm shocked! I was only thinking about my poor friend, alone, hurting, and probably hungry.

Kathi: Don't play innocent with me. We talked about this.

Mary: So? You're in your house and he brought you pizza. You had dinner with him the other night, so what's the harm?

Kathi: I'm in my jammies and don't have a bra on!

Several smiling devil emojis came flying across my phone.

Mary: If you ask him, I'm sure it won't bother him!

"You ready to eat?" came floating out of the kitchen. I tapped my phone keys again.

Kathi: This isn't funny. I am so going to get you for this.

Mary: Loosen up. Have fun. Oh, one more thing.

Kathi: What?

Mary: He likes his eggs sunny-side up for breakfast.

Kathi: You are so dead to me right now.

A string of laughing emojis came back in response as I snapped the phone shut. I made a mental note to plot Mary's death as I walked back towards the kitchen. Pausing at the doorway, I took in the sight before me.

I had a small breakfast nook in the back of the kitchen. Its bay windows let me look out over the backyard. During the winter, I would have my morning coffee and gaze out over the snow-blanketed grass, a glimpse of the mountains off in the distance. It was always a great way to start my day.

There were several small does that lived in the area and in the spring, it wasn't unusual to see them and their new fawns grazing, tails flicking lazily.

Tonight, though, Mark had set it up for dinner. Boxes of pizza and plates were still on the island, but glasses, silverware and napkins adorned the table.

As I stepped into the kitchen, Mark looked up from the island.

"I brought beer. Didn't know what you would want to go with your pizza. I did see you had some sodas and an open bottle of red in the fridge," he said. "What do you want to drink?"

"You've already rifled through my fridge?" I tried unsuccessfully to look indignant. His lips twisted up in a sheepish smile.

"Well, duh. I had to figure out what there was to drink. Word to the wise, there's something in a bowl in the back that's beyond the science experiment stage. I think it waved at me, but I'm not sure. I'm not ashamed to admit it scared me," he said, shuddering.

"But," he continued, rubbing his hands together and waving them at the island. "I got pepperoni with Italian sausage. You didn't tell me what crust you liked, so one's thin and one's traditional."

Mark looked at me expectantly and I gave myself a mental 'huh'. He'd remembered my favorite pizza. He'd really been listening.

"Traditional. I'll have some of the wine."

He crooked an eyebrow at me. "Taken anything for the pain?"

"Huh? Oh. Yeah, a couple of Advil two hours ago, before my soak."

"Good. Those shouldn't be a problem then," he said, nodding. He flipped open the boxes and, using a spatula, moved slices from boxes to plates. He closed the box lids and took the plates to the table, placing them at seats that were across from each other.

As I sat there watching, he went back to the kitchen to finish his prep, moving with familiarity around my kitchen. He plucked a wine glass from the storage slots under the cabinet, then pulled the wine from the fridge. Spinning back to the table, he sat the glass and bottle near one of the plates, which I assumed was mine. Returning to the fridge, he pulled out two beers, then bumped it closed with his elbow before returning and setting the beers down near the other plate.

I watched him move around my kitchen without a care in the world. It looked so... domesticated, as if it was something he did every night. And if I was honest with myself, I had to acknowledge it was nice having someone to share a meal with other than Simon.

"Good thing you have cushions in your chairs. Let's eat," he stated as he pulled a chair out from the table and waited expectantly.

I stood at the island, multiple confusing thoughts running through my head. This was a bad idea. A *very* bad idea. He shouldn't be here, should he? He shouldn't be in my kitchen. Not to mention, I wasn't wearing a bra, and I really didn't want to put one back on. I considered this. Luckily, or unluckily, depending on the point of view, I hadn't received the same blessing from the boob fairy as others. Given that my shirt was dark, and I wasn't planning on reenacting any scenes from *Baywatch*, it should be okay.

Mark gave my hesitation a bemused look before walking over to the island. He took my hand, gently tugging me over towards the table. Closer to the food, I got a full whiff of the pizza. My stomach gurgled loudly in anticipation. Mark's eyes shot to my middle and my neck flamed.

He chuckled. "At least your stomach approves. Let's feed that thing before it escapes and eats the villagers."

I snickered, but let him guide me to my chair and sat. He pushed my chair up to the table before moving around and picking up the bottle of wine. He worked the cork out with a slight *pop* and deftly filled my glass half way. He re-corked and sat the bottle down near his plate before taking his seat. He leaned over and took an appreciative sniff of his pizza before popping off the cap of his beer.

He took a large bite of his slice, crunching the thinner crust. I still hadn't touched my food, and my stomach wasn't happy about that, but I had to say something first.

"Mark, you really didn't have to do this," I said.

He pointed at his mouth, chewing slowly, and shook his head. He inclined his head towards my plate, indicating that I should eat my pizza. *Fine.* I picked up my slice and bit into it. *If you can't beat them, eat their pizza.* My stomach flipped in happy circles as its favorite food came sliding down.

I must have been hungrier than I thought, because it seemed like I inhaled the first two slices in no time and Mark quickly got me more. As we ate, he kept watching me, eating in silence. I liked that he didn't feel the need to fill the void with small talk.

I eyed the box, debating a fifth piece. I glanced up to see Mark grinning at me. He lifted his napkin up, wiping at a smear of sauce at the corner of his mouth. He nodded towards the box.

"Go ahead, I won't judge. You've got some serious pizza-eating skills. I am impressed and a bit in awe."

I grinned. "It's a gift." I looked around, suddenly uncomfortable. This was a little too relaxed and cozy. I know what Mary said, but this felt like more than friends. Handsome and attractive aside, it was giving me a weird vibe. I needed to gain control of this situation.

I clapped my hands together. "Well, Mark, this was nice. Thank you, really, for bringing the pizza. You can tell Mary that you fed me and all was good. I know you have a big day tomorrow, so I can understand you needing to leave."

Mark smiled, polishing off his beer. He pushed his chair back, then stood up slowly. Still smiling, he walked over to the island. He popped open both pizza boxes and started consolidating the slices into a single box.

I waved at him, getting him to stop. "You don't have to do that. I'll take care of it before I go to bed." He nodded at me and kept working. Finished with the pizza, he came back and grabbed his empty beer bottles.

"Garbage?" he asked

"Recycle. Under the sink. Mark, didn't you hear me?"

He turned towards the sink, bottles in hand. "Yes, I heard you. Under the sink. Got it."

I grumped. "I meant about not needing to do anything. You can go home now."

He tossed the empty bottles in the recycle bin and came back to the table.

"Nope, can't leave yet. Be at least a couple of hours, maybe longer," he said, picking up the pizza and heading for the fridge.

"Why not?"

"Well, I had several beers with dinner. Gonna have to give those time to clear my system."

He flashed me that devastating dimpled grin again. "You wouldn't want me to get DUI or anything, would you?" He tried to look innocent, but no jury in the world would buy it.

He had set me up.

I rose out of my chair, huffing slightly. "Fine, I guess you can stay. This changes nothing about the situation, Mark."

"Of course not, Kathi," he agreed. Deep down, I wasn't sure I was happy with how fast he agreed to that.

I gathered up the plates and silverware, bringing them over to the sink. I popped the dishwasher open and began loading while Mark was putting the pizza in the fridge. Turning, he clapped his hands and rubbed them together.

"So, what should we do? What were you doing before I got here?"

"Well, I was going to watch a movie."

"Perfect," he said, clapping his hands together. "We're gonna need popcorn."

"But we just ate?"

He snorted at me. "What's that got to do with anything? It's not a movie without popcorn."

He turned and started raiding my cabinets again until he found the pantry and my bags of microwave popcorn. A few beeps later, the microwave was humming. Once the bag of corn started popping, he opened the fridge and pulled out another beer. I stepped forward and took it away from him, sticking it back in the fridge. I pulled out two sodas and closed the door.

"No more beer for you," I said, handing him a can. He chuckled and sat it on the island. He rummaged through the cabinets to find a bowl.

"Butter?" he asked.

I shook my head. "No, thank you."

He nodded and turned back to the microwave as the popping sped up. Wandering into the den, I set my soda on the end table next to the couch before making my way to the TV. I plucked a DVD from the shelf next to the TV and pried open the case. I put the disc into the player's tray, touched the close button, and went back to the couch.

I'll show him.

Mark came over and plopped down next to me, setting his soda on the coffee table. Before I could tell him to slide over to his side, Simon hopped up onto the vacant end of the couch, did several circles, and laid down.

Great, now my cat is helping shove us together.

"Nice couch. Big and comfy. What are we watching?" he asked as he stretched his legs out and propped them on the coffee table, crossing his ankles. The bowl of popcorn sat between us.

I said nothing, touching the play button on the remote. The disc began whirring, and in a few moments, the main title screen came up.

Mark tossed several pieces of popcorn into his mouth and started chewing. When the opening scene started, he turned, grinning at me.

"*Sleepless in Seattle*? Cool. This is one of my favorites."

I stared, open-mouthed. "You said you didn't like this movie."

"I never said I didn't like it. I said that *You've Got Mail* is a better movie."

"You really like rom-coms?"

He nodded. "I love rom-coms." He turned to look at me directly. "Some of us guys are more cultured than others, you know."

He laughed at me as I rolled my eyes. He grabbed some more popcorn and turned his attention back to the TV.

As the movie played, he didn't make any commentary, didn't point out any corny lines. I was thankful. People had ruined movies for me in the past by telling me how silly or unrealistic something was. But Mark took it all in and enjoyed the movie.

At one point, I looked out of the corner of my eye and felt my heart flutter. Simon was stretched out along Mark's thigh, legs extended forward, eyes closed. Mark was absently rubbing the traitorous cat's head, who was purring hard enough I could feel it through the cushions. *I bet he could make me purr like that.* I was startled by thought that ran through my mind unbidden and shook my head. *Get a grip, girl.*

Still, I knew it was Mark, and I knew all the reasons this situation was wrong, but maybe… maybe there were worse things. I missed this, missed the closeness. Seeing him move around my kitchen with familiarity was one thing, but here, on the couch, hanging out together and watching a movie, I was reminded of the other important things missing in my life since I lost Jeremy.

Hell, if I was honest with myself, those things were missing *before* Jeremy passed. He and I had settled into life, each of us with our own routines, not necessarily revolving around each other. We said we loved each other, but had they been just words we were expected to say?

I sighed to myself, snuggling back into the couch, letting myself relax and my head to fall back against the cushions. It had been a long day. The hot tub, the full stomach, the wine, and yes, the company, all combined to make me really relaxed. Mark moved the empty popcorn bowl out of the way and sat back against the couch, head back as well, silently watching Annie plot to find Sam.

Try as I could to stay awake, my eyelids were dragging down. The last thing I remember is Sam seeing Annie walk off the plane and into the airport before the blackness pulled me down into its comfort.

THIRTEEN

W*arm.* That was the groggy thought swimming through my brain. I was warm, and I was holding a very warm pillow. I sighed, pulling it in closer. The warmth was all-encompassing.

The heat from the pillow I was hugging lulled me back into the depths of sleep as it moved. Its steady, deep breathing let me know it was sleeping as well, which made me feel good. Pillows deserved a good sleep, too.

I sighed, snuggled my pillow and let myself drift. My pillow snuggled back, and I sighed again, content.

My eyes snapped open with a clarity fueled by fear. Fear which stemmed from an unmitigated truth.

Pillows. Don't. Snuggle.

My brain raced as I tried to get up, but my pillow snuggled me tighter, preventing me from getting up. I stilled, slowly settling back down against the pillow-that-was-not-a-pillow.

The moonlight streaming in from the kitchen gave me barely enough light to make out vague shapes. Looking up, I could tell by the ceiling and the general shape of the light I was in the front room. Which meant I was on the couch.

Why was I on the couch and not in my bed? I rarely slept on the couch. What reason could I have for sleeping on the couch?

Oh. My. *God.*

Memory crashed into me like a rogue wave at the beach. Mark. Movie. Couch. I was on the couch. With Mark. I was on the couch with Mark. Mark and I were snuggling on the couch, and dear God, I wasn't wearing a bra. I hoped that this was a dream. A dream brought on by pizza, wine and an overabundance of Advil.

My not-a-pillow sniffed and pulled me in closer.

Fuck a duck. It wasn't a dream.

I took silent stock of the situation, now that I had an inkling of what was going on. My right arm draped over what I can only assume was Mark's chest. Given the warmth on the side of my face, my head must be laying slightly on his chest and shoulder. Which meant the fiery streak down my back was Mark's arm.

I was in Mark's arms. Well, *arm* at least. But the fact remained, I was sleeping in Mark's arms. This was wrong on so many levels and had so many questions attached. What would he think? Would he think we were dating since we'd done the snuggle dance on the couch? Wait. Did he hear me snore? Or worse, what if I've drooled on his chest?

A quick tongue flick confirmed the lack of drool. At least I had that going for me.

Mark shifted slightly, his hand on my lower back, pulling me tighter to him. He sighed softly as his other arm, which must have been between him and the couch, drifted up and over his chest. His hand landed on mine, covering it easily. He squeezed lightly and then seemed to relax and drift deeper into sleep.

I laid there, unsure. What was I going to do? How was I going to escape this very warm, very nice snuggle? This was an intimate situation. My first time laying next to a man since my husband died. I shouldn't be doing this. It didn't matter how much I missed this, or how solid Mark's chest was, or how touching it was that he was holding my hand in his sleep, or even how comforting it was to be held, to be in someone's arms. *God, how I've missed that.*

What's the harm here?

That small thought pole-vaulted over my concerns. What was the harm? We were both clothed. Well, mostly, since neither of us was wearing a bra. Mark wasn't pawing at me, we weren't doing any couch surfing. We were just laying here, sleeping, one of us laying on a very warm and firm chest, being held in a very, *very* nice cuddle.

What *was* the harm? Long day, full tummies, bound to happen. No harm, no foul. The best course of action would be to just ignore the situation, deferring it till morning.

Yes, that was the thing to do. Be embarrassed in the morning, laugh about it, and go with it. Perfect. In that case, there was no reason not to go back to sleep and make full use of this perfectly good snuggle.

Satisfied with my rationalization, I pulled myself even closer to Mark, adjusted my head so it was more comfortable on his chest, and let myself drift off.

Consciousness came with the heavenly aromas of bacon and coffee. My nose twitched in anticipation even as I blinked my eyes, trying to clear the sleep from them. I sniffed again, and my stomach gave a little gurgle. It wanted some of the bacon. Wait. Bacon?

My thoughts slammed on the brakes even as my stomach revved up for the bacon. I was on my couch. Meaning I wasn't the one cooking. Either my cat had developed skills that were going to make me famous, or someone was in my kitchen cooking bacon.

Understanding exploded inside me, both in my head and in my stomach as the fear hit.

Mark. Mark, my cuddle bunny, my not-a-pillow, was still here, and he was cooking bacon in my kitchen. I recalled the process I worked through to rationalize staying next to him last night. I also ignored the fact it had been some of the deepest and most stress-free sleep I'd had in years.

Pushing the blanket away, I swung my feet off the couch, pulling myself up to a sitting position. A low groan escaped my lips as a pulse of pain came from my lower back, even as I wondered where the blanket had come from.

From my kitchen, an entirely too chipper male voice rang out. "Rise and shine, breakfast will be ready in about 10."

It wasn't a dream. I so hoped it had been one. A pleasant one, but a still a dream. Now it looked like it was about to be a nightmare.

I pulled myself up and headed to my bedroom and a much-needed bathroom visit. Washing my hands, I looked in the mirror and shuddered. My hair was going every which way, and I wasn't wearing any makeup. I picked up my brush and attempted to wrangle my hair into a semblance of order. Dropping the brush, I grabbed my mouthwash, took a healthy slug, and swished it around for a few seconds before spitting in the sink. That should smother any lingering morning dragon breath.

Another memory punched me in the gut. No bra. I hadn't been wearing a bra. How could this situation get any worse? I snagged the bra off the end of my bed and wrangled it on as Simon sauntered in and began rubbing against my leg.

"Traitor," I said, wagging my finger at him as he jumped up on the bed, staring at me as I fought with my bra. "I saw you cozying up to him on the couch last night. You were supposed to be on my side."

He stared up at me, head cocked to one side. His look screamed *hypocrite*.

As I finished adjusting my bra, I stared back at him. "Don't you judge me. You don't understand," I said. Simon turned, jumped off the bed with a resounding thump, flipped his tail up, and stalked out of the room. A cat had just judged me. Great.

I wandered back into the kitchen, pausing at the doorway to take in the sight before me. The morning sunlight was streaming in through the windows, casting hazy rays around the room. Mark was working on something in a pan, using a spatula to move things around. He was wearing the same clothes from last night, but his hair looked wet. Did he shower? A momentary image of a steamy shower with a naked Mark inside flashed into my thoughts, thoughts I quickly squashed. *Oh no, brain. We can't go there.*

As if he heard my thoughts, he glanced up at me, smiling, his eyes raking over me before he spoke. "Morning. Hope you like your eggs sunny-side up."

Pausing his spatula, he reached over and pushed the lever down on the toaster before resuming his egg preparation.

I crossed my arms, watching him move about my kitchen, unsure how to proceed. *Remember, laugh it off. No big deal. Act casual. No reason to freak out just because the young man whose arms you slept in is now cooking you breakfast. Nope, no freak out needed.*

Yeah, that wasn't working so well. The freak out was sitting right there, ready to jump into action at any moment.

Mark was moving between the fridge, stove, and table like a well-trained dancer. He opened the microwave, pulled out a plate of bacon, and sat it on the table.

"Sit," he said, looking over at me again before turning back to his meal preparation dance. I sat gingerly, trying not to jar the parts of my body that were still a little sore this morning.

Mark appeared next to me, placing some Advil next to my plate, along with a glass of water. "Here, I thought you might need these this morning."

"Thanks," I replied, genuine relief in my voice as I scooped up the painkillers. I threw them into my mouth and gulped the water.

Like magic, Mark appeared again, this time holding the skillet. He tipped it, using his spatula to slide some eggs onto my plate, dumping the rest on his plate. The toaster popping in the background drew him back to the stove. A moment later, the toast appeared on my plate and the butter tub appeared in front of me, along with a knife.

One more lap of my kitchen and a welcome cup of steaming coffee appeared in front of me. I looked up as Mark slid into the seat to my right, placing a large glass of juice next to his plate.

"Sorry, I'm not a big coffee drinker, so I exercised chef's prerogative and scarfed the last of the juice, if that's okay?" he asked, gesturing at the glass.

"Um, sure," I said before waving my hand at the table setting. "This looks amazing. But you didn't have to do all of this."

He shrugged. "Yeah, probably not. But I was hungry and figured you might be, so, fix for one, fix for two, no big difference. But fair warning, I love bacon, so better snag yours quick."

He speared a slice of bacon off the plate, shoving it into his mouth, whole. I rolled my eyes, and he grinned. We both focused on our eating, but even while chewing, I let the normalcy of the moment settle. Again, the simple act of eating breakfast with someone was comforting, and reminded me again of the things I missed since Jeremy's passing.

I sipped my coffee, enjoying the post-breakfast fullness. I stared at Mark over the rim of my cup, my thoughts flowing back over the events of last night. For an evening, it felt... normal. I hadn't been alone. Someone had been there, eating dinner, enjoying a movie. Yes, even sleeping in someone's arms, all made more perfect by the breakfast he'd fixed.

My head knew dating Mark would be wrong, but my heart? My heart was having different thoughts. These last hours had been... nice. For a short time, the aloneness had faded.

My plate sliding away from me pulled me back from my thoughts. Mark was clearing the table, placing dishes in the sink. I stopped him as he pulled the dishwasher door open.

"Mark, please, leave them. I'll get them later."

Looking over at me, he wiped his hands on the dish towel he held and dropped it on the cabinet.

"Okay. Guess I'll head out. Oh, I texted Mary and told her you'd be running late. She understood you were sleeping in and might be stiff and running slow."

I felt the blood drain from my face as a sick feeling hit the pit of my stomach.

"You told Mary you stayed here last night?"

He nodded. "Yeah, told her I crashed on the couch when it got late."

Shit. Now I could expect the Mary Inquisition.

He walked over and sat down on the couch. He grabbed his shoes and slipped them on over his socks. I followed him as he strolled to the front door, opening it. He paused and turned back to me.

"Thanks for the pizza, breakfast, and, well, everything," I said. My heart was pounding in my throat. It was like it being in high school again, my date dropping me off at the house, me wondering if he was going to kiss me or not.

Grinning, his hand shot out, taking mine. My eyes widened as he brought it up to his lips. Keeping eye contact with me, he kissed my knuckles lightly, like a butterfly lighting on a flower, before letting go of my hand. I held it there for a moment, stunned, then let it slowly fall to my side. He studied my face before speaking. And when he spoke, his voice was deep and gravelly, despite the light dancing in his eyes. "See you at Mary's." With that, he turned and was gone, the door closing behind him.

I stared at the door, rubbing my hand over my knuckles, still warm from the lingering heat of Mark's lips. Simon head-butted my legs before winding through them.

"What do I do, Simon?" I asked, still staring at the door.

Simon meowed and head-butted me again, winding his way back through my legs before jogging off to wherever he goes during the day.

"Some help you are," I muttered before heading to my room to get dressed.

FOURTEEN

I parked my car next to Mary's and got out slowly, making sure there were no twinges. I'd done some light stretching after my shower this morning and rubbed some balm on my lower back to help with the soreness. If I stayed off a horse today, all would be well. Thankfully, Mary's schedule had me working with a group in one of the round pens this afternoon. I would spend most of my time leading them around, which would keep my back loose and relatively pain free.

The EMTs were sitting at their picnic table near the house. One of them glanced up as I walked to the gravel path leading to the barn, then slid off the bench and came to meet me. I recognized Brenda, the EMT who had helped me yesterday. I smiled and waved.

"Morning."

"Hey," she said, stopping in front of me. "How ya feeling this morning?"

"Good," I said, my hand instinctively going to my lower back and rubbing. "Bit sore, but other than that, fine."

"Mind if I check?" she asked, holding up her small light. I nodded, and she clicked it on, flashing it through my eyes again. Done, she slid it back into her shirt pocket and grabbed my hands.

"Squeeze," she said. I squeezed both her hands for a few seconds before she stopped me.

"Blurred vision, double vision, headaches?" she asked.

"No, no, and no." She nodded, dropping my hands. "Take anything?"

"Hot tub soak last night with Advil, more Advil this morning."

She smiled and winked at me. "Good. Take it easy today and try to stay on your horse. Not that I don't mind the work, but a bored EMT is a good thing in this situation."

I laughed and nodded. "I'll let someone else entertain you today, if that's okay. Thank you for everything you did yesterday," I said, smiling as well. She nodded, heading back to rejoin her partner while I continued the path to the barn.

The clear blue sky promised another good day as the gravel crunched under my boots. The footing turned to hard-packed dirt as I moved from the sunlight into the coolness of the barn. I paused, taking a deep breath, filling my lungs with the familiar smells. Hay, wood chips and shavings, horse, and the inevitable horse poop.

Most of the stalls were empty. Mary probably had the horses and their owners out helping with the kids. I glanced at the closed tack door as I walked by, smirking at the memory of Mark and his attempt to scare Mary.

A gray head stuck out from the last stall and snuffled, blowing out loudly. I smiled, always amazed that he sensed me without fail when I arrived at the barn.

"Morning, boy," I cooed, rubbing his head. I twitched his forelock into place and scrubbed the skin under it. Ringo responded by snuffling softly, tossing his head and trying to nip at my hair. I laughed and moved my head back out of the way.

"Stop that. Be nice."

After rubbing his head and patting his neck a few more times, I headed to the back entrance of the barn. I paused before stepping out into the sunlight, surveying the grounds.

Jake had set up two smaller round pens on the back side of the barn. Mary held court in the right pen, pacing around in the middle of the enclosure like a queen in her court. She had a small whipstick and was using it to point out corrections to six older riders who were plodding around the ring. As the riders went by, I noted their seats and posture. I spotted corrections that were needed, which were very ones Mary was pointing out.

Glancing at the left pen caused my pulse to speed up. Mark had his equipment setup in the middle of the ring. He wore his worn leather work apron over a pair of well-faded blue jeans. A weathered red ball cap sat backwards on his head, holding his hair out of his eyes.

Next to him was what appeared to be an old, five-gallon pickle bucket. I wasn't sure what it was filled with, but it had what appeared to be a huge tie-ring mounted on the top of it. The mare's lead rope looped through the ring, keeping the horse in place without Mark holding the rope.

Around him, adorned in their helmets, were another five kids, all watching Mark work. They were close enough to see what was going on, but far enough away that even if the horse kicked out, hooves wouldn't come close to them.

His back was to the mare's head as he had pulled her front leg and hoof up between his leather-clad thighs. This made the bottom of the hoof visible to the watching kids. I watched as he used a farrier's knife to trim away at the frog of the hoof. As pieces flipped off from his work, he would glance up at the kids, his mouth moving. I assumed he was telling the kids what he was doing and answering questions they were throwing at him.

I crossed my arms and stood silently, taking him in. He was wearing a black t-shirt, which made it easy to watch as the muscles in his forearms flexed with each cut. The muscular cords of his neck rolled each time he completed a stroke with the knife.

The mare stomped one hind hoof and attempted to pull the front one out of Mark's grasp. He clamped his thighs down on her leg and kept his grip on the hoof, shushing at her. The mare settled back down, flicking her tail. Without missing a beat, Mark kept working and answering more questions from the kids as he used his rasp to smooth the hoof and even the trimmed edges. He was fantastic with them, smiling and taking the time he needed, addressing each kid directly as they asked questions.

He finished the hoof and gently lowered it to the ground. He stood up and stretched, working his back. As he twisted his neck, he spotted me and his eyes lit up. That intense look ignited a warmth in me that spread like wildfire. He winked at me before moving to the horse's back hoof.

I couldn't take my eyes off him. It was as if he had enthralled me and I couldn't escape. What I was seeing was mixing with the images from earlier this morning, being in his arms. The hairs on my arms were tingling and standing up and warmth washed over me. A hand with a red handkerchief appeared at my arm, tapping it against my skin.

"Here."

I started as my breath caught in my throat. I looked to my left into Jake's easy smirk. His eyes were dancing with suppressed laughter, even as they squinted against the sunlight. He'd opted for a well-worn tan stetson today instead of his normal ball cap. Guess he was going for the full cowboy look.

"You startled me. What's that for?" I asked, looking down at the handkerchief.

"Well, Mom mentioned you might need this. And sure enough, you got a little drool there on the side of your face," he said, flicking a finger at my chin.

I felt the heat explode up my neck and my face flame up. He broke out laughing as he danced out of the way, the swing I flung at his arm missing, causing me to stumble. He kept laughing even as moved out of my range.

He chuckled, waving his hands at me in surrender, now that he was sure it was safe. "You made it too easy, Kathi." I turned away, embarrassed. Jake came back up beside me, slipping an arm around my shoulder.

"Sorry," he said, squeezing me. I turned my head away, still embarrassed that I'd been caught like a schoolgirl watching her first crush.

His gaze flicked between me and Mark. "You wanna tell me what's going on with you two?" he asked. I could feel his eyes on me without looking back at him.

I shrugged. "Nothing," I said, still not looking at him.

"Really?" he asked, his hand rubbing over his jaw. "You want to take a few moments to think about that? Come up with something else?"

I considered for a moment, then shook my head. "No, nothing else to think of, since it's the truth."

"Uh huh," he hummed. "Come on." He grabbed my arm, pulling me back through the barn until we were standing outside the tack room. He leaned back against the wall. Taking his hat off, he wiped through his hair with the red handkerchief before setting the old hat back on his head and stuffing the cloth back in his pocket. Crossing his arms across his chest, he cocked his head to one side, looking me in the eye.

"Mom tells me you and Mark had dinner the other night. That doesn't *sound* like nothing to me."

I crossed my arms, feeling slightly defensive. "It was just dinner," I said. "As friends. Friends can have dinner."

"If you say so," he said, smiling. A thought flitted through my memory, a conversation from another time. I stepped forward and poked him in his chest, glaring at him.

"You *knew* he liked me. That night in my kitchen you told me I needed to 'swim in a new pool'," I said, air-quoting the last few words. "You guaranteed me there was someone out there for me, that he wouldn't care how old or young I was. You *knew*!" I poked him in the chest again. I really should stop doing that, as it was as useless as poking an oak tree. The boy had some serious muscles under that shirt.

He shook his head, still smiling. "All he wanted to know was if you were dating or seeing anyone."

I started to poke him again, but halted. "You should have *said* something. I would have been prepared instead of getting blind-sided at Scott's."

He shrugged his shoulders. "Why? He asked questions about you, nothing more. Besides, what's the big deal? He likes you. So what?"

"The *big deal* is I'm old enough to be his *mother*, Jake," I argued.

"But you're *not* his mother." He took my arm, giving it a squeeze, and looked me in the eye before he continued, his voice serious. "And Kathi, *he* doesn't care."

I stared at Jake and he held my gaze, not breaking away. I pulled out of his grasp and turned away, heading back towards the opening.

His voice sounded from behind me. "Kathi."

I paused, looking back at him as he closed the distance between us. He laid a hand on my shoulder, gripping it gently as his eyes studied my face.

"It's your call, either way. He's a good man, no matter his age. Life's too short to be alone, Kathi. Don't let a damn number keep you from something that might be a good thing."

He squeezed my shoulder again before heading out towards the pens, leaving me standing in the barn, alone with my thoughts.

The movie on the TV droned on, but I didn't know what it was about. Ensconced on my couch, I finished my glass of wine, grabbed the bottle from the table and refilled my glass. Setting the bottle back on the table with a clink, I let my hand drop to Simon's head. His rumbling purrs let me know he appreciated my attention.

I never got the chance to talk with Mark, or even see him again, for the rest of the day. When I finished up my work, I went looking for him. Mary let me know he'd left after his last demo. His uncle was covering their normal jobs while Mark helped us with the kids, so he'd left to help.

I swirled my glass, watching the liquid move and flow as Mary and Jake's words rolled through my head. I'd spent this bottle of wine going over the pros and cons of dating Mark.

Every worst-case scenario I could think of had been imagined and analyzed, and I was still no closer to an answer. Not to mention, if Samuel found out, I'd barely have time to collect my things before they would escort me out the front door of my job. The job that I loved. I looked down at my furry friend, rubbing between his ears.

"Why is this so hard, Simon? I make big decisions all the time at work. I have a budget, staff, responsibilities. Why is this one simple decision so hard?"

Simon looked up at me, furry head cocked to the side, eyes slowly blinking at me.

"Meowwr."

I nodded at his astute observation. "Yes, he's fun and interesting. Lord knows in those tight jeans and that shirt, he's damn attractive, not to mention sexy as hell. That smile. God, that smile lights me up inside every time. What am I going to do?"

Simon remained unresponsive, apparently thinking I was smart enough to figure this out.

I raised my wine glass, gesturing to the otherwise empty room. "Like Mary said, what's the harm in going out with him? Worse that happens is I find out we have nothing in common and I chalk it up to a lesson learned. Best case, I have a great time."

"And," I continued, "If I went out with him, would he expect a kiss at the end of the night? Of course he would. What would a kiss with him be like?"

For a moment, I let my imagination take flight. Would he have soft lips? Would he kiss hard, or tentative? What would his tongue feel like as mine slid against it? God, I haven't kissed a man in years. Would he think I was awful?

I groaned, letting my head lay back against the couch.

"Why can't the universe give me a sign to—"

My phone chimed with an incoming text. I picked it up from the end table. I swear my heart paused for a beat as I read the contact name on the screen.

Mark. *Big freaking sign, universe.*

With a slightly shaky finger, I pushed the button and read the message.

Mark: Hey. Watcha doing?

A simple, friend-type question. Shouldn't the answer be simple? I slugged back more wine, setting my glass on the table. I could do simple.

> Kathi: Just watching a movie, having some wine.

> Mark: Cool. What movie?

Shit, I had no idea. I glanced up at the TV screen. Nothing. No clue. I started typing.

> Kathi: No idea. It's whatever was playing when I turned it on.

> Mark: Everything okay?

No, everything was *not* okay.

> Kathi: Yeah, fine.

> Mark: You sure? Not hurting, are you?

> Kathi: No, it's good. I'm just spacy tonight. Probably the wine.

> Mark: lol. Okay. Sorry I wasn't able to chat today. Was helping my uncle.

> Kathi: Yeah, Mary told me.

> Mark: Ok. Well, guess I will see you tomorrow.

> Kathi: Sure. Tomorrow. Night.

I sat there for a moment, waiting to see if any other message were coming. It was obvious after a moment that no other text was incoming. I grabbed my drink and polished it off. Maybe it was the wine, maybe it was the universe. But I needed to ask him something. My fingers moved before I could change my mind.

> Kathi: Hey Mark?

It was a few seconds before the text alert dinged. He must have put his phone down.

> Mark: Yeah?

Sweat popped out on my neck and my stomach launched acid missiles.

> Kathi: Um, you doing anything tomorrow night, after Mary's?

> Mark: No, not really. Need help with something?

My fingers froze. *Get over it Kathi. You're a grown-ass forty-year-old woman, not some ninth grader. Act like it.*

I tapped out my message, fingers hammering the screen, and hit send before I could chicken out.

> Kathi: Was wondering if you wanted to have dinner and hang out. Maybe do something?

I waited for what seemed like hours before Mark responded.

> Mark: Kathi, did you just ask me out on a date, or are we just hanging out? Heck, I'm alright with it either way. I just want to make sure we're both on the same page.

I grabbed the wine bottle and took a big slug. Setting it between my legs, I tapped out my response.

> Kathi: Yes, I did. I mean, yes, I'm asking you
> out on a date. If that's okay.

No response came flying back. I was thinking I scared him off when the phone in my hand started ringing, scaring me. Once my heart settled down, I glanced and saw it was Mark calling. Fear building, I hit the answer button.

"Hello?"

"*Sorry for the call, but I had to hear the words. You're really asking me out? You seemed pretty adamant the other night that it wasn't what you wanted.*"

"Look, if you don't want to...."

He blew out a breath. "*No, Kathi, I do. Like I said, I need to make sure we're on the same page. Wait, this isn't the wine talking, is it?*"

"Maybe a little, but we can talk more tomorrow night, okay?"

"*Sure. Jeans okay, or are we doing something more dressy?*"

"Jeans are fine. I'll pick you up at 5."

"*Wow, asking me out and picking me up. I could get to like this.*" His chuckle came through the phone speaker. It sounded like graveled honey, and I felt a tingle rush up my spine.

"*And for the record,* " he said, "*I want it known that I am not easy, nor do I put out on the first date.*"

I snorted into the phone. "Try not to get too cute, okay?"

"*I'll try, but I've been told I'm very cute, especially my butt.*"

I couldn't help it. I giggled softly into the phone, trying to cover the receiver, feeling like that high school teenager again, as I felt the flush blow up my neck. If Mary or Jake had said anything, I was going to kill them dead, bring them back to life, and kill them again.

I let out a small sigh and regained my composure. "I guess I need to go. I'll see you tomorrow."

"*Okay. Oh, and Kathi?*"

"Yes."

His voice lowered. "*I'm really looking forward to our date. Night.*"

I didn't get a chance to respond before he hung up. Glancing at the time, I punched in another contact. Mary picked up on the third ring.

"Kinda late for you, Kathi. Everything okay?"

"Yes. No. I'm not sure. God I have no clue."

"What happened? Do you need help?"

"Other than having my head examined, no, I'm okay."

"Then what's the problem?"

"I… that is, I… well," I paused, clearing my throat.

"Spit it out girl, it's late, and I got a four-year-old granddaughter who is up at the crack of dark, fully charged and ready to go."

"IaskedMarkoutonadate" I know I said those as individual words, but that's not what I heard, nor did Mary, apparently.

"Break that down for me. You did what?"

I took in a big, calming breath.

"I asked Mark out on a date. God, what have I done?"

"How much wine did it take?" I held the bottle up, sloshing it around. It was almost empty.

"Almost the full bottle." On the other end of the call, Mary snorted, muttering something I couldn't make out. Then she spoke again, clearly this time.

"Okay. Get here early tomorrow, before the kids. I gotta get some sleep. Oh, and Kathi?"

"What?"

"Don't be dreaming about his ass or what he's filling the front of those jeans with."

I groaned, putting my hand on my forehead. "I hate you so bad right now."

She was still laughing when she hung up. While I had not planned to think about Mark's ass, now that she had mentioned it, it was the only thing I *could* think about.

FIFTEEN

The next morning, an hour before the volunteers were supposed to show up, with a stomach full of churning acid, I knocked on Mary's back door. I kept glancing around, like I was stepping up to an illegal speakeasy. I just knew that any minute, someone would slide back a small opening in the door and ask for a password.

The door opened before I could contemplate possible passwords. Mary, grinning like the cat who'd eaten the canary, practically yanked me inside.

In the kitchen, Julia was wrestling shoes onto Sarah, who seemed to be dead-set on being barefoot. Sarah's little head jerked up when I came in and her face lit up.

"Aunt K, Aunt K!" she shrieked happily. Somehow she escaped the chair and flew across the kitchen floor, slipping and sliding on her sock feet. I dropped to one knee and barely got my arms open before she leapt into my embrace, her hands going around my neck and squeezing for all she was worth. I got a whiff of syrup along with soap. She must have had her favorite breakfast of syrup with a side of waffles. I thanked the stars that someone got her reasonably clean before I got there.

I pulled back and gave her a sloppy kiss on the head. She beamed up at me and my heart tugged a little at how much she looked like her mother. She was the spitting image of her mother, Nikki, at that age. Time had dulled the pain of her loss some, but we still all missed her ferociously.

"Momma Juwea is taking me shopping for shoes and clothes. Then we're gonna go get pessa and meet Becky and Sally and play games and get in the ball pit!" Her words came out all jumbled and all in one breath, which was actually quite impressive.

"We're not going *anywhere* unless you come put your shoes on, young lady," said Julia, waving a small purple and red shiny shoe. Mary came over and pulled Sarah off of my neck, shooing her towards Julia.

"Get your shoes on and mind momma Julia," she said.

"Yes, Gamma," said the small angelic-looking hellion as she rushed back to Julia.

Some minutes later, Julia was leading Sarah, now sporting both shoes, towards the back door. She let Sarah run ahead and swing for a second while she stood in the doorway. Turning to me, she grinned. "Heard you have a date tonight. Gonna get that pic you wanted?"

I felt my face flame up again at the reminder of my drunken call to Mark. Julia just laughed as she headed off after Sarah, the screen door slapping shut behind her.

I whipped my head around to where Mary was sitting at the well-worn wooden kitchen table. Sandwich fixings and chips occupied the tabletop. I pointed at Julia's retreating form. "Seriously? You just had to tell her?"

She grinned over her coffee cup. "She wormed it out of me, threatened to make me bathe Sarah for the next year."

"Yeah, I can understand how that horrific fate would have you quaking in your boots."

I sat down in the chair next to her. Mary pushed a plate and the loaf of bread at me.

"My bet is you were too nervous to eat breakfast this morning and your stomach's churning like a volcano. Put something in there to soak up the acid so you don't feel too sick to go out tonight," she said, pulling her own sandwich together.

I nodded, my hands already moving of their own accord. My mind was too occupied with other thoughts to give too much attention to sandwich construction.

Not sure if I was hungry or nervous, because the sandwich and the chips were gone after a few minutes. Mary filled up my tea glass, refusing to let me have any coffee to add to the volatile concoction my stomach was brewing up.

"Okay, spill it. You look like you're heading in for a double root canal, not out on a date with a handsome young stud."

I stared at her like she's sprouted a second head.

"I told you last night, I asked Mark out."

"So?"

"So?" I said, wringing my hands. "Didn't you hear me? I asked out someone who's fifteen years younger than me on a date. I'm old enough to be is *mother*. What will people think? God, this was a mistake." I knew I was babbling like a flooding brook.

Mary rapped the wooden table with her knuckles, stopping me my rant before it really got started. She held up her hand, fingers closed except for one finger pointing up.

"One, you're not his mother." The second finger went up. "Two, asking someone you like out on a date isn't a mistake." Finger three joined the group. "Three, what does it matter what others think?"

"What if someone I know sees us? If that gets back to Samuel, he'll blow a stack. He's just looking for a reason to dump me." I groaned, thunking my head down on the table. Maybe the pain would bring me clarity and guidance.

"Get a grip, girl. Answer me something," she said, pushing at my shoulder with one finger. I moaned into the tabletop, sounding like a wounded cow. Why was this such a hard decision? Why was I even dwelling on this?

"What?" I said, not raising my head.

"When you told me about the dinner the other night, you were all about the nice things he did, the fun you had, how it was the best non-date you'd had in months. Was that all a lie?"

I lifted my head to look at her. She reached over to pluck a small piece of what appeared to be lettuce from my forehead. She looked back up at me expectantly as she flicked it off onto her plate.

I thought back, remembering the night. The conversations Mark and I had engaged in had been light and fun. We had learned about each other's families. That was nothing like my other dates. Unbidden, that face of the little girl at the restaurant surfaced in my head. Remembering the pure joy on his face as he played with her brought a pleasant warmth to my feelings.

"No," I said.

"You find him attractive?"

"That's got nothing—"

Her knuckles rapping on the table broke into my response.

"Girl, don't lie to me. That call you made the night of your birthday wasn't nothing. All that tequila did was loosen up those walls of yours."

Stupid tequila.

"Yes, fine, he's attractive. I mean, that smile and those arms…" I said, trailing off into memory of laying in those arms. Arms that had held me tight, his hand on mine.

"Last but not least, that ass," she said, grinning. I nodded, then shook myself. Before I could resume my denial, she reached over and gripped my hand.

"Stop it, Kathi. You found someone attractive who's also engaging, funny. You asked him out on a date. Yes, yes, I know it wasn't a date. Keep telling yourself that, if it makes you feel better." She let go of my hand and leaned back. "There's not a damn thing wrong with that. Jake tells me Mark wanted to ask you out last year, but he got called out of town."

She dropped my hand and tapped at the table, making sure she had my full attention. "Kathi, you're forty years old and have been alone for long enough. We both know Jeremy wouldn't want you to be alone. This man *likes* you. Put on your big girl panties and woman up."

I let her words sink in, letting them soak into my thoughts. I hadn't lied when I'd told Mary that it had been the best non-date I'd been on since I started dating again. If I was being honest, it was better than the last dates with Jeremy.

"Besides all that, you're missing one very important thing," she said, toying with the remains of her sandwich.

"What's that?" I asked.

"Bet you could ride him all night long," she said. She broke out laughing when my face lit up like a match.

"Keep your heels down, Meredith. Just like that. Good," I said, watching the new rider make the correction yet again. I spun slowly around in place, watching each pair as they worked their way around the ring at barely above a walk. Six eager young equestrians were doing their best to master the art of not falling off a horse.

What they didn't realize was that the horses they were on were some of the most dead-broke, gentle creatures that Mary owned. Veterans of years of lessons, the horses knew the routine. They plodded along, almost tail-to-nose, not requiring any input from their charges.

"Lisa, don't grip your knees so tight. Relax."

Something moved on my right as I glanced at the last horse and rider. A flutter of butterflies swished around my stomach. Mark stood near the metal pen gate, watching. He nodded, smiling. All the butterflies launched into flight as that smile heated me up and melted me at the same time. Mentally shaking myself, I willed my stomach to settle down and returned my attention to my charges and not the stud gracing the fence line.

I caught Mark watching each time I followed the girls around the pen. His grin was constant as our eyes met. I found myself willing the girl's horses to walk faster. He was like some sexy school crossing guard. Arms crossed on his chest, his shirt pulled tight.

The alarm on my phone started chiming softly, signaling the end of the lesson. I shut it off and moved across the ring so that I was well ahead of the horses and all the girls could see me.

"On three, ladies, let's come to a stop. One... two... three." At three, most of the girls managed to stop their horses. The rider at the end didn't give enough pressure and her horse took a few more steps, veering out past the horse in front of her.

"Sorry," she cried out, looking worried and embarrassed.

I held up one hand, shushing her worries. "It's okay. It's all part of the learning. Now, remember how we click our tongues to get the horse's attention?"

"Yes, ma'am," she said, nodding, causing her helmet to bob slightly.

"Great. When I tell you, I want you to click at him, say 'back up' and pull back on the reins. Not too hard, just enough to let him know what you want him to do. The horse is going to step back. When you're back in line, stop him again. Do you think you can do that?" She nodded again.

"Perfect. Ready? Go."

The horse tossed his head a bit as she applied pressure, but eventually backed up. She got him stopped and reasonably back to the spot she needed to be at.

"Okay girls, time to dismount. I'll come along and help you down, if you need it."

Only two of the girls needed help. Once they were all down, I got their attention.

"Good ride today, ladies. Very good. You'll be trotting like pros before the camp is over. Now it's time to get our horses untacked, brushed, and put away."

As the girls started walking to the gate, Mark opened it, positioning himself so he could guide them to the barn in case someone had problems. Once in the barn, he helped me clip the horses halters to the short leads that Mary had installed near each stall.

Mary and Jake were there waiting for us as well. The four of us got the saddles, bridles, and blankets off and set out of the way. We handed out curry brushes to each girl and then worked with them as they brushed their mounts.

Once we brushed the horses and returned them to their stalls, we walked the girls out to the front and collected their helmets. They all washed and dried their hands at the basin near the barn entrance. They said their goodbyes as the chaperones led them off to their bus.

With my charges handed over, I turned back to the barn to help with the tack cleaned up. Mary held a hand up, stopping me in my tracks.

"Jake and I've got this. You take off."

"I can…" I started, but she shook her head as she stepped up closer, gripping my arm.

"Kathi, go home and take a shower, and get ready. Oh, and don't do anything I wouldn't do," she said, grinning.

I glanced over my shoulder to see Mark waiting near my car. I turned back to Mary. "Thanks. If I don't puke on him, I'll call it a win."

Mary pulled me in, hugging me tight. "You got this," she whispered. Releasing me, she pushed me towards the path before turning back into the barn.

As I got near the car, Mark started chuckling as he pushed up off the door to meet me. "You look like you're going to your own funeral, Kathi. If you don't want—" I quickly cut him of then took a short, stress-relieving breath and cursed myself for my insecurities. I looked up at him and smiled. As Mary had said, time to woman up.

"No. I want to. Really, I do," I said, keeping my eyes locked to his. "I'd be lying though if I said I wasn't a little nervous."

He stepped closer, his presence almost overwhelming. He took my hand in his, squeezing it softly. An electric current shot up my arm at his touch; a tingle that spread up and out to the rest of me. I looked down at our joined hands, feeling the heat and callus of his grip.

"I get it," he said. "I really do. Don't overthink it. You, me, dinner, a movie. We've already done it once. Only thing different this time is adding a movie to the mix."

"That time wasn't a date."

He shrugged. "Alright, let's call that one a practice date. Got us ready for this one."

He let my hand drop. I missed the feel immediately, and I had to keep myself from reaching out and grabbing his hand back. He pulled his phone off his belt, flipping it open, and began tapping at it. My phone pinged, and I pulled it out of my pocket. A text alert was on the screen.

"That's my address. I'll see you soon." I looked up from my phone, but he was already heading for his Jeep. His engine rumbled to life. He backed out and headed to the highway. He waved out the window as he drove off.

My hand still tingled as I opened the door to my car.

———

As I neared the address Mark gave me, the pep-talk I'd given myself earlier was fading. I gripped the steering wheel and repeated the earlier words I'd spoken to myself.

"You can do this, Kathi. He likes you, you like him. You've had one dinner already. This is just a longer one." I continued my pep talk as I drove, watching the telephone poles go by. The car's navigation system sounded off, telling my turn was coming up in three hundred feet.

I had expected to find myself in a rural area filled with ranches and livestock. It surprised me when the directions led me into a more scenic suburbia. Scatter houses, some close to the size of my place, were spread out on larger tracts of land, none butting up next to another. Well maintained yard with trees dotted the landscape in spots along the road. This was not what I was expecting at all.

I took what my GPS said was my last left before Mark's. I passed by five more modest sized homes before reaching the address he gave me. I turned into the driveway and parked. As I shut the car off, I took a moment to take in his house.

It was a single-story ranch with a three-car garage. Mark's Jeep was parked in front of the rightmost door. The exterior was a darker red brick. The roof lines were clean, not filled with dormers or extensions along the front. Landscaping was subtle, but nice. It accented the house without being overbearing. Given the lush green grass, he must use a lawn service and possibly even an irrigation system.

The only oddity compared to the other houses was the dark brown metal roof. I had to admit that it gave the house a little character, setting it apart from the others. Once again, my assumptions were shattered. I had expected a little farmhouse, perhaps older, and not as nice. I obviously had a lot of preconceived notions I needed to work on letting go of.

The front door opened up, interrupting my perusal, and my heart sped up. Mark came out, pausing, locking the door behind him. He turned back, waving once before making his way down the steps and onto the sidewalk, heading to the car. I couldn't help but admire the view as he moved towards me. He was wearing a long-sleeve gray Henley that showed off his shoulders and chest, as well as his tapered waist. Worn jeans and black Converse completed his outfit. I knew that if Abby was here, her word would be 'yummy'. I wouldn't have disagreed with her.

He walked around to the passenger door as I popped the lock. He climbed in and faced me, giving me that dimple-powered smile that sent shivers through me. That smile should be illegal.

His eyes roamed over me. "Hi. You look fantastic."

I smiled, waving my hand at him. "Thanks. You look nice yourself. That gray looks good on you."

Nodding at the house, I continued, "Nice place, too. I really like the area out here. Not what I was expecting."

"Oh," he said, one eyebrow twitching up. "Making assumptions again? Let me guess." He tapped his chin with one finger. "Ramshackle old farmhouse with a junked truck in the side yard. Round pens with a dirt-packed lot all snugged up to an old barn?"

When I dropped my eyes, he snorted. "That's a pretty close description of my uncle's place. I bought this place three years ago. I like my comfort and having a nice place to entertain."

I felt a flash of jealousy at the thought of Mark entertaining some young skank. *Down girl, down.*

Oblivious to my internal fight with the green-eyed monster, he clapped his hands together. "So, I am completely in your hands. I think I should tell you that this is the first time a woman has asked *me* on a date. I'm looking forward to it, especially the company."

My cheeks heated up as I started the car and backed us out of the driveway. We drove for some time in silence. When I dropped my hand to the gearshift, he slid his hand underneath mine so that our fingers intertwined. That touch again not only sent sparks up running up my arms but it also made me smile. I hadn't fully realized how much I missed holding hands. It was a simple act of intimacy between us. I squeezed his hand lightly, and he tightened his fingers around mine in response.

Then he spoke up. "So, where are you taking me for dinner?"

I glanced over at him. "Do you have a taste for anything?"

He shook his head, laughing. "Oh no, that's not the way this goes," he said. "*You* asked *me* out so you are in charge of dinner selection and movie picking."

I glanced over at him again, my lips quirking up into a smile. "Really? *That's* how we are playing this?"

"Oh yes. Told ya. I've never been asked out before, so I want the whole first date experience. Points off for no flowers when you picked me up."

I know my mouth popped open. I stared at him again and he just flashed me that dimpled smile, innocence dancing in his eyes.

"You seriously expected flowers?"

He inclined his head. "Well, I brought *you* a flower when I picked you up."

Damned if he hadn't.

I glanced at him again. His eyes twinkled and his lips were compressed as he fought off his laughter. I shook my head, staring back out at the road.

"Please excuse my oversight, Mark. I can only hope that I've not ruined the evening for us. I'd hate for you to have a terrible first date." He lost his battle and burst out laughing, and I soon joined him.

We spent the rest of our drive talking about the songs we heard on the radio and a serious discussion on which of the Pink Floyd albums and tours were the best. I was delighted to find out that musical taste was yet another thing we had in common.

I pulled us into the parking lot of a small strip mall across from the theater and parked near a deli. Pictures of sandwiches, bags of chips, and bottles of drink covered their front windows. Online reviews had given it high marks for its cozy atmosphere and great food.

"Wait, please," he said, touching my arm. He got out, rounded the car, opened my door, helped me out, and then held the deli door open to allow me to go in before him.

The inside of the deli was indeed cozy and perfect. One wall housed the prep area and coolers of meats and cheeses. The other wall had pictures of famous people. I recognized several movie stars and even a few athletes I had seen on the TV.

We ordered our sandwiches at one end of the counter. I got a club with pepperoni and extra tomatoes. Mark settled for a cheesesteak with peppers, no onions.

He winked at me as he ordered it. "Never know when onion-free breath might be important."

I laughed at his confidence even as I wondered what kissing him with or without onion-breath would be like.

We sat at a small table about midway back in the store. As we ate, we read off the names of the people in the pictures and talked about where we had seen them or what movies they had been in.

After that, we talked about the event at Mary's. We both agreed we'd been having a fun time, even with my accident. Mark finished his sandwich and upended his small bag of chips into his mouth, crunching on the crumbs.

Mark wiped his mouth as he finished chewing and crumpled his bag up. "You're really good with those kids."

I hid my smile by taking a drink. "Thank you. I can see why Mary likes it so much. I've helped her occasionally over the years, but this is my first time doing it in a concentrated setup like this and I have to say, I'm really enjoying myself."

"The kids are having a blast," he said, picking up his drink.

"You've gathered quite the fan club yourself," I said, laughing when the slight blush appeared on his cheeks.

Mark had quickly become the favorite of the young female students, all of whom wanted to see his demos. Repeatedly. Mary and I laughed as we watched the adoring faces follow his every move, vying to ask him questions. We both chose to ignore that *we* were also staring at Mark.

He locked eyes with me, the intensity and the heat in those eyes boring into me.

"What can I say? Women of *all* ages find me attractive."

I couldn't form words, could only keep staring as he drank me in. That warmth spread through me again and it was everything I could do to not drown in that look. Blinking, I grabbed my napkin, wiping at my lips.

"So," I said, dropping my napkin back to my lap. "What movie would you like to see?"

He laughed, wagging a finger at me. "Nope. You're in charge here and as such, that puts all the decisions on you."

"Your male ego is going to allow me, the lowly woman, to decide?" I quipped.

He pulled himself upright, sitting straighter. "I will have you know I am a firm believer that a woman can do anything a man can do. Besides," he said, "I'm kinda curious as to what you will pick."

"It might be a chick flick," I said. "You sure you want to take that chance?" I asked, quirking up an eyebrow and grinning.

"I'm not scared," he said. "Bring it on."

"Ready?"

"For you, always," he said, winking. I gathered up my plastic sandwich basket and other trash. Mark followed suit, and we dumped everything in the trash bin near the door. Once on the sidewalk, I turned left, heading for the crosswalk. Traffic was light, only the occasional car and city bus.

The parking lot of the theater complex wasn't empty, but wasn't jam packed. Mark took my hand as we navigated through the lot, moving between cars and trucks.

When we stepped up to the ticket window, he let my hand go as I stopped behind a family of four, arguing over their choice. The family distracted me and I didn't realize Mark was no longer next to me. I glanced around and saw him standing next to the lobby door, twiddling his thumbs and looking very pleased with himself. I rocked my head towards the movie board, wanting him to help me pick. He just grinned and wiggled his fingers at me. Sighing dramatically, I turned back to the selection, perusing the titles. Fine, if that's the way he wanted to play it.

The family in front of me made their choice, the dad griping about the cost. The mom started herding kids to the door. The excited kids were already calling out their order for sodas, popcorn, and candy.

By the time I stepped up to purchase our tickets, I'd decided on my selection. Mark held the door open as we stepped into the air-conditioned chaos of the movie lobby. Posters for upcoming feature films dotted the walls in their metallic cases. The buzz of orders at the snack bar mixed with the low roar of those milling in the lobby, waiting to enter their selected shows. I looked at Mark while flipping my hand towards the menu.

"Hmmmmm," he hummed. "Decisions, decisions."

When he remained quiet, I shook my head and stepped up to the counter. After the young teenager manning the counter gave me her opening sales pitch, I ordered a large soda and popcorn. Paying, I turned back to find him grinning.

"Excellent choice. Cheaper if we share."

"Uh huh," I said, handing him the popcorn to carry. I made my way to the ticket-taker guarding the entrance to the theaters like a goalie on the ice. He took our tickets, tearing them in half, and then handed me the stubs.

"Theater 3, down the hall on the right."

It didn't take us long to make the trek down the carpeted hallway lined with other doors to our theater. Once inside, Mark headed up the stairs to the top row, where he snagged two seats under the projector. Once we settled down, I noticed there were hardly any other people in the theater. In fact, the three rows in front of us were empty, as well as two or three of the seats on either side of us. We were like a small island in the sea of seats. My aversion to others might not be a factor tonight.

He took a drink from the soda and pointed at the screen with the straw. "So, *The Proposal.* I read some reviews on this one the other day. Sandra Bullock is one of my favorite actresses."

Stunned, I turned my head towards him. "Really? One of your favorites?"

"Yep. What can I say? I have a thing for older women."

I gave him my best glare, which only caused him to smirk quietly.

"Do you mind if I raise this?" he asked, tapping the armrest between us. "These seats are kind of cramped."

I snorted softly. "Is that the best line you can come up with? Are you going to yawn and stretch later when you try to put your arm around me?"

He chuckled and wiggled his eyebrows. "Think it would work?"

"Guess we will find out," I said, smiling, and settled back in the seat. Mark raised the seat arm and settled back as well, just as the lights dimmed and the movie advertisements started scrolling across the screen. We were soon laughing at the on-screen antics.

We were enjoying the movie, laughing quietly and making fun of the characters. I was caught up in the bachelorette party antics when I felt Mark shift, and his arm settled around my shoulders, his hand laying on my arm. I stiffened for a moment, then let myself relax as Mark my shoulder, encouraging me to tuck into his side.

I can do this. There is nothing wrong. I can do this.

I shifted and relaxed, settling in closer to Mark and letting my head lay back against his shoulder. I inhaled lightly, filling my lungs with his scent, something light and fresh. Good, but not overpowering. His warmth, even in the cool air of the theater, blanketed me. A feeling that had been absent for several years blossomed in me.

Contentment.

SIXTEEN

Multiple movies let out together, filling the lobby and all the exits with a rush of people. Excited conversations discussing the movies seen hashed out around us as we moved with the crowd towards the exit. I glanced at the women's restroom, needing to go but not willing to stand in the long line that already stretched out into the lobby.

Mark took my hand and began wading through the crowd. Our hands fit perfectly together and a pleasant warmth infused my hand. His hand felt natural and comfortable in mine.

Once on the sidewalk, we broke free of the crowd as everyone scattered to their vehicles. I beeped the locks on my car and Mark was there to hold the door open for me.

A few minutes of stop and go traffic finally got us out of the parking lot and on the way to Mark's place. We traveled in comfortable silence for a few minutes before Mark spoke.

"Interesting choice of movie," he said, grinning over at me.

I gave him a quick glance. "How so?"

"Well, she's the older boss, making the moves on her younger assistant, even if it was fake. Any particular reason you chose that movie?"

"I didn't... that is, it wasn't..." I stuttered. I glared at him as he started laughing, trying to be upset but failing.

"Relax, I'm yanking your chain. But I have a question, if you don't mind?"

I waggled my fingers at him, keeping my eyes on the traffic. I was also regretting not taking advantage of the restroom at the theater before leaving. The pressure in my bladder was becoming noticeable.

"After that first dinner, you were very clear that we couldn't date. That you wouldn't date me. What changed? I'm not complaining, far from it. Just curious."

I should have known this question would come up.

"It was a culmination of several things, not just one thing," I said. I scrubbed the steering wheel, my nerves twitching at saying the words out loud.

He tilted his head, curiosity in his eyes, and studied me. "How so?"

"I've been by myself for more than a few years now. I've only started dating again in the past few months. To say it's not been going well would be an understatement."

I glanced over and his gaze was still focused on me. He remained silent, waiting for me to finish my answer.

"Our dinner the other night, well, to be honest, was better than any of the dates I've been on," I said. His eyebrows shooting up almost had me laughing again.

"You're kidding me, right? It was a burger, in an old airplane of all places."

"True. But it was fun, and I had a good time. Then, there was my fall and what you did, or rather, *didn't* do."

Confusion crossed his handsome face. "What didn't I do?"

"When I said I needed to get back up on the horse and ride, you didn't tell me no, or try to plead with me. You didn't rush me off to a hospital like the others wanted to do. You understood what I was doing and why, and you supported my decision. That meant a lot to me."

He didn't respond, so I kept going.

"Then, you came over to make sure I was okay, brought me food, and then... the couch."

"Kathi, nothing happened, I swear. You fell asleep, and I didn't want to disturb you."

"Oh, come on Mark. You could have carried me to my bed or even woken me up and then left. You did neither."

He nodded. "Okay. Guilty. I could have, but I didn't *want* to. But nothing happened."

"Yes, something did happen," I said before changing lanes to go around a slow-moving semi.

He sat back, looking at me, concerned. "Kathi, I swear I didn't ..." My soft laughter cut him off.

"I know *that* didn't happen, Mark. But what *did* happen was enough."

He blew out a breath. "Okay. I'm *really* confused right now."

"For the first time since Jeremy died, I woke up in someone's arms, and it felt safe, cared for. Okay, I admit, I freaked a little at first, but then I accepted it for what it was and just let myself relax and enjoy."

"I have to admit," he said, "I hadn't expected it, but, for whatever reason, it felt... right."

My bladder began to express its displeasure at its fullness, causing me to shift in my seat. The larger soda had really been a big mistake.

Of course, being the man that he was proving to be, he picked up on my discomfort. "You okay?"

Hopefully, he couldn't see the embarrassment on my face. "Yeah. Just, umm, need to go to the bathroom."

He chuckled, patting my hand. "Good thing we're almost at my place."

When we pulled up in his driveway, Mark was out of the car in a flash, hurrying up to his door. By the time I'd gotten unbuckled and out of the car, he had unlocked his front door and was holding it open for me. I dashed up the steps and into the house in an awkward walk/run, the pressure almost at a critical level.

"First door on the right," he said, hitting the lights.

With a wave of thanks, I hurried past him, down the hall to the indicated door. I entered the bathroom quickly, closing and locking the door behind me with one hand while undoing my jeans with the other. I slipped pants and panties down and sat, sighing with relief as the pressure released.

I gave the bathroom a cursory once-over as the pressure flowed away. Basic white tile, nothing fancy. No floral soaps or any cute décor. Plain white shower curtain, small gray rug around the toilet. There was only a walk-in shower, no tub. Gray towels hung on the towel bar. Definitely a guy's bathroom. Clean and well-kept, but still a guy's bathroom.

After what seemed like ten minutes, but was really only a minute or two, I finished and cleaned up, resisting the urge to snoop in the small mirror-covered medicine cabinet over the sink. I unlocked and opened the door, stepping out into the hallway. As I entered the living room, Mark came out of the kitchen.

"Feel better?" he asked, eyes twinkling.

"Much. Thanks," I said, glancing around and taking in the front room. As with the bathroom, it was clean, functional, with a nice comfortable looking couch and a big TV, but not a lot of personal items. I turned my attention back to Mark and found myself captured by his eyes. Eyes full of fire, as if they were lasers burning through me. My whole body begin to heat up and tingle as he took a step towards me.

Like a deer in the headlights, I stood there, watching as he stopped in front of me. His presence was almost overpowering, wrapping around me like a blanket.

"I had a great time tonight, Kathi," he said, keeping his eyes on mine, holding me with the force of that gaze.

I took in the small lines around his eyes, a ruggedness which sat well on him. But my gaze kept falling on his lips.

Desire bloomed inside of me, filling me to the point I thought I was going to explode.

"Kathi?"

Hearing him say my name seemed to be the key. I crashed into him, throwing my hands around his neck and pulling his lips to mine. The minute our lips met, the heat in me exploded like a sun. Mark's arms went around me, pulling me to him. The intensity forced a moan from me at the contact. My tongue pushed at him, pressing until his lips parted, allowing me in. He groaned as my tongue met his.

Mark broke away first, panting. "God Kathi, we—"

I pulled his head back to me, latching my lips back onto his, cutting off whatever he was going to say. He growled deep in his throat and dropped his hands to my ass, pulling me close and then lifting me. My legs wrapped around his waist as he staggered backwards. We spun and crashed into a chair. He shifted, and I heard the chair hit the floor as he sat me down on something.

He dropped his mouth to my neck, sucking and nipping at my neck and jawline, leaving a trail of heat as he went. I wrapped my hands around his head, pulling him tight to me.

His mouth returned to mine. I'm not sure which of us moaned as I forced my tongue deeper.

His hands grasped the bottom of my top and pulled, yanking it out of my jeans. I grabbed it, pulling it up and over my head and tossing it away. Once it was gone, his hands slid up and under my bra, cupping my breasts.

I hissed as his rough hands caressed and squeezed my flesh. Electric jolts went through me as his thumbs flicked my achingly hard nipples. I pulled his mouth back to mine, devouring him as he twisted a nipple between his fingers, sending pleasurable pain coursing through me.

All of my senses were flaring alive, sensations awakening that had been asleep for years. I ached all over, and I knew I was dripping wet already. Everywhere he touched me branded me. I wanted more. Damn the consequences.

He pulled at my bra and I grabbed it, working it up and off, tossing it away as he yanked his shirt up and over his head, dropping it to the floor. I ran my arms around his muscular back, drawing him to me, his skin against mine, his heat washing over me.

Panting, he dropped his hands back to my waist and slid them back under my ass, lifting me back up. I kicked off my shoes and locked my legs around him again. I ran my hands behind his neck and into his hair, my lips working from his jaw to his ear, where I sucked the lobe in between my teeth and nibbled.

His breath hissed warm against my neck. "Fuck, Kathi." He stumbled once as he walked down the short hallway. I went back to his mouth, sucking his tongue out and swirling mine around it.

He grabbed my waist and pulled me off him. I dropped my feet to the floor, barely registering the fact that we were in his bedroom. My hands yanked at his belt, jerking it open so I could work at the buttons of his jeans. He was busy doing the same to mine. We were interfering with each other, each wanting the same thing. If I hadn't been so desperate for him, I might have broken out in laughter.

Growling, he moved my hands out of his way and unsnapped his jeans, shoving them down. He yanked at his boots, kicking them across the room. I hooked my thumbs in the waistband of my jeans and shoved them down, stepping out of them and kicking them out of the way. Mark managed to kick out of his jeans without falling, but it was a close thing. Free of clothes, he melded back into me.

I shoved my hand into his boxers and grasped him, stroking him, causing him to suck in his breath in a harsh rasp. He was big, hard, and hot. I kept pulling, stroking.

"Too much," he panted, pulling my hand up and out. I threw my hands back around his neck and sucked at his lips. He pushed me back until my knees hit the bed, causing me to fall backwards onto my back. He dropped to his knees, hands roaming to my waist. When he reached my panties, he grabbed them and ripped them off and used his hands to spread my legs.

His face rubbed up my inner thighs and managed a strangled "Mark" when his tongue flicked my clit just before his tongue speared into me.

I came. Hard. My orgasm shot up my stomach to my nipples, rippling my muscles as my neck and shoulders went rigid. I collapsed back against the bed, but his mouth didn't stop. I had never, ever orgasmed that fast. That thought barely registered because his tongue never stopped swiping up and down my drenched slit before plunging back into me.

"Oh God… more," I panted. I dropped my hands to his head, gripping his hair and trying to pull him inside me.

My next orgasm was building like a rising wave, ready to crash down and engulf me. I grabbed my breasts, squeezing and pulling my nipples as Mark feasted on me like a man starving.

Then his mouth sucked hard on my clit and I came again.

"MAAARRKKKKKKKKKYessssffffuccckkkkkkkkkk!" I screamed, my whole being exploding outward. I had a death grip on the sheets and I shoved my ass up, pressing myself against Mark's face and his unrelenting and oh so talented tongue.

My orgasm didn't stop, only ebbing before peaking again as he licked and sucked my clit. I bucked, pushing up and collapsing back to the bed.

"Stop… stop…" I panted, squeezing my legs and pushing at him. Mark pulled back and I let my legs fall to the bed, my breath coming in big gulps. He moved up and kissed my stomach, causing me to jerk at his touch. His tongue continued dragging up my body, swirling across my skin. He kissed my breast before blowing lightly on the nipple. My skin pebbled as his tongue flicked out, licking my nipple before covering it with his mouth. I inhaled sharply and arched my back up to press into those lips as he feasted on me.

Moving from one breast to the other, he suckled me, sending waves of heat through me and, incredibly, I felt another release building. It teetered, hovered, keeping me on edge as he continued ravishing my nipples.

I hissed and fisted the sheets. "Maarrkkkkk…" As I inhaled to urge him on, he bit one nipple lightly. My release gushed through me, curling my toes and taking my breath.

I collapsed back onto the bed, my body tingling. Mark raised up over me, staring down at me. He started to say something, but I growled and shoved him over. He yelped in surprise as he rolled over to his back, taking me with him and letting me throw my leg over him. Once settled, I planted my hands on his chest and dropped my swollen center right on top of his cock, hovering there. I smashed my lips to his, taking them in a hard kiss.

I pulled back, panting. "Condom." He pointed to the nightstand. Leaning over, I ripped the drawer open, seeing the foil packages laying in a pile. I grabbed one and moved back onto his legs, freeing his cock.

It took me two tries to grab one corner of the package and rip it open so I could pull out the slick latex. I grabbed his cock, gripping and jerking it upward.

He sucked in a harsh breath. "Not a pull toy," he hissed. His eyes were closed and the look on his face spurred me on.

I dropped my head, licking the crown once before kissing it, sucking gently, pulling another long gasp from Mark. I rolled the condom on and moved forward, kneeling over him as I grabbed the encased flesh and lined it up, letting just the tip push into my aching heat. My pussy was leaking like a river. He locked eyes with me as I sank down, taking more of him inside me. My head rolled back at the sensations washing through me.

"Fucckkk... Big... God. Bigggg..." I moaned, the pleasure gripping me stretched me, filling me. God, how much more of him could I take?

My hands dropped to his chest again as I rose an inch or two before dropping again. I gasped as more of him filled me, pushing the air out of my lungs.

Unable to wait any longer, I lifted and drove myself down, taking him all the way in.

"Fuccckkk, Kathi."

Never in my life had I been this full. Another small orgasm rippled through me as Mark's hands dropped to my hips. I started rocking, moving, rubbing my clit at the base of his cock as he helped me move forward and back.

Heat built and flowed inside me like a river of lava. Unable to take it anymore, I leaned over, letting my hands fall to the bed on either side of Mark's shoulders. I moved forward a few inches, then drove back hard, grunting as the air pushed out of me.

I picked up speed, riding him hard. He grabbed my breasts, squeezing and mashing as he tugged at my nipples, sending another small ripple through me.

Mark pulled me to him and rolled us over. Once I was on my back, Mark pushed my legs towards my chest and thrust into me, burying himself. I flung my legs up, locking them around his waist as he began to pound into me. The slapping of our flesh and our panting was loud in the silence of the room as I urged him on.

"Harder... harder... More Mark... More... Moorrreeee..."

"Kaattthii..."

My name came out as a growl as he buried himself in me, throwing his head up and arching his back. I felt each pulse of his release, squeezing him as hard as I could as he filled the condom.

He gave a final ragged breath before resting on his elbows, his weight pressing down on me but not smothering me.

He dropped his lips to mine and kissed me softly, deeply. Our tongues played gently before he pulled back. He climbed off me and the bed and went to the bathroom, pulling at the condom. He was back in moments, tugging the covers open and crawling into the bed and laying next to me.

I turned on my side and pushed back into him. He draped the covers over us, threw one arm over me, pulling me in close. He kissed my neck several times before laying his head next to mine on the pillow. My last thought before sleep pulled me down was how nice his breath felt on my neck.

SEVENTEEN

The feeling of feathery kisses along my neck and shoulder pulled me from sleep.

"Mmmmmm."

The kisses lingered longer, working up my neck. Lips nibbled at my ear. I shifted till I was on my back. Twinges of pain reminded me of the night's activities. Parts of me that hadn't been used in a while protested the overuse while asking when we would do that again.

I looked up at Mark's ruffled hair and sleepy face. He kissed me before pulling back to stare back at me, a soft smile gracing his lips. He brought a hand up and caressed the side of my face and jawline, sending small shivers through me.

"Good morning," he said.

I smiled. "Hey you."

"Sleep well?" he asked before bouncing his eyebrows at me.

I snorted. "Sleep? I don't recall getting much *sleep*," I said, reaching up and running a finger along his jawline. The light scruff he was sporting gave him a rugged, sexy look, which I found pleasing.

He kissed my finger as it came to rest on his lips. "How can you blame me? I had a beautiful, sexy, very naked woman in my bed. What was I supposed to do? Play dominoes?"

I let my hand drift down his chest, my eyes following my fingers as they dragged across his very wonderful pecs. I looked back up at him, smiling.

"You let her sleep instead of wearing her out."

His face tightened and some of the twinkle left his eyes.

"I wasn't sure if last night was a fluke or a start of something. So sue me for wanting to take advantage of it."

"Given the wet spot I'm laying in, and that my body thinks it's run a marathon, you most definitely took advantage."

It was the wrong thing to say because I could see the immediate hurt flick through his eyes and his face drew tight. *Oh crap.* I rushed to reassure him.

"I'm sorry, Mark. That's not what I meant. I attacked you, remember? *I* took advantage of *you*."

He shook his head. "You can't take advantage of the willing, Kathi. Last night was…"

I put a finger to his lips, halting his speech.

"Mark, we shouldn't have. *I* shouldn't have, and I have no idea what came over me. Mark, we…"

"Don't, Kathi," he said, stopping me. His eyes narrowed as he looked at me. "Don't say what you're about to say."

"Mark, we…" I said before several realizations exploded in my brain. I stiffened, glancing around the room as my heartrate ramped up, and not in a fun and bed-romping kind of way.

Mark raised an eyebrow, puzzled. "Kathi? What's wrong?"

"What time is it?"

He leaned back, glancing over his shoulder before turning back to me.

"Little after 9."

I shot upright, almost smacking Mark in the face with my head as my heartrate exploded.

"Shit! I'm late!"

I kicked at the covers, succeeding only in getting more tangled up in them. Mark started laughing. I shot him a glare that would have melted steel. He shut his mouth, but I could still see the mirth in his eyes as he watched me struggle. He finally took pity on me, or was more likely worried I was going to kick him, because he grabbed the sheets, tugging them up and away, freeing me.

I rolled out of the bed, my feet smacking into the bare wood floor. Standing up, I looked around frantically for my clothes. My jeans and shoes were off in the corner on the floor. Leaping over to them, I bent over to scoop them up even as I was looking for my panties. Then I caught a whiff of myself. Sex and sweat. I needed a shower in a bad way.

"Nice ass."

I whirled back around, one finger spearing at him. He was out of the bed, leering at me as I tried to get dressed.

"Not. Helping," I said. My gaze swept over the floor, taking a brief note of the condom wrappers scattered around the room. My eyes widened at the number before continuing my search, flipping his clothes around and tossing the covers off the bed.

"Where are my panties?"

"These?"

He was twirling them around his finger. I rushed over and grabbed at them. He laughed, shaking his head and holding them out of my reach.

I hissed at him, trying again to snatch them from his hand. "Mark, I don't have time for this. I'm late. Give. Me. My. Panties."

He stared me down, grinning as he held them up high. "Trophy. I *earned* these."

"Mark," I growled, snatching at my panties as he dangled them out of my reach. I reached for them again and saw he was watching my tits bounce. God, he was so juvenile.

I groaned. "Arrghhhh. *Men.*"

Giving up on getting my panties back, I fast-walked into the kitchen, looking for the rest of my clothes. My bra was hanging off a chair arm. I snatched it up, dropping my pants on the table. I untangled the straps and fastened it around my chest before twisting it around, sliding my arms through the straps, adjusting it until it properly encased the girls.

A male voice sounded from behind me. "So that's how you do that."

I turned, my breath halting for a split second as my gaze fell on Mark, leaning against the wall, grinning at me. He was still naked and even as I rushed around, I couldn't help but take a moment to admire the view. I felt myself slipping into memories of last night, the bed, the multitude of dead condoms, the fullness when he... I shook my head. Nope, couldn't go there. *Focus, Kathi.*

I grabbed my jeans and slid them on, wincing when the rough denim rubbed against my overused equipment. Going commando in jeans was overrated at the best of times. When you have a sore and worn-out pussy, it was just plain hell.

I yanked my top on, looking around for my purse. A ringing sound led me to the couch. I dug my phone out of my purse and snatched it open. Abby. Thank god it hadn't been Samuel. I punched the connect button.

"Yes?"

Her voice sounded slightly frantic. *"Where are you? Samuel has been asking for you, and I'm running out of excuses."*

And the hits just kept on coming. I thought quickly. "Tell him I'm cramping and bleeding. That'll shut him up. I'll be in as quickly as I can get home and shower."

The silence on the other end should have warned me. Then I realized the words I had said. I was so screwed.

"Home? Shower? Those words imply you're not at home and I know for a fact you were bleeding like a stuck pig two weeks ago. Where are you and..."

Mark spoke up from beside me. "Hey Kathi, here are your shoes."

I sighed, knowing there was no way Abby hadn't heard him.

"Who was that?" Abby drew that last word out for about three years. *Fuck a duck.*

"Abby, gotta go. See you soon." I hung up before she could utter another word. I turned and poked Mark in the chest, which started it throbbing. Jabbing his chest was worse that smashing my finger into a brick wall.

"Did you *have* to do that?"

The smug asshole held out my shoes.

"I hate you right now," I said, snatching them from his hands. He kept chuckling as I finished throwing on clothes, hopping to the door. I yanked it open even as I was slipping on a shoe, already thinking about my shower and what I was going to tell Samuel.

"Kathi."

"What?" I snapped, turning away from the open door. My nose smacked into a hard, naked pec. Fingers gripped my chin, raising it up. I took in a breath, ready to rip Mark a new one, when his lips landed on mine.

I struggled to get my words out, but those lips kept working, moving lightly. My arms moved as if controlled by someone else, wrapping themselves around his waist as my lips got in on the action.

What seemed like hours later, he pulled back and then kissed my nose. It was corny and sent a shiver right through me.

"I'll call you later," he said, stepping back.

My voice was breathless. "Um, yeah. Right. Call you... I mean, sure, talk with you later." I stepped back, running into the door. I slid around it, shaking my head as I stepped backwards out the door. Mark grinned, crossing his arms, then waggled his hips at me. The blush exploded on my face as his erection shift back and forth like a sexy metronome. Tearing my eyes away, I dug in my purse for my car keys.

As the elevator reached my level and the doors opened, I locked eyes on my door. I marched straight to it, doing my best to ignore the guardian stationed at the side. Unfortunately, the guardian was not having any of it.

Abby stood up, moving between me and my office door. With one hand on her hip, she stared me down as I got close to her.

"Do you..." she said, but her words trailed away to a whisper, her eyes widening as she stared at me. Still staring, she moved to the side, allowing me to continue into my office. I'd just set my purse down on my desk when she came back in, holding her purse. Backpacks were smaller that what she called a handbag. I always teased her she could live out a zombie apocalypse using just her purse's contents.

Closing the door behind her, she sat down across from me, digging in for a moment before tossing a small container of something onto the desk so it landed in front of me.

I picked it up and turned it in my hands, noting it was a concealer she and I both used.

"What's this for?"

She gave me a smirk, touching a place on either side of her neck where it joined her shoulder.

"Someone seems to have had a bit of fun?" she said, a self-righteous smirk stretching her lips.

I touched my neck where she had pointed and started swearing quietly. Dropping into my chair, I yanked open the side drawer, reaching in to grab the small mirror I kept there. A quick glance confirmed my suspicion. Love bites.

"He's a dead man. I'm gonna kill him," I hissed. I twisted the top of the concealer, dabbed some on the first of the two hickies I now sported.

Abby snatched the makeup from me. "Give me that." Working swiftly, she dabbed, quickly spreading the concealer. Shit, I felt like I was back in junior high, covering up my first hickey to hide it from Mom.

"Sooooo, boss lady, want to tell me about last night? Got some sore parts we need to discuss? Or, you could give me a running total of the orgasms. More importantly, who was the stud?"

She set her elbows on the desk, interlaced her fingers, and propped her chin on them, waiting expectantly. I groaned, laying my head back against my chair. I didn't really want to have this conversation at this moment. Abby had other thoughts.

"I already cleared your calendar for the next three hours and informed Mr. Harrison of your delicate feminine state. He was muttering something about how inconvenient female problems were for business when I hung up. So. Dish."

I stared at the ceiling of my office, trying to find some guidance or wisdom. Unfortunately, all I saw were some cobwebs the cleaning crew obviously missed.

"Abb, I don't know what came over me."

"Forget what came over you. Let's talk about *who* came *in* you."

I dropped my chin and rolled my eyes her way, only to have her smile brightly at me and raise one eyebrow.

Still staring at her, I grumped. "Can you *try* to be serious for just a second?"

"Sorry," she said. I knew she was not even remotely sorry.

"Look," I said, leaning forward, a sober expression crossing my face. "This has to stay between the two of us. I'm serious, Abby. I need you to swear it."

She gave me an intense look before nodding and resuming her wait. I leaned back in my chair and laid out the night.

"The short of it is that I decided I wanted to date someone." I waited to see her reaction, but she wiggled her fingers at me before resuming her statue imitation.

"Last night was our second date. Well, our first time where we both agreed it was a date. And, I asked *him* out."

"Wait," she said, sitting up. "Is it the dentist you went out with last month?"

"No, it's not him."

"The lawyer?"

I shuddered. "No, definitely not him."

Abby waved her hand at me. "As much as I would like to keep playing this game, I have work to do. So how about we get to the name of the guy who gave you those little love bites?"

"Mark."

"Mark? Mark who?"

I glanced up to the ceiling, then back at Abby. "I went on a date with Mark. Last night was our first actual date."

"Mark?" she asked again. I waited, watching her face as she started working through her mental database of information about me. The minute her eyes lit up, I knew she'd made the connections.

The smile started slowly and then enveloped her face and eyes. "Mark? As in Mark, the horse guy? The one who wanted dinner from you for helping with the kids' project? That Mark? Flowers Mark?"

I nodded.

"But, didn't you tell me that…" and her words trailed off as the last piece of the puzzle fell into place. Her eyes flew open wide and then she leaned forward, the grin on her face almost meeting at her ears.

"Boss, did you take that young stud to bed and ride him like the stallion he is? Holy *shit*, Kathi. When you jump, you jump big."

She got up and moved her chair around the desk until it was next to me. She swung my chair around to face her, then plopped down in her seat.

"Okay, I want *all* the details. How did you go from not even giving a kiss to those old dudes to swapping bodily fluids with your young cowboy on your first date?" She paused, sitting up straighter as she waited for my reply.

"I don't know what happened, Abby. We had dinner, went to a movie. It was great. I enjoyed every minute of it. When we got to his place, I went to the bathroom. When I came out, I started to say good-night, and then…"

I stopped talking as my mind got lost in the memories of last night. Abby smacking me brought me back from the memory of being tangled together in the sweaty sheets.

"Hey, don't leave me hanging. What happened? Goodnight? Then what?"

"I was looking at him, and his eyes, and those lips. He said my name and the next thing I knew, I was kissing him. It kinda went out of control from there."

Abby was shaking her head, the grin still stretching across her face. She got up, pulling her chair back around my desk and setting it back in its place.

I cringed. "Abby, you can't say anything to anyone. You know how Samuel is. If he finds out I'm dating a man as young as Mark, it will give him the ammunition he needs to remove me from the company."

She leaned closer, one hand on the desk. "Boss lady, your secret is safe with me. So, can I assume it was good?"

"Oh, *so* good." My thoughts cast back to last night, bringing a smile to my reddening face. Abby laughed as she walked back to her desk. I sighed, wincing as I shifted in my chair before flipping open the folder and began reading Samuel's latest event idea.

I eased down into the deep soaking tub, letting the water slide over me as the bath bomb's vanilla fragrance filled my senses. I could feel the heat from the steaming water wrapping around me, soaking into aching muscles that hadn't been used in that manner for quite some time.

Once I had my back settled against the small pillow I had fastened to the tub, I picked up my glass and took a sip of my wine, setting the glass back down next to the bottle. I glanced at the phone laying on the ledge, silently cursing myself. No response had been forthcoming from Mark from the several texts I'd sent him. Even my call to him when I got home went straight to voicemail.

Simon was curled up on my folded towel, dozing in the heat of the bathroom. I stared up at the ceiling, contemplating.

"Guess he got his trophy and is moving on, but I suppose that's how the younger generation works these days, Simon. Meet up, casual sex, move on. God, I'm a fool."

I drained my wine glass, refilling it with the last of the bottle.

"I mean, we hadn't talked about it. Maybe I just read it wrong. Maybe what we did was all he wanted. Casual. If so, I can do casual." I shrugged, trying to be nonchalant, glancing over at Simon, who was glaring at me with a look of disbelief. I groaned, letting my head settle back against the vinyl pillow.

"Who am I kidding? I don't do *casual*. I've never done casual. And I've never had sex on a first date. Well, technically, it was a second date, but still. That's not the way I work, Simon. Hell, I made Jeremy wait three months. But I jumped Mark right in the doorway. It was like I was someone else. All I wanted were those lips on mine. One kiss and poof, instant slut. Maybe I was channeling Abby. All that time working around her affected my subconscious. That must be it." Simon remained mute, staring at me emotionlessly, obviously not believing my reasoning.

I drained my glass, contemplating its emptiness. "But oh God, it was *great* sex. Simon, I loved Jeremy, I did. But he never did to me what Mark did. Mark was gentle sometimes, not gentle others. God, he fucked me, but he also loved me, worshipped me and I couldn't get enough of him, or that lovely, huge cock. And he should insure that tongue of his. I've *never* had a night like that, and I think he may have broken my vagina. I'm in pretty good shape for my age, but God help me, I feel like I ran a marathon and got into a fight when it was over."

I turned over to stare at the lounging, judgmental tomcat. "Regina may be right. There's definitely something to be said about youth."

I put my head back on the pillow, staring at the ceiling again, letting my memories take me away as I sank further into the steaming water.

EIGHTEEN

"I'm a fool, Mary."

I was sitting at Mary's well-worn kitchen table, having stayed for dinner after I'd finished riding Ringo. Jake and Julia had taken Sarah into Denver for a family dinner with Sarah's other grandparents, the Petersons. At the trial, Julia had promised the judge that she and Jake would ensure Sarah spent time with her other grandparents. There were still hard feelings about the attempt to break the conditions of the will that granted Jake custody of Sarah.

Mary picked up our plates and dropped them in the sink. She opened the fridge and grabbed two of Jake's longnecks. She popped the tops off them and sat one in front of me before sliding down into her chair, turning to face me.

"Here's to old fools," she said, holding up her beer. I clinked it and we both drank.

"So," she said, wiping at a spot on the table, "what monumental thing have you done this week to make you into a fool?"

I launched into what happened Sunday night and the following morning, leaving out most of the graphic details. She remained silent, letting me spill my guts. When I finished, she stared at me, giving me no indication of what she was thinking. After several long seconds, she cleared her throat and leaned towards me, her face the picture of seriousness. I moved closer, not sure what to expect from my best friend, but prepared for a chewing out.

"So, is his dick really big?"

I swear my jaw cracked from my mouth flying open so fast.

"Seriously? All of that I spewed out, all those heart-wrenching worries, and *that's* what you key in on? His dick size? *Really,* Mary?"

Mary shrugged, a twinkle in her eye. "Hey, it's been a long dry spell for me. I'm living vicariously through you."

She took another pull from her beer. "So," she said, bouncing her eyebrows at me. "Is it?"

I glared at her for a few seconds before breaking out in a grin.

I couldn't help but let out a contented sigh. "So big and so perfect. God, I was so sore later."

She laughed and lifted her beer bottle to me. "Here's to those perfect dicks and our enjoyment of them." We finished our toast and set the bottles down on the table with a thunk.

"So, tell me, why are you a fool?" she asked, bringing us back on topic.

I sighed. "Because I thought he was different. The way he talked, telling me how long he'd wanted to date me, the fall and him coming over to take care of me. Then I finally get up the nerve to ask him out and it was just… amazing. I just didn't expect him to screw me and run."

She shook her head. "That just doesn't sound like the Mark I know," she said, tapping one finger on the table. "I've been around that boy for years. He's not one to date around. From what little Jake has told me, Mark rarely dated since before he left last year to help his friend."

I shrugged. "Yeah, but he sure has ignored me since that night. No text, no phone call. I mean, I'm not some clingy freshman sitting by the phone waiting for the quarterback to call. But no call, no text. It kinda hurts." I paused, trying to quell the fear and hurt. "It took a lot for me to ask him out, Mary."

She patted me on the arm. "Yeah, I know. But maybe, and hear me out here, maybe this isn't a bad thing."

"Excuse me?" I said, staring at her like she'd grown a second head.

"Let me ask you something. If you and Mark date seriously, are you going to tell Samuel and all your friends up in Denver that you're dating someone fifteen years younger than you? Invite him to the company parties?"

My shoulders slumped as I dropped my eyes to the table, her words cutting through me like a knife. That, right there, was the crux of my holdup. I know how what my friends and Samuel thought about Regina. Would I keep Mark a hidden, guilty secret? I'd like to think I was better than that, but I was afraid I might not be and that admission made me sick to my stomach.

I looked up at Mary, who was giving me a half-smile.

"That's just it, Mary. I don't know."

She nodded at my words. "At least you're honest about it. Maybe, before you get so upset about him not calling, try to figure out the answer to *that* question. If you and Mark talk about it, and he only wants a casual thing, problem solved. But if he's interested in a relationship, then you've got to be honest with yourself and him. He deserves it."

I dropped my head to the tabletop and let out a frustrated groan. "Why couldn't I have screwed one of the older guys I dated? Why did it have to be Mark?"

"Maybe because those older guys didn't have pecs, a six-pack, and a big dick?"

I rolled my head to the side and glared at her. "You're not helping."

"Truth hurts," she replied. "But I've got another question."

"I shudder to think what it might be," I said, sitting back up.

"Did he *really* claim your panties as a trophy? I gotta admit it's kinda juvenile, and hot, all at the same time."

Before I could answer, her phone made a chiming sound for an incoming text. She touched her phone and stared at its screen.

"Huh," she said, before tapping out an apparent reply. Finished, she put her phone down on the table and turned to me, a bemused look on her face.

"Do you believe in fate? In signs?" she asked, peeling at the label on her bottle.

"Maybe. Why?"

She touched her phone with one finger. "That was Mark. Seems he had to go out of town with his uncle unexpectedly. Had a brain-fart and left his phone at home. He finally broke free and borrowed someone's phone. He only had time to get one message out, and he knew my number. Wanted me to relay a message to you."

Despite myself, my heartbeat quickened at her words. I waited expectantly, but instead of continuing to speak, she picked up her beer, finished it, and stood up. She dropped the empty in the trash. She pulled out a glass from the cabinet, filled it with water from the sink and drank half before sitting back down at the table. I waited for her to say something, but she simply sipped her water and stared off at the barn.

"Well, what's the message?" I asked, trying not to sound too eager. Mary chuckled, letting me know I was failing miserably.

"He's sorry for being out of touch. He'll be back Friday and wants me to tell you he can't wait to see you and to make sure you're gonna be here."

I sat back in the chair, surprised at the immense sense of relief. Even more surprising was the anticipation building in me. It seems I was worried about nothing. *He couldn't wait to see me.* And I had to admit, I couldn't wait either.

She laughed out loud at my obvious relief. "Guess you're gonna have to wait until Friday to suck face with him. Oh, and one other thing..." I raised an eyebrow at her.

"Try not to screw him in the tack room. There'll be kids present."

She burst out laughing as my face flamed red.

I've given speeches in front of an audience full of corporate CEOs. Hosted countless dinner parties for all levels of dignitaries, including senators and congressmen.

Yet I'd never been as nervous as I was on Friday waiting for Mark to show up. After my tenth trip through the barn to look down at the parking area, Mary threatened to force-feed me a horse tranquilizer to calm me down. To occupy my time, she loaded me up, making me work with both groups and single kids who needed additional instruction.

Working with the kids opened my eyes. I felt imbued with a sense of purpose, something I hadn't realized was missing in my life. Helping these kids discover the joy I'd known for years; the love of riding. Very few things were more freeing and fulfilling than riding. Galloping down a trail, the wind in your hair, and the life and power you sat astride.

To watch that love of riding come alive in a young one's eyes made it even more alive and real to me and me understand why Mary stuck with it. It might not be the most lucrative gig in town, but the rewards were beyond price.

Lunch time came and still no Mark. Too nervous to eat, I camped out at one of the unoccupied tables. Every argument about being with Mark, or starting something with him, began replaying through my head as I stared at the tabletop. I relived every moment of time with Mark. Every touch, every sensation, both in bed and out.

He was attractive, sexy, and intelligent. I also found him engaging, exciting. The sex was good, there was no denying it. But, I also enjoyed the time we spent just talking and spending time together. It was a closeness and intimacy that I had always cherished and enjoyed.

Lost in my thoughts, it startled me when someone set a plate in front of me and plopped down next to me on the bench.

"Thank you, but I'm not hungry," I said, turning to see the food bringer and stopped, my pulse going from calm to racing in a single heartbeat.

"Pity," Mark said, arranging his plate and setting down a soda. "I was hoping we could share lunch." Grinning at me, he brought a finger to my chin and pushed up to close my open mouth. He stared at me, and I saw a slew of emotions go through those eyes. Regret, sorrow, heat, and something else I couldn't identify. A molten warmth spread through me from where his finger touched my skin.

"Kathi?" His eyes captured mine.

"Yeah?" I said, my voice breathy.

"For the last five days, all I could think about was you. We didn't get a chance to talk about Sunday, and I know things might be weird, but if it's okay, I'd really, *really* like to kiss you."

I stared at his lips and nodded.

He closed the distance to us, pausing before his lips connected with mine. I waited for two seconds before it hit me what he was doing. He was giving me an out. I didn't need it. I closed the gap between us and our lips met.

The minute we kissed, my world snapped back into focus. All the doubts and misgivings flowed out of me like sand slipping through my fingers.

There was no urgency, no massive jolt of lust or heat, just the need to acknowledge, to make the connection. I inhaled deeply, his scent wrapping around me like a warm coat that I never wanted to take off.

A series of whoops and cheers interrupted our moment. Our lips parted as we pulled back. We turned to find everyone, kids and adults alike, focused on us. Lots of grins and smiles were aimed our way, not to mention a few wistful looks among the older girls. I felt the blush start up my neck. Mark chuckled and turned to face me again.

"How about we find a quiet spot to eat and talk?" he asked. I nodded. Standing up, we grabbed our plates and drinks and started walking past our admirers, who began clapping. As we reached Mary, she held up a hand, halting us in place. She gave me a knowing look and pointed a finger at me, humor with a touch of seriousness dancing in her eyes.

"Remember what I told you."

I grinned and nodded, acknowledging her warning. As we started walking, Mark leaned over.

"What was that about?"

"Tell you while we eat. Come on."

We walked through the barn and with a malicious grin, I nudged Mark towards the tack room. Mark shot me a look of concern. Probably thinking about the last time he and I were at this very spot. Laughing, I walked past him and popped the latch on the door.

Since Mary had planned her barn with the future in mind, the tack room was actually rather large, close to four hundred square feet. In one corner was a bookshelf filled with binders, one for each horse. Mary used these to document the care and issues associated with each animal. Next to it was a small table, a couple of folding chairs tucked up under it.

On one of the side walls was a metal storage system for tack. It was a fancy setup with sections for saddle trees, hooks for hanging bridles and halters, and shelves for helmets, boots, and various other sundries. It always reminded me of school lockers for horses.

The back wall was a series of metal trash cans storing feed and grain for the stabled horses. Mary always supplied hay and a basic sweet feed, but if owners wanted their horses fed something else, they could purchase it and have it stored here for use.

She'd actually put in good decking for the floor, giving it a sturdy surface able to handle the weight of all the tack and supplies.

Mark set his drink down on the dusty tabletop and handed me my food.

"Here, hang on a sec."

I took his plate, curious. He grabbed several shop towels from a rag bin and ducked back out of the room. When he came back in, he flopped a wet rag down and began wiping off the table. He pulled the chairs out and washed them down as well. He tossed the now dirty wet rag to the side, then used the others to dry off the table and chairs.

"There," he said. I sat the plates and drinks down before reaching for my chair only to have my hand intercepted. Mark pulled me to him, enveloping me in his arms even as his lips crushed mine. I inhaled sharply as his tongue found mine, turning up the heat.

I moaned as our tongues danced and I ran my hands up his back, pulling him as close to me as possible. He dropped his hands to my ass, pulling me tight against him. His desire for me was clear by the hardness pressing into me.

I pulled away before I climbed him like a tree. Mary's words of warning about losing control in the barn while kids were present were blaring in my head. I took a couple of deep breaths to lower my heart rate.

Mark chuckled. "Man. Just when it was getting good." He stepped back, shoving his hands in the pockets of his faded jeans, his eyes scouring me from head to toe and back up again.

I sat down, taking a long drink of my soda, trying to cool down the fire inside me. I shook my head at him, my grin turning up the corners of my lips as I looked at him sideways.

"Mary told me I'm not allowed to screw you inside the tack room. She's afraid we'll corrupt the kids."

He laughed, plopping down into his chair. His face softened as he reached out to lay his hand on my arm.

"Sorry about not being able to answer all your calls and texts. I can't believe I was stupid enough to leave my phone at home."

I dropped my hand on top of his, squeezing lightly before letting go.

"Thanks. As you may have guessed by now, Mary knows. I let my imagination work me up like a teenager after her first date. Not to mention I was feeling weird about Sunday."

"Weird?" he asked, his eyes narrowing as he searched my face. The tone of his voice let me know a ton of feelings were wrapped around that word. I shook my head as I realized what I said sounded wrong. I hastened to soothe his worries.

"No, no, no. Not weird like that. Mark, I'm good with what happened. I really am." I saw the tightness around his eyes lessen and his shoulders relax as I spoke.

I took a deep breath. "Look, before our first dinner, I'd been on six or seven dates. And I use the word 'date' loosely. No chemistry or connection. I didn't even kiss anybody after the date. I got more action petting Simon when I got home at night."

His lips quirked up, and I smacked his arm. He wiped the grin off his lips, but not from his eyes.

I continued. "I don't know what happened, or why I attacked you. That was so out of character for me. I don't do that. Ever. But regardless, I did it. I don't regret it, and I most *definitely* enjoyed it, and I really enjoyed being with you."

I took a drink, clearing my parched throat, willing my nerves to calm down enough to get me through this.

"Mark. I like you. A lot. There's something between us I haven't felt in a long time, and I want to explore that. But I'm also sensitive to the age difference and how others will perceive us, especially my boss. Friends, associates, and everyone else in my business world. Having a reputation as someone who chases young men, or boys, does not bode well in my corporate world."

"Wait," he said, holding up a hand. "Are you saying you would be *ashamed* to be seen with me, or to have these so-called 'friends' see you with me? Does how they think of you really matter *that* much? True friends don't care about stuff like this. True friends support you."

I rubbed the bridge of my nose, the tension settling like a weight. I looked back at Mark. The tension was back around his eyes. *Damn, this was not the way I wanted this to go.*

I exhaled, trying to make my words gentle. "Yes, and no. I'm trying to be honest with you and let you know my fears. This has all been sudden for me, but I want to try this with you, so I want you to be aware of some things I will face, that *we* will face. I'm sure your friends are going to have something to say when you tell them you're dating someone old enough to be your mother."

He shook his head. "First, you're not old enough to be my mother. That's just... *ugh*," he said, shuddering. I stifled a giggle at his discomfort. But knowing he didn't see me that way also made me feel better.

He continued. "Second, most of my friends wouldn't bat an eye. I *may* have already mentioned something to a few of them about being interested in this incredible, beautiful, sexy woman who was a few years older than me."

I looked at him, my eyes wide. "Mark—"

He grabbed my hands, lacing his fingers with mine. That zing started up my arms again. It was amazing to me that just his touch was enough to get me going.

"Kathi, I only care about one opinion. *Yours*. I don't live my life or rotate my world around what others think of me. I've been on my own for the last seven plus years and I'm pretty grounded in myself and what I want. Maybe that's why I'm drawn to you. You're intelligent, beautiful and well aware of your own wants and needs. I want to date you, and not just casually, okay? And if my friends can't handle that, then fuck 'em. They're not my friends anymore."

His gaze didn't wander from mine as he gave me the time to process what he'd said. He meant every word. No hesitation, no lies, no evasions. This incredible young man in front of me... wanted *me*.

I finally found my voice. "Okay." I replied, still reeling from his declaration.

"Look," he said, giving my hands a light squeeze. "I'm not going to lie to you. I think you're worrying over nothing. But," he said, before I could speak, "they're your concerns and I'll respect them and work through them with you."

"Mark—"

He interrupted me, squeezing my fingers again.

"That said, I need you to promise me something. Should we run into your friends, explain who I am and what I am to you. *Acknowledge us*. I'm not demanding dinner with Samuel next week, but I also don't want you to lie about us."

He paused, searching my eyes as I worked to quell the fear churning in me, the fear of discovery.

"Kathi, you tell me you feel something for me and you want to try this. All I ask is that you give *us* your best shot."

I cocked my head, looking at him. "Mark, I'm fifteen years older than you. Does that truly not bother you?"

His response was immediate and decisive. "Nope."

I stared into his eyes. His gaze was intense but steady. Everything in me told me he meant every word he had spoken. He was committed to me, to us, and he wanted the same from me. He remained quiet, leaving the ball in my court.

Several seconds passed, the comforting, familiar sounds of the barn filtering in, the snuffles from the horses, hooves pawing the ground, the jingle of a halter as a head was shook.

I nodded, never breaking my gaze with him.

"Okay, Mark. I know I've had reservations. Trust me, I've had a thousand arguments in my head, but I have to be honest. I want this and *I want this with you*," I said. I could feel the weight of the decision flowing off my shoulders. A new one replaced it, one that had been becoming stronger as Friday approached. One that I now had to acknowledge and act on.

I stood up, flicking my fingers at Mark and his chair. Puzzled, he pushed his chair back and started to rise. but I put one hand on his shoulder, stopping him. Throwing a leg over him, I sat down on his lap. I draped my arms over his shoulders, letting my fingers run up into his hair. His hands grabbed my waist, holding me tight.

I met his gaze, seeing the heat and want in his eyes. The intensity was like a blowtorch playing on my desire. I leaned forward slowly, grinding myself against the growing stiffness beneath me, bringing a small groan and a smile from him.

I placed my cheek next to his, inhaling him like a drink of water in the heat of the desert. My lips nipped at his earlobe, and kissed lightly against his ear. He shuddered in response.

"Mark," I whispered.

"Hmmm?" he replied as he pushed my shirt up enough that he could put his hands on my bare skin. His touch sent shivers up my spine.

I put my lips right on his ear. "My pussy was sore for two days. I'm way out of sex-shape. Since we appear to be in a relationship now, is there something we can do about that?" I punctuated my question by running the tip of my tongue around the edge of his inner ear.

He growled and pulled me tighter to him. His hands started pushing up under my bra. I bowed slightly, anticipating his hands on my breasts, my nipples hard in anticipation.

A loud bang broke us apart as the tack room door exploded open, smacking against the outside wall. Before I could utter a word, water sprayed on us for several seconds. Ice cold water. Mark and I both jerked upright. I shrieked as the water hit my bare skin before my shirt could drop back down. We stared at the door as we both sputtered and blew water out of our faces. Mary stood in the entryway, water dripping from the sprayer and hose she held in her hand.

"I swear to all that's holy. I'll drown both of your horny butts. This is a tack room, not a hangout for horny juveniles," she growled.

"But…" was all I got out before she raised her hand, pointing the sprayer at me and a 'go ahead, make my day' crazed look in her eyes.

Laughing, I slid off of Mark's lap. I picked up my now soaked food dish and headed for the door. I was almost to Mary when I realized Mark was still in his chair.

"Mark? You coming?"

He glanced up at me, grinning. He was hunched over slightly, his hands in his lap. "Gonna need a sec. Go on without me."

Mary held up the hose. "I can help with that," she said. The smile she gave him was sweet in a totally evil kind of way. Mark shot a hand up, shaking his head.

"Nope, I'm good. Just need a minute."

Mary and I giggled like two teenagers. We started back to the front of the barn, leaving Mark to take care of his issues.

We hadn't taken more than a few steps before a new voice called out to us.

"Mary, wait up."

We turned to see Ty Richardson, one of the local vets, striding towards us. Ty had joined old Doc Ferguson's clinic several months ago, a much-needed addition to the large animal staff. Even though Bare Ridge was a small, out of the way town, there was a large population of horses, goats, cattle, and a few other larger animals in the area. Doc Ferguson was hard pressed to keep up with the demand for his services.

Doc had been searching for a year or more to find one or two more vets to join his staff. Given the pay and benefits offered by some of the larger vet clinics in the Denver area, his efforts had failed for a long time.

Then Ty showed up. He'd taken over almost all of Doc's large animal work. He'd proven to be good with the horses here at the ranch, and Mary was pleased with the work he'd done so far. I'd seen him around but hadn't had a chance to speak with him yet.

"What's up, Doc?" asked Mary.

I snorted as Ty rolled his eyes.

"Wow, haven't heard that one in about an hour or so. Good one, Mary."

She shrugged, grinning at him. "Hey, it's an oldie, but a goodie. What did ya need?"

"I checked on those two rescues you wanted me to look at. They're coming along nicely. Keep up the exercise and feed program we set up and I think by summer they will be ready to adopt. The mare has an abscess on her front left hoof, but she's still a bit skittish around me, so I couldn't get a good look at it. Can you and Jake keep an eye on it?"

"Sure." She glanced over at me as Ty smiled in my direction. "Oh, where are my manners? Have you met Kathi?"

He nodded to me, smiling and holding out his hand.

"Haven't had the pleasure. Ty Richardson."

I shook his hand, liking that he gave me a firm grip. "Kathi Harrison, and it's nice to meet you. Glad to see Doc Ferguson finally found some help."

"Yep, I'm really glad he hired me. I'm loving it here, Mrs. Harrison," he replied.

I shook my head. "Kathi, please."

He smiled, tipping his head to me. "Thank you. Folks normally call me Ty, or Doc, when they're making a *terrible* pun," he replied, giving Mary a mock glare. She tried looking all innocent but failed miserably.

"Well, gotta run. Gotta meet Doc Ferguson for a rousing afternoon of cattle checking over at the Gleason Ranch. Ladies." He tipped his head at us again and hustled out of the barn towards his truck. We both turned and watched him leave, taking a moment to admire the view. I elbowed Mary and lifted my chin at the retreating vet.

"What?" she replied, still watching the vet walk away.

"Single guy, good looking, employed. Looks to have all his teeth.

Might enjoy a woman of your… maturity, guiding him through life. Help you end that long dry spell you were talking about."

Mary's head snapped back to me as I used the same words she had said to me not so long ago. I grinned, waiting for the explosion, but her before she said anything, a throat cleared behind us.

"Wow, already scoping out my replacement."

I whirled to find Mark standing behind us, arms crossed, sporting a shit-eating grin. The grin morphed into an exaggerated hurt look on his face before clutching his hand to his heart.

My face blazed red. Mary started laughing.

"Busted," she cackled before walking towards the house, leaving me red-faced and sputtering. I walked to Mark, grabbed his shirt, and yanked him forward until I could throw my arms around his neck. I pulled his head down and devoured his lips. He pulled me in tighter and did his best to swallow my tongue.

A sing-song voice came dancing back up the pathway to us. "Don't make me get the hose again." Smiling against his lips, I gave him a final kiss before pulling away from him. Mark slid his arm around my waist and we followed the still cackling Mary. I couldn't have been happier than I was at that very moment.

NINETEEN

I was on cloud nine as Mark and I sped down the highway, heading back towards my house. Trees and grass were greening up and our day trip up into the mountains of Colorado had been wonderful. We'd set no destination, letting the road guide us as we went from small town to small town.

The idea of me taking a whole day off before our two major events did not thrill Samuel. To appease him, Abby and I had given him and the other board members a full briefing on both events, highlighting the status and readiness of all parties. After the presentation, I told him I needed the day to recharge and be ready to host our gala and dinner. After some grumbling, he finally agreed, but again warned me he would not tolerate any slip-ups. That phrase was almost becoming a mantra for him now.

I glanced at Mark only to find him staring at me, something which happened quite often. We had spent every moment together that we could since our talk in the tack room. We spent much of our time simply enjoying each other's company and making up the lost time in my love life. Within reason, nothing was off the table. Today was a great example. I was still tingling from making love on a blanket beside a mountain lake. There was something freeing about being naked on a blanket under the open sky.

I wasn't a virgin when I met Jeremy and we had an active love life for most of our marriage... or so I thought. Mark showed me what I didn't realize I was missing.

The time we spent together gave us the opportunity to learn everything we could about each other. Even with the age difference, we still found we had many of the same likes and dislikes. Maybe it was the newness of the relationship, but we never lacked for something to do or talk about.

We finished up the final weekend events with the kids at Mary's ranch. The Councilman had been ecstatic at the feedback he was receiving from the families and kids. He was pressing Samuel to make it a more permanent event. He wanted to do more weekends throughout the year and even expand into multiple programs during the summer. Samuel was more than pleased to agree.

The wrinkle was Mary and Jake. Their place was not setup for this kind of sustained event activity. Occasional weekends were fine, but anything more than what we had done required a different setup. Logistics, more horses, more staff, etc. Mary had been fine with helping us out, but a few times I could tell she seemed stressed. I would follow up with her after the gala.

Work had exploded the Monday after we wrapped up at Mary's. Final touches to the two big events, ensuring we had parking and other logistics covered, had kept me hopping. Unfortunately, this had limited my time with Mark. That was why today had been so important. A chance to spend time with each other after the rush of work.

The first sponsors' dinner was tomorrow night, followed by the larger dinner on Saturday. Once the events were done, I planned to work next week doing wrap up while Abby took some time off, then I would take the following week off. Mark and I had discussed taking a mini-vacation if he could get his schedule arranged.

Mark finally broke the comfortable silence.

"Kathi, I just want to say again how fantastic you were with those kids. I think you missed your calling."

His praise washed over me, warming me like a hug. "My calling?" I asked.

He nodded. "Yeah. I think you should have been a teacher. Like Mary, teaching others to ride and jump."

I started laughing, but he stopped me.

"I'm serious Kathi. Over these last few weeks, I got to see two different Kathi's. Corporate Kathi working for Harrison Enterprises, and another Kathi, teaching others about her love of horses. You were way more happy when you were with the kids."

With a quick glance, I could tell he was serious. I pulled my attention back to the road, maneuvering around a minivan doing about twenty miles under the speed limit.

"And how did you come to this conclusion, oh mighty seer?"

"Easy. I watched you."

"I'm going to need a bit more than that. You watch me all the time." I glanced over at him, grinning. "Some people might even think it's a little stalkerish."

He waggled his eyebrows. "It's only stalkerish when I stare at your ass."

Laughing, I let his hand go just long enough to smack his leg. Smack delivered, I recaptured his hand, entwining my fingers with his.

He continued, his voice serious. "Look, when you were with those kids, your face was glowing and you were always smiling. You got lost in the fun of teaching those kids and they fed off it. You made it better for them."

I felt my heart warm at his words. "I have to admit, I enjoyed it more than I thought I would. I've covered for Mary before, but this was so much more involved."

"That's what I mean," he said, squeezing my hand to emphasize his point. "This last week or so, when you've been talking about these work events, your mood is different. I think you like the challenge, just not the environment or people.

"And yeah," he continued, "I know you like Abby and a few others, but the pressure that Samuel is putting on you to sell him your shares is borderline abusive. Not to mention he's like a vulture circling a carcass, watching for a reason to fire you."

He let the silence stretch, the sounds of the tires meeting the road and the subtle roar of the engine fill in for words before he spoke again.

"One last thing. A wise man once said if you are doing what you love, it's not work. That applies here. You love horses and riding, and it seems you love teaching others. I think you would love teaching way more than planning events."

I had to admit, his words weren't far from the truth. When Jeremy died, work was safe. It was comfortable, like a favorite robe. Harrison's had been a big part of my life for years and I had assumed it would be my entire career. And now, unexpectedly, Mark's words were making me reconsider that choice.

All too soon, our drive was over and we arrived back at my house. I dropped my purse on the kitchen island as Mark closed the front door. I slipped off my shoes as he opened the fridge, pulling out a beer.

"Want anything?" he asked.

"A glass of the white, please?"

He pulled a stemmed glass from the sliding rack under the cabinet. It was eerie how easily he moved around my kitchen now, having spent more than a few nights fixing me dinner. He grabbed my favorite Riesling from the wine fridge under the island and poured me a half-glass.

"Thanks," I said when he handed it to me. He took a sip and stared at the tabletop.

"Mark? Everything okay?" I asked.

He jerked his head upright, fixing me with that dimpled grin. "Um, yeah, everything is great." I don't think he believed himself anymore than I did. I sat my glass down on the island.

"To quote Mary, 'horseshit'. What's up?"

He scrubbed at his hair before dropping his hand back to the island. His gaze dropped to the bottle he was fiddling with.

"I know you have the events tomorrow night and the night after. But how would you feel about going out Sunday evening?" he asked, still not looking at me.

That's odd. Why is he so worried about asking me out?

"Sure," I replied, laughing. "Why is asking me out worrying you so much? We've been out several times already. It's called dating."

"Because of where I want to take you," he said, his head coming up, so that he was now looking straight at me.

I felt a small tendril of fear creep up my spine. "Where?"

"I scored two tickets to the first part of Wagner's *Ring Cycle*."

Shit.

I set my wineglass down, sighing. "Mark, honey, we talked about this."

"I know," he said, leaning forward on the bar. "It's all we ever do about it, Kathi. Every time we've gone out over these past weeks, it's been someplace other than Denver. Or anywhere close to Denver. All because of your fear of Samuel or being seen by your society friends."

I could feel that aforementioned fear welling up inside me, along with a flare of anger. "We talked about this, Mark. It's not that simple. You agreed to give me time."

He came around the bar to my side. His gaze locked with mine, and there was no mistaking the intensity in his eyes.

"Yes, it is. It's just that simple, Kathi. And I think I've given you plenty of time."

"Mark—"

"I wanted to take you to that symphony last week, but you said no because Samuel's wife is at every performance."

"I know Mark, but—"

"I wanted to take you to the art display at the museum, but you said it was too risky."

"Yes, but—"

"Every time I try to take you some place that I know you would like, you've said no because of who might see us."

His continuous interrupting before I could explain only ramped up my anger. He knew I hated it, knew I thought it was a huge type of disrespect.

"Dammit, Mark. It's not that simple," I growled, matching his stare with my own.

His hand smacked down on the island, the sharp crack echoing like a shot through the house, causing me to flinch.

His voice was firm. "Yes. It. *Is*."

This was getting ridiculous. I waved my hand at him. "Shit Mark, it's not. We've talked about this."

"Why Kathi? Why can't you do this?"

"I told you—"

He cut me off again, leaning forward. "Why?"

I was seething. I didn't like being treated like a child.

"Why Kathi? Why? Why?"

He didn't give me a chance to reply, just kept punching that one word back at me. I was pissed and reeling from his verbal assault. The words were out before I registered their meaning.

"BECAUSE I DON'T WANT PEOPLE TO THINK I'M REGINA PARADING MY BOY-TOY AROUND."

The blood drained from his face as my words ripped into him. He stepped back from me as if slapped. The hurt in his eyes almost dropped me to the floor.

Good lord, what had I done? Where did those words come from? I stepped forward, one hand reaching for him.

"Mark, I'm so—"

He held up his hand, freezing me in my tracks. My lowered by hand slowly as his face tightened, then settle into an emotionless stare.

"Your boy-toy. I see," he stated, his voice dead and emotionless. "Thank you, Mrs. Harrison, for clarifying that for me. If you'll excuse me, I think I'll call it a night and head home. You have a lot on your plate with your *friends* the next couple of nights."

I stood there numb as he pivoted sharply and walked out the front door. My head was screaming at me to say something, anything, to get him to stay and let me explain. My body refused to listen, rooting me to the spot. When that door slammed, my heart broke in my chest, bleeding and worthless. I barely registered the sound of his Jeep's engine roaring, followed by the bark of his tires as he fled.

I stumbled back to the island, gripping the edge for some support. Why had I said that? Where did those words come from?

As the tears flowed down my cheeks, I reached into the wine fridge to pull out the bottle of wine that Mark had poured from earlier. I filled my glass and drained it. I filled it again and downed half of it. I slid down to the floor, letting my back rest against the fridge. I beat my head slowly backwards, thunking the door. Maybe the pain in my head would cancel out the pain from my heart.

The thoughts tumbled wildly through my mind. What was my problem? Why couldn't I take this last step? I liked Mark. I liked everything about him. When I told him I wanted a relationship, I meant it. I couldn't understand why I was so hesitant about letting my work friends and family know we were dating.

I don't know how long I sat there, the same thoughts going back and forth in my head like a tennis match. I was only vaguely aware the sun had set. With no obvious reasons blasting into my head, I decided I needed help.

I wiped my sleeve across my face to clear away the tears as I fumbled my phone out of my pocket. As I blinked rapidly to stop fresh tears from falling, I punched my speed dial, tapped the speaker icon and sat the phone on the floor. Taking another drink from my almost empty glass, I waited for it to connect. Three rings later, Mary answered.

"*Hey girl. Thought you were on a date with Mark. Taking a breather between make-out sessions?*"

I sobbed and snorted a laugh at the same time. Mary's voice immediately changed from playful to laced with concern.

"*Kathi? What's wrong? What happened?*"

"He's gone, Mary. I screwed up and chased him away." The sobs overtook me again.

"*Shit, Kathi. What happened?*"

In between my sobbing and hiccuping, I told her the entire story, including our conversation about teaching and work. I barely choked out those terrible words I had uttered about Regina. By the time I was done, my throat was raw.

Mary let out a low whistle. "*Girl, when you decide to screw up, you sure don't mess around, do you? Give me a moment to think about this. Wait, where are you?"*

I snorted before answering her. "Sitting on my kitchen floor, drinking wine."

"Put the wine away. You need a clear head for this."

I nodded, even though she couldn't see me. I reached up and grabbed the fridge handle, using it for support to pull myself upright. I put the almost empty wine bottle away before I stumbled into the front room and collapsed on the couch. A few moments later, Mary chimed back in.

"Okay. Any reason, other than the age, keeping you from telling Samuel and the others?"

I wiped my hand across my face again, snot smearing across my sleeve. Lovely. "I can't think of anything. It's all I have been thinking of since he left."

"You think it would be that bad if you told Samuel?"

I took a breath, hiccuping. "It would be bad, Mary. He's as straight-laced as they come and looking for a way to remove me from the company. Hell, he doesn't want to invite Regina to any of the events, and she's our biggest private sponsor. Everything in his world is prim and proper. There is no gray, just black and white. I'd lose my job and everything I've worked for at Harrison Enterprises would be gone."

"So? It's not like you need to work."

I protested, weakly. "But I've worked there for years. It's all I've ever known. It was everything for Jeremy and me. What I would do if Samuel fired me."

"Hmmmm." Then she fell silent.

After a moment, I couldn't stand the silence. "What? Don't give me a 'hmmmm' and leave me hanging."

Her voice was gentle as she spoke. *"You're pretty comfortable at Harrisons. Lots of time spent with Jeremy. Work was a surety."*

If she had been here, she would have seen the confusion on my face. "Yeah, so?"

"Even with Jeremy dying and the fallout from that, you've always had work to fall back on. Maybe that's part of the issue."

"You've lost me," I said, sniffing.

"Okay, just a guess here. I'm not one of them therapists. That said, think of this. For twenty-plus years, you had Jeremy and work. Then you lost Jeremy. The two of you had no kids, but you had work. Work was your anchor and your connection to Jeremy. Are you following me?"

I nodded, sniffling again. "Yes."

"Along comes Mark, and he starts to filling in some of these voids in your life. You get a glimpse of a future with him, something not tied to work or Jeremy. But to move forward with Mark, you have to introduce him to the work and social side of your life. That means Samuel firing you. Which means you lose work. An anchor for you, and a last link to Jeremy."

Her words hit me like a freight train. Was she right? Her words vibrated across my brain, breaking loose old thoughts and fears. At an instinctual level, I knew she had hit on something. Other than the house, all I really had left of Jeremy was work. Was I holding on, not letting him go?

After a few beats of silence, Mary spoke. *"Did I lose you?"*

I shook my head, realization falling into place. She was right. I repeated her words back to her. "If I tell Samuel, I lose work, and lose one of the last pieces of Jeremy. And I do it by gambling with Mark, not knowing if we would ever be a couple, or if he's a short-term thing."

"Pretty much. I think you're scared of losing that last link to Jeremy. I think it's what's holding you back. And Kathi, I don't think he's a short-term fling. Not the way he looks at you. Definitely not with as happy as I've seen you lately."

The ringing of the doorbell interrupted me before I could answer. How did anyone get past the gate?

A chill ran through me, followed by a rush of excitement. Only three people had my gate code and I was talking to one. Abby was out with her girlfriends tonight, clubbing. That left only one other.

"Mary, I have to go."

I didn't wait to hear her answer before hitting the disconnect button. I scrambled to my feet and rushed to the door. Throwing it open, my heart flew to my throat at the sight of the man standing before me, a sad, hurt look on his face.

Mark.

With a strangled cry, I threw myself into his arms and started sobbing all over again as his arms gathered me to him in a desperate embrace.

TWENTY

"Sorry, so sorry, sorry," I sputtered as I sobbed into his chest. He tried gently prying my arms from around his neck, but I hung on for dear life as I continued to babble and sob, soaking his shirt in tears and snot.

He gave up trying to detach me and lifted me up, walking both of us back into the house far enough to close the door behind him.

For what seemed like hours, he leaned against the door and held me, rubbing my back as I cried and told him how sorry I was. It was when the hiccups started that he finally reacted, his chuckles rumbling inside him.

I punched his chest weakly, my misery giving me no strength. "Don't... hic... don't... hic... hic... laugh... hic at me... hic."

He walked me over to the island, lifted me up, and sat me down on it. Once he got my arms unlocked from his neck, he opened drawers until he found a small dishcloth. He flipped on the faucet and let the water run for a few moments before wetting the cloth and wringing it out.

He held my shoulder and gently used the cloth to wipe my face, cleaning away my tears and other obnoxious bodily fluids. He handed me the cloth, got a glass from the cabinet, and filled it with water from the fridge door.

He handed it to me, taking the now disgusting cloth from my hand as I hiccuped again.

"Drink," he said, breaking the silence between us.

I drank, breathing deep between sips, trying my best to make the hiccups stop. While I did, Mark rinsed the cloth out and leaned back against the sink edge, watching me.

Finished, I sat the glass down. He came back and again wiped my face. Finished, he tossed the cloth towards the sink and looked at me. Sitting on the island, I could look him in the eye. Experience from a couple of weeks ago also told me spreading my legs allowed him to step right up to me and kiss me without bending his head. I didn't know if I'd ever experience that again, but I knew wanted to.

I grabbed his arm and squeezed.

"Mark, I'm—" He cut me off with a single finger to my lips. I couldn't help myself. I gently kissed it.

The corner of his lip jerked up slightly, and a flash of desire filled his eyes before it faded. As it left, my heart sunk as I realized this was one time I couldn't read the emotions swirling in those eyes.

His mouth turned down. "Kathi, I'm sorry."

I'm sure my eyebrows climbing over my head was amusing because he chuckled. Then the unreadable look was back, and he placed both hands on my legs, causing a tingling heat to bloom where they touched.

He looked me in the eye, unblinking. "What you said hurt."

My stomach flipped as shame washed over me again. "Mark..."

He shook his head, and I fell silent. "Let me finish," he said, squeezing my legs. "You hurt me. I got pissed, so I ran away from the problem and the hurt. I ran away from *you*."

He stepped closer, his focus on me so strong I trembled.

His eyes studied mine intently. "I'm sorry I ran. This thing between us differs from anything else I've ever felt. It's scary. That said, if I'm going to date an incredible woman who also happens to be a few years older than me, and has a ton more experience being in a long-term relationship, then I guess I need to learn how to talk first before I take my toys and go home."

He stepped closer and nudged my legs apart. He looked at me again and I'd swear those eyes were parsing my soul, looking for answers to the questions I'm sure were hurtling through his head.

"Kathi. Talk to me. What's holding you back? I told you I would depend on you to tell me where we were, but today made it seem like we were nowhere. Are you embarrassed by me? Ashamed? What do I need to do to fix this?" His eyes searched mine. "I can wait. I *will* wait. However long it takes, you are worth it."

My heart jumped into my throat at his pleas as I heard the underlying fear in those questions. Fear that I had put there.

My eyes teared up again. I realized I had *really* hurt him with my unthinking words. He stood before me, begging me to help him fix this.

I shook my head vehemently. "God, *no*. Please, if you believe nothing else I tell you, believe that I'm neither ashamed nor embarrassed by you. I told you in that tack room that I wanted this. I just suck at showing it."

I took a couple of deep breaths, trying to maintain focus and control and not become a crying mess again. Mark waited, not filling in the silence.

I took a deep breath, letting it out slowly before continuing. "This is all on *me*. I talked with Mary after you stormed out. No," I said, holding up a hand as he started to speak. "Don't apologize to me again. I hurt you. You got pissed. I get it. I don't blame you. Not at all."

I looked at those eyes again and a need flashed through me so strong it scared me.

"Mark, I… before I go on, can… can you please kiss me?"

He pushed forward, closing the distance between us. He grasped my chin and then his lips were on mine, and with that touch, I was whole again.

The kiss was full of love. It was the only word that fit. It wasn't a word, or words that I could say right now, but that didn't mean I couldn't recognize the feeling. His lips were soft, the kiss gentle and unrushed. It was a balm to my soul.

I pulled back, reluctantly, letting his lips slide away. He looked at me, that panty-melting smile forming on those unbelievable lips.

He ran his hand down my arm. "What did Mary say?"

I recapped all the things Mary had said while I cried to her. He only nodded a few times, not interrupting me.

"What do you think?" he asked, rubbing one hand along my arm, sending tingles up my arm and pebbling the skin.

I shrugged slightly, glancing over his shoulder before I looked him in the eyes again. "I think, maybe, she's right. When Jeremy died, I had my work and this house and our friends. Other than Jeremy not being here, my life didn't change. Hasn't changed. It's comfortable. Safe. Jeremy's dying scared me. Maybe I'm still scared. As long as nothing else changed, I... I would always have some small piece of him."

He pulled me into him, wrapping his arms around me. I nestled my head into this chest, filling my lungs with him. He whispered into my ear, his breath tickling. "You can't ever lose him, Kathi. He'll always be a part of you."

"I know," I whispered, nodding into his chest.

He let his hands run lightly up and down my back, kissing the top of my head.

Laying there in his arms pushed forward another fear that had been quietly building in me in the last week. Thoughts I only allowed to surface when I woke late at night and found myself in Mark's arms. A fear that beat at me to let it out. Mark must have sensed something. He pulled back far enough to look at me, searching my face again.

"Kathi? You went all tense. What's wrong?"

Damn the torpedoes…it's time to be honest with him. I at least owe him that.

I glanced down as I spoke, my worries and fears causing my voice to shake. "I think… I think I'm falling for you and it scares me."

Of all the reactions I expected, laughter wasn't one of them. But laughter bubbled out of Mark. My eyes shot up, and I gave him a startled look. He shook his head and looked at me, laughing again at my apparent confusion. He brought one hand back up to cup my face and then kissed me again.

"Kathi Harrison," he said, our foreheads touching. "I fell in love with you the first time I saw you, almost two years ago. I left for a time because I didn't think you would ever see me in that way, so I tried to forget you. It didn't work. I loved you while I was gone, and I fell for you all over again that day in the barn, and I've loved you every day since."

He kissed me again, his love pouring out to me, washing over me like a shower. My hesitancy in the face of those emotions floored me. I wasn't worthy of that from him.

"Mark... I..."

He quickly pecked my lips with his, cutting off my protest.

"It's okay. You don't have to say it." He gave me a soft, crooked grin as his eyes bounced back and forth between mine. "I've been in this relationship for almost two years longer than you. It might take you a while. And as much as it kills me to say it, you might never get to where I am. But that's a risk I'm willing to take because you are *so* damn worth it."

I gazed intently into those searching eyes, overwhelmed by his words.

He *loved* me.

My heart was racing, and I swear I could feel the blood moving through my veins. It had been years since someone had spoken those words to me. Red hot flames roared through me, filling me with desire for *this* man.

I wanted him, and I wanted him now. His eyebrow popped up when I grinned at him.

"So, we've had our first fight, correct?" He nodded slowly. I could see the wheels turning in his head as he worked to figure out where I was going. I continued, my voice dropping a lower. "And we've made up, right?" A slow smile began spreading over his face as he caught on to my line of thinking.

I cocked my head to the side. "Well, it's been a while for me and the relationship rules may have changed, but I thought after lovers fought and made up, there was *make-up* sex."

I punctuated my statement by rubbing the front of his jeans. He kissed me again and the intensity of it melted me.

"Hell *yes*, there's gonna be makeup sex." I laughed as he pulled me off of the counter and stood me up. I squealed when he bent, and with a quick flip, tossed me over his shoulder.

"A *lot* of makeup sex," he declared loudly as he carried me off to the bedroom, my laughter echoing off the walls.

I drifted up from sleep. A very sated sleep. I took a moment to languish in the feeling of warmth and tranquility that infused me.

Mark was spooned up to me, his arm draped over me, his hand firmly attached to my boob. Even better, his morning hardness was pressing between the cheeks of my ass. I pushed back against him, gently rubbing up and down his manhood.

When he stirred, I increased my efforts. He groaned, pulling me back tighter, keeping me from teasing him further. His lips nibbled where my shoulder and neck met, sending shivers through me and igniting a fire between my legs.

"Woman," he said in a sleepy, breathy cadence. "Stop that. We used the last condom sometime after two."

I started slowly grinding again.

"Kathiiiii," he whined and moaned at the same time, a sound I'm pretty sure I'd never heard before. I giggled, pushing my chest out against his hand. He squeezed me firmly, twisting my nipple.

As I flipped around to face him, I noticed his mussed hair and the sleepy smile on his face. His eyes softened as met mine.

He brought his hand up to cup my cheek, then shifted it to behind my head and pulled my lips to his. The first kiss was soft, almost hesitant. I slid my hand to his waist and let it drift slowly up his side, caressing as he shivered at my touch.

He kissed me again, and I opened, meeting him. Our tongues

danced and explored, the rush of last night replaced with a tenderness of contentment.

He pulled back, letting his hand come up to brush the hair out of my face.

"Hi," he said, reaching up and running his fingers lightly through the hair over my ear.

"Hi," I replied, my fingers making small circles on his skin.

"If last night was an example of make-up sex with you, I foresee a lot of fighting in our future," he said.

He yelped when I pinched his nipple. I scooted up, propping myself on his shoulder so I could look down at him.

"Listen clearly, buster. I'm not saying we will never argue or fight, but I want us to work real hard on not having make-up sex. I'm good with the sex part." As I talked, he began tracing one finger down my side, then sliding it over between my legs and tickling at a spot just above my clit.

"Stop that. I'm trying to talk to you," I said, not sure if I was mad at him for not going further or for stopping. He grinned, but only pulled his hand back to my stomach.

I kissed him deeply before pulling back to gaze down at him.

"I love you," he said. Those words set my soul on fire. I looked at him, a man who had proclaimed his love for me, who's been honest with me from the start in telling me my age had nothing to do with it. A man who had awakened feelings in me that had lain dormant for years.

"Come with me to the dinner tonight." I blurted the words out before my brain could engage.

I'd never seen eyebrows go up that high. "What? Are you serious?" he asked.

I needed to show him what he meant to me, so I pushed on before I could think about it fully. "Yes. Tonight. Come with me."

He gave me that intense gaze, the one that seemed to look deep inside me.

"Kathi, if I come tonight..." he started, but I kissed him hard, interrupting whatever point he was about to make.

"I know. Come tonight." I kissed him again. "Please? Let me show everyone my boyfriend."

He studied me with intense eyes, and I met his gaze. Satisfied with what he saw in my face, he slowly nodded. "Okay, Kathi. I'll come."

I grinned and kissed him again, harder. I kissed his jaw, nipping along the edge.

"What are you doing… fuckkkkk." His last word ended in a groan as I grabbed his shaft and began stroking him slowly, loving the feel of his heat and girth in my hand.

"Kathi, we don't have any condoms left," he hissed as I kept gripping and stroking him.

I trailed kisses down his chest, flicking his nipple with my tongue. I kissed and licked my way across his abs as he gasped and moaned.

I held his cock up, giving it another stroke. It was so warm and hard and I could feel the blood pulse in time with his heartbeat. I lowered my mouth, letting my tongue lick around the crown before dropping my lips around it.

"Fuccck meeee," he groaned as he gripped the sheets.

I pulled back up slowly, letting him go with a slurping pop.

"Wrong verb, lover."

I paced outside the doors to the event area, the sparkling-red evening gown that I wore brushing against my legs. My stomach was churning and I think I had a groove started in the carpet.

I knew what Mark was expecting tonight and he was right. It was time to face those fears and let the chips fall where they may. Mark was worth it. *We* were worth it.

It was a given that the minute I introduced Mark to Samuel, my time at Harrison Enterprises would be over. Samuel would fire me and install one of his other cousins in my place. I'd still have all my stock, but I'd have no job. Thankfully, Jeremy had left me comfortable, and I always had the option to sell my stock. Work wasn't really a necessity, just something that helped me fill the day. I kept telling myself that over and over.

I glanced left as the doors opened and Abby poked her head out.

"Boss, why are you out here? I thought you would be inside rubbing elbows with our benefactors?"

"I'm waiting for Mark," I said. Abby's eyebrows jumped skyward as she stepped closer, letting the door close behind her.

"Are you serious?" she hissed, looking around. "What about Samuel?"

I shrugged, not wanting to give voice to my fears.

"Look, Kathi, I know this is a big step and - oh... my."

Her last words confused me. I started to say something, but stopped when I realized she was focused on something over my shoulder. I turned and completely understood her reaction as my entire body began humming.

Mark had entered the lobby and was heading our way. He was wearing a black suit that fit him like a glove. The coat was open so you could see the black shirt he was wearing. The top button was open, and he wore no tie.

The belt buckle sparkled silver from across the room and looked like a smaller version of those buckles awarded to rodeo riders. Black cowboy boots rounded out the ensemble.

Every woman in the lobby snapped their eyes to him like they had some dick-seeking radar, but he was looking only at me.

"Boss..." Abby started to say, but I cut her off.

"*Mine,*" I hissed through my smile, my eyes never leaving Mark's. His gaze never wavered as he approached me.

I had watched a lot of wildlife shows as a kid and always wondered what the gazelle thought when it spotted the lion. At that moment, I knew exactly how it felt. I was Mark's prey, and he was stalking me, ready to devour me. He covered the final gap between us, pausing in front of me. He didn't even glance at Abby as he captured my hand before bending forward and kissing me lightly on the lips. A nova exploded inside me at that intimate touch.

"You look beautiful." Those words and the sultriness of his tone sent shivers down my spine.

A slight throat clearing reminded me I wasn't alone.

"Mark, this is my assistant, Abby. Abby, Mark Danlock. My... my boyfriend."

Mark's eyes flared with pride at those words, and the look he gave me caused my body to heat up like the sun.

He smiled at Abby, holding his hand out. She quickly grasped it, hitting him with a smile that had reduced other men to putty.

"Hello, Abby, a pleasure to meet you."

She leaned closer, her smile reaching out to pull him in, like a spider pulling a fly into its web.

"No, the pleasure is *all* mine." She smiled again before dropping her eyelids down, hitting him with her version of bedroom eyes. Mark glanced over at me with an amused look on his face, and I rolled my eyes at my assistant's antics. She and I would have to have a talk later, but now wasn't the time.

Mark smiled politely at Abby before releasing her hand and turning his entire focus to me. His eyes burned with passion and admiration as he studied me.

"Abby, I think you should go check on the bar and make sure everything is going smoothly," I said, smiling. However, the tone in my voice was anything other than smiling. Abby sensed it and immediately backed down. She gave me a brief hug.

"Lucky bitch," she whispered in my ear before straightening up. She glanced once more at Mark, raking her gaze over him from top to bottom before sighing and reentering the event hall.

I turned back to him, chuckling at my crazy assistant. Mark immediately caught my hand and squeezed it while giving me another of his panty-melting smiles,

"Ready?" he asked.

I paused, willing the acid in my stomach to quit erupting in geysers. The pause was long enough to worry Mark.

"Hey," he said, searching my face and eyes for a glimpse of my feelings. "Second thoughts?"

I smiled and squeezed his hand as I drew in a deep breath.

"No. It's just a big step. I know it's silly and I know we've talked about it."

He stepped in front of me, one finger then tilted my face up to his.

"Are you embarrassed by me?"

I gripped his arms, my words sharp and clear.

"No. Never. It's nerves, that's all. I promise, Mark. I *want* to do this. I want *us* to do this. No more secrets."

He smiled back. "I love you, Kathi."

He had said it several times already, but those words still crashed through me, wrecking me, adding to the maelstrom of emotions within me.

I remained silent, smiling at him. Nodding, he stepped back beside me and offered me his arm. I slid mine through his and took a deep breath.

He pushed open the doors. As they swung open, he released my arm and let his hand drop to the small of my back, guiding me through the doorway and into the room full of people. Multiple heads turned as we entered to give us the once over, several eyebrows raising as we passed by, others registering only a slight surprise before they returned to their conversations.

My anxiety ramped up and Mark's hand on my back felt red hot. I couldn't catch my breath and I needed some distance. I needed to breathe and get a handle on the moment. When I turned slightly towards him and his arm fell away.

"Would you get us a drink?" I asked. My nerves were jittering as I realized that a good majority of the eyes in the room were focused on us.

"Sure," he said, giving me a smile. He leaned in to give me a kiss and, like a stupid woman, I turned away, pretending to scan the crowd. I chose to ignore his small sigh. I turned to apologize, but he was already heading to the bar at the other end of the hall.

I began working through the room, saying hello and exchanging pleasantries. Halfway into the room, Regina Vaughn cornered me.

She spent several minutes asking about the event and a few more mundane things before getting to the question I knew she was dying to ask. As she talked, Samuel had appeared behind her, a slight frown on his face.

My worst fears about tonight were coming true. Here we go.

Regina smiled, not bothering to lower her voice as she asked the questions I'm sure were foremost in her mind. "So, Kathi, dear, you must tell me about that *delicious* young man you came in with? He looks like he would be *most* entertaining. Tell me, is he good in bed?"

Samuel, only a step behind Regina, was staring at me, arms crossed, awaiting my answer. I opened my mouth and lied before I was conscious I was doing it.

"Who? Mark? Oh heavens no, it's nothing like that. He's just a friend. Actually, a friend of a friend. He helped us with a recent event. I was lamenting about coming alone to these parties and he overheard and offered to accompany me. I thought it would be a nice way of saying thank you for the help he provided us."

My heart raced. *Who the hell was this crazy woman making up all these lies?*

Regina's disappointment came through in her voice. As did a hint of interest that made my hackles stand up. "So, nothing at all? No late-night rendezvous after these last few years? No one would blame you, darling. Women like us have... *needs*," she said, emphasizing that last word. Samuel's scowl was so heated it should have reduced Regina to ashes.

We both shared a quiet laugh at her statement.

"Oh, dear no. Just a friend, Regina." Over her shoulder, Samuel gazed at me for a few seconds before someone tugged at his elbow and he turned away. Even still, I knew we would be talking on Monday.

She flicked her eyes over my shoulder before concentrating back on me.

"Well, you must introduce me then. I would *love* to get to know him better. Oh, hold that thought dear. I see Vivian and I *must* ask her where she got that divine dress she is wearing. Would you excuse me?"

I nodded. "Of course."

We exchanged a fashionable air kiss and then she was gone, a whirlwind of scents in her wake. As she walked away, the reasoning side of my brain kicked in and highlighted what a stupid bitch I was. The first and probably best chance I had to explain mine and Mark's relationship and I had chickened out. What the hell was wrong with me? Not to mention it would be a cold day in Hell before I introduced her to Mark.

I turned away and began scanning the room for Mark. Not seeing him right off, I started mingling, chatting with others as I made my way through the crowd. I was thanking my stars he had not been there when I had talked to Regina. Those stupid words would have probably ended our relationship before it really got started, especially after our last talk. I needed to find him and start introducing him. I needed to do this right.

I exchanged pleasantries with several of the other benefactors as I approached the bar. I looked among the patrons but didn't see Mark. I grabbed a small flute of champagne and kept searching. I was walking by Regina again as she was talking to Abby.

Regina reached out to tap my arm. "Kathi, dear, you seemed perplexed," she said.

I gave her a small smile. "Oh, it's nothing really. I was looking for my escort." Abby shot me a sharp look at the mention of the word 'escort'.

Regina nodded. "You mean that delicious young stud? He left, dear, right after our little chat."

"Oh, did he say where he was going?" *Left? What chat? What had she said to him?*

She looked perplexed, and then her face brightened.

"No, dear, he and I didn't talk. It was after the chat you and I had earlier."

"But why would…" and my voice trailed off as I remembered Regina's eyes flicking over my shoulder when she had asked me to introduce her to Mark. A coldness seeped into my stomach and spread out through me like a rushing river.

"He was *behind* us?" I gasped. *Please God, tell me he wasn't behind me. Please don't let me have been that stupid.*

She nodded, her hand waving her empty flute around like a small wand.

"Of course, didn't you know?"

The bottom drop out of my world. "Would you excuse me, Regina?"

I didn't wait for her to answer. I was already pulling my phone from my clutch and hitting the speed dial for Mark as I walked to the door. Two rings and it went to voicemail. Fear started worming its way into my stomach and brain.

Please. Please no. Nonono

I hit redial and went straight to voicemail again. He'd blocked me.

Abby caught my arm, pulling me into an empty corner. Concern was written all over her face. "What's wrong? You're white as a sheet."

I was frantic. "I have to go. God, what have I done? Abby, cover for me. I have to go find Mark."

She studied me for only a moment more before nodding.

"Go. I got this."

I hugged her before fleeing from the room, the silence of the hotel lobby deafening after leaving the buzz of the ballroom.

I rushed out the front doors of the hotel, stopping at the valet stand. The young man on duty turned to me, hand already out for the ticket. I held it out but did not let go when he pulled on it.

He paused, confused. "Ma'am, would you like me to get your car?"

"There was a young man who came out about twenty or thirty minutes ago. Black suit, wavy brown hair. Did you see him?"

I waited anxiously as the valet pursed his lips, thinking.

"Yeah, there was a guy. Man, he looked like someone shot his dog. Kinda pissed and sad, all at the same time, you know?" My heart sunk.

The valet's words knifed into me, cutting deep. *What had I done? What had my foolish fears done?*

"Did you see where he went?"

He shook his head. "No ma'am. I brought up his car, and he left. Burnt rubber going out of here."

With that, I let him have the ticket, and he hustled off for my car.

Ten minutes later, I was working my way south. I couldn't stop the tears as they flowed.

What was I thinking? Especially after what we had said that morning. How could I possibly do what I had done to a man that had told me he loved me? I told him I was falling for him. How could I possibly utter those words?

It was like a near death thing. I saw myself say those words, and they appalled me.

I had hurt a good young man.

"Stop it!" I screamed, gripping the steering wheel so hard my hands began to hurt. "Stop calling him young. That's what got you in this situation, you cow. He's a good *man*. You stupid bitch, he was *your* man."

My man. I had hurt the first man who had treated me like I was his everything. I had hurt the man I loved.

That word crashed through me with all the force of a speeding train. *Love*. I *loved* him. I had told him I was falling for him, but I now realized those feelings were so much more. I loved him and I had hurt him, and maybe lost him completely, before I could tell him.The tears ran down my cheeks, following the line of my chin to drop off into my lap.

Where would he go? I was pretty sure he wouldn't return to his house, since I knew where he lived. Mary's place was out. I didn't know where his uncle lived, but I'd bet I could find out. He probably knew that, so doubt he would go there either.

I wiped my cheeks with the back of my hand as I grabbed my phone from the seat, flipped it open and hit a speed dial. The phone started ringing. Three rings and it connected.

"Hey, Kathi. Thought you and Mark were at the party?"

"Mary, is Jake there? I need to speak to him," I sobbed.

"Kathi, are you crying? Jesus Christ girl, every time you call me lately you're crying. What the hell happened now?"

I tried to hold back the sobs, but couldn't.

"Mary... Mary, oh... oh God, I... I did something so stupid. Again."

"Oh no, Kathi, what did you do?"

I took in several ragged breaths, trying to control the agony.

"Mary, I need to talk to Jake. Is he there?

"He left about thirty, forty minutes ago. Got a phone call, grabbed his keys and left."

"If he comes back, please tell him… no, forget that. I'll be there as fast as I can."

"Kathi, please be careful."

I disconnected from Mary and tried Mark again. Voicemail.

I sped into the night, dialing over and over, only to get the same response.

TWENTY-ONE

"Nooo. Mark."

My breath heaved and my heart raced as I pulled myself out of the nightmare. I was chasing Mark through a dense fog, knowing he was there, but never seeing or getting close to him. My only clue to his location were his howls of pain.

I blinked my eyes open, or at least I tried. My eyelids felt like they were caked in sand. After three attempts, they finally cracked open. I blinked several times to clear them, finally able to see. Sunlight was streaming in from somewhere, and someone had spread a blanket over me. Looking over my shoulder, a horrible brown fabric told me I was on Mary's couch.

Why was I on her couch? Like a dam bursting, the events of last night came rushing back into my consciousness. I took a ragged breath, trying to sob, but nothing came out of the rawness that was my throat.

I must have croaked out something or made some other sound because Mary was soon kneeling at my side. A warm cloth began gently wiping my face, clearing the grit from my eyes. She smiled softly at me, putting her hand on my arm, giving it a gentle squeeze.

"Come on, hon. It's almost noon. Time to get up."

Mary pulled the blanket back and helped me up off the couch.

Someone had dressed me in what appeared to be more of Julia's sweats. It was disheartening to me that waking up in distress at Mary's and dressed in Julia's clothes was happening way too often.

Mary held my arm as I stumbled into the kitchen, helping to ease me down into a chair at the table. She stepped to the counter and came back, setting a cup of coffee and some pieces of dry toast in front of me. I ate and drank mechanically, my mind numb.

The back door opened, and Jake stepped in, dusting off his jeans. He looked at me and I swear I'd never seen eyes more dead and emotionless than those that stared back at me. I tracked him as he made his way to the burbling coffee pot. He poured a cup and turned to face us, leaning back against the counter. His gaze never wavered from me as he sipped his drink. I'd never been more judged in my life than at that moment.

I took a shaky breath, calming myself before I spoke. "Jake, please tell Mark—"

"No."

That single word from him stopped any further words from me. It was so embedded in ice it could have been a piece from a glacier. I didn't have the energy to sob anymore, but tears obviously still flowed easily.

Mary was at my side, ready to rip into her son. "Jake, what the *hell*?"

As Mary glared at her stony faced sun, I glanced around the room and noted one person missing this morning.

"Where's Julia?" I croaked.

Mary waved a hand at the door. "She took Sarah into town for a playdate and lunch." She kept glaring at Jake, taking affront to his apparent indifference to my pain, not to mention his poor manners, one of Mary's biggest peeves.

I tried one more time. I looked at Jake, my eyes pleading.

My voice was contrite, full of pain. "I need to talk with Mark. *Please*, Jake. I need to explain. To apologize."

His face was like stone, showing and giving me nothing.

"He doesn't want to talk to you. Frankly, I don't blame him. You hurt him, Kathi. Bad." The coldness of his tone was merciless. My heart exploded, the pieces fluttering in my chest as those words stabbed into me. *God, what have I done?*

Mary was looking between both of us before gripping my arm, pulling my reddened eyes her way.

"Can you *please* tell me what happened? I feel like a third wheel on a blind date. My son is acting like a horse's ass and you look like someone shot your cat. You came in here last night bawling and damn near catatonic with grief. I thought I was going to have to sedate you."

I looked back at Jake, surprised.

"You didn't tell her?"

He took a long drink of his coffee, staring at me over the cup. He finished his drink, and, lowering the cup, shook his head. "Not my story to tell. That's on you."

I nodded, understanding. He wasn't going to make this easy on me, and I didn't blame him. He was right. This shitstorm was all on me.

My heart breaking all over again, I hesitantly told Mary about the events of the previous evening. When I recited those stupid words again, I almost puked.

Her hand fluttered at her lips before she let it drop to the table to grab my hand. Her eyes bored into me, filled with confusion.

"Why, Kathi? I thought you liked him. Hell, I thought you were falling for him. What would possess you to say something like that? Especially after what just happened the last time you called me in tears?"

I dropped my forehead into my free hand, not wanting her to see the shame in my face. "I froze, Mary. Samuel was hovering behind Regina, glaring at me, and I froze. I zoned out and lost my damn mind. I said those hateful, stupid words, not knowing Mark was behind me."

Mary reached over and gave my shoulder a light squeeze. I leaned my cheek against her hand, appreciative of her love and support for my bone-headedness.

"Okay. You panicked and slipped. I'm sure it's not the end of the world. Mark will understand," she said, squeezing my shoulder again. I grabbed at her words, willing her to be right. *If only that were true.*

I stared up at her, my face and heart crumbling on the table. I could see the concern building in her eyes as she gazed at me. My continued silence finally caused her to raise one eyebrow.

"There's something else, isn't there?" she asked softly. I nodded as I took in a couple more ragged breaths.

"Yesterday morning, we were in bed, holding each other. He... he..." My throat tightened again, unable to force myself to finish the sentence. It was just too painful.

Mary laid her hand on my arm. "What did he do?"

I sniffed hard before clearing my throat. "He told me he loved me."

Mary gripped my arm and squeezed, her smile lighting up her face. "Isn't that a *good* thing? He told you he loves you, and you told him you loved him. What's the issue? You two can talk and work through this."

"I... I didn't tell him I loved him. I told him I was falling for him. It wasn't until I was driving here... after... that I realized I *do* love him."

I started sobbing, letting my grief consume me.

"God, I've fucked this all up. I wasn't ready. He told me it was okay that he was in a different place than me. He said he's been in love with me for two years, Mary. Two years!"

Mary inhaled sharply, her eyes widening and cutting over to look at a still impassive Jake before returning to my face. "I didn't know, Kathi. He never said anything, to me or Jake, that I know of."

"That's why he left town last year. To get over me. Then he said he came back and fell for me again." I drew in a ragged breath and looked at my friend. "What have I done, Mary?"

I blew my nose, wiped my eyes as I tried to gain control of my emotions.

I shook my head. "I can't just sit here. I need to find him. I need to apologize to him, beg for his forgiveness."

Jake's coffee cup banging into the sink pulled our attention back to him. He turned back to us, arms crossed over his chest, eyes jumping between Mary and me.

"Maybe it's a guy thing, but I don't know how you can fix it," he said, emotionless. "He told me about the incident yesterday. You invited him last night. You were going to introduce him and explain to everyone who he was. But the very *first* time you got called out by one of your society friends, you sold him out. You tossed his love on the floor and shit on it. You can't unsay the words, and he can't unhear them."

Unsay the words. My subconscious latched onto that phrase. Can't unsay the words. I didn't have a time machine, so I couldn't unsay the words Mark had heard.

A tickle at my thoughts, a wisp floating in the turmoil and anguish that was flowing through my brain. I couldn't *unsay the words*.

But.

Wisps became threads, threads became patterns, patterns became thoughts. I couldn't unsay the words, but I could do something almost as good.

A plan burst into being, and with it came hope and possibility. I pulled myself up out of the chair, took the four steps over to Jake, and stared up at him. His eyes met mine, still cold as stone.

"Kathi?" came from behind me. I turned to Mary and smiled, a smile I meant. I wiped the tears away and nodded at her.

"He's right, Mary. I can't unsay the words, so I won't try. I have to do something else."

I turned back to Jake, pulled myself up straight, and looked him in the eye.

"I'm calling in my marker."

I saw him stiffen, and his eyes flicked over to Mary, then back to me.

We had spoken little about that night and the events that surrounded Jake's blowup at Julia and his subsequent arrest. He'd been unwilling to call Mary for help that night. He was too embarrassed, and she was watching Sarah. So, he called me instead to bail him out.

He had also hidden at my place for a few days after the arrest, avoiding both Mary and Julia. He later pled guilty to the charges and got a suspended sentence and a promise of expungement if he kept his nose clean for six months, which he did.

For my help that night, he had given me his marker. Jake, like his father, was a man of his word. Didn't matter what the cost, he kept his word. His marker was a promise to help me with anything. Legality could be discussed, but was not a show stopper to him repaying his debt.

He stared at me in silence for a few more moments, his eyes searching mine, peering into my soul. I counted five heartbeats before he nodded slowly.

"I'm listening."

For the first time since last night's nightmare, I felt hope. If Jake pulled this off, I would get the chance I needed and so desperately wanted.

"I want you and Mark at the banquet tonight. I'll have two spots for you at the farthest table from the stage and the head table, where I will be."

"Kathi…" but I held up my finger, stopping him, before laying my hand on his arm.

"He doesn't have to be there for the whole thing, just for my closing speech. I *need* him there, Jake. Please. I'm *begging* you," I said, squeezing his arm.

He looked out the kitchen window and I could tell he was working through the angles. People always underestimated how intelligent Jake was. To most people, he was just a simple rancher, working the farm and taking care of the horses. But I knew better than to underestimate him. He was one of the more intelligent people I knew, and he didn't undertake anything lightly.

He took a deep breath and blew it out before looking back at me. I hoped he could see the desperation in my eyes and the determination to fix this.

"Okay, Kathi. He'll be there. But hear me on this. If you do anything else to hurt him…" He left the threat unsaid, letting my imagination run with possibilities.

"Jake, I promise you that hurting Mark is the furthest thing from my mind. Thank you."

His face was serious, his voice firm as he spoke. "This squares us, Kathi."

I wrapped my arms around him and hugged him tight. Unwrapping my arms, I stood on my toes to kiss his cheek before stepping back. Nodding, I turned and gathered Mary to me as I walked to the back door. I hugged her hard.

"Thank you for being there for me when I needed it," I said. She brushed the hair out of my face and held my cheek for a second before she smiled.

"Always, and you know it. What are you going to do?"

"Get my man back."

Those words echoed through my soul and lit a fire in me. My man. Mark was *my man*, and I was going to shout it to the world. Literally, if my plan worked.

We hugged again. Mary handed me a bag with my clothes and opened the back door. I headed for my car, my mind bouncing through my plan. I had a lot to do and very little time to do it.

The banquet went off smoothly, even though I was a nervous wreck. The crews from the local stations had captured a multitude of goodwill and the best of human kindness. Now it was time for the closing speech and the end of tonight's event. If it went like it had in the past, these last words and comments would never make air time. Maybe tonight would be different.

My plan had to work. *Had* to. If it didn't, I lost everything and had no one but myself to blame. If it worked, I had a chance to win back what I had foolishly tossed away.

The head table was located at the front of the room on a small stage with the standard plain podium to one end. From my chair, I scanned the crowd as dinner was finishing. It had been a sumptuous meal, prepared by some very talented chefs. I'd not touched any of it. As nervous as I was, if I ate anything, it wouldn't stay down. Two flutes of champagne over the course of the night barely calmed my nerves, but didn't even make a dent in the dive bombers racing around my stomach.

Ten minutes before I was supposed to speak, I sent Jake a text. My eyes kept darting back to the table where two chairs remained empty. From her table, Abby kept watching me. I had filled her in on my plan and she was prepared to help, either to congratulate me or help me pick up the pieces of my shattered world.

When the MC called my name to give the closing remarks, those seats were still vacant. Jake must not have been able to convince him. My heart sank as I pushed my chair back and rose. I quietly thanked the MC as I took my place at the podium. I adjusted the microphone and took a deep breath before looking back at the audience, plastering a fake smile on my face.

"Good evening. My name is Kathi Harrison and on behalf of Harrison Enterprise, I would like to thank..." and the next words died in my chest.

He was here.

It took everything I had to not scream in happiness. Jake and Mark were now sitting at the table. Mark met my gaze and immediately looked down. My resolve took a hit, both from the avoidance and the pain I saw in his eyes.

He was *here*. That's all that mattered. I let that fill me with the strength I was going to need.

I laughed softly and cleared my throat. "Sorry, I forgot to imagine you all in your underwear, so I wouldn't be nervous." A polite round of laughter for the old joke drifted through the room. Taking another deep breath, I began speaking, knowing what I was about to do would cost me everything I'd worked for and my spot in the company. But, if it worked, I would gain a reward worth more than gold itself and a future I now so desperately wanted.

"I'd like to take this time to thank all of you for coming out tonight and to celebrate another prosperous year of giving. Harrison takes pride in their employees and friends who helped many in need throughout the year. The love they have shown for their fellow men and women is truly inspiring."

I paused, more for nerves and another round of polite applause. It was the same basic speech I had given for the last several years. Until now.

My hands shaking, I pulled the wireless mic from its stand and started walking towards the stairs at the side of the stage. The murmurs began immediately. The MC flipped through his notes, glancing at me and then back at them. I smiled at him and kept walking. I passed Samuel, whose icy stare promised me death if I messed this up. I looked at Abby as she mouthed something at me. I couldn't make it out, so I just smiled and nodded at her.

I was trembling, but I had to do this. I had to get him back. I stepped down the stairs without breaking a leg and walked to the front row of tables. Pausing at the first table, I looked out at the sea of faces before me and then focused on the one face that meant everything to me.

"Love is an amazing thing. As human beings, we sometimes take love for granted. A simple act of love, or kindness, pays benefits far beyond what any amount of money can do. Money can't buy love. Yes, I know some folks in Nevada and a few other places who might disagree."

A nervous round of laughter and some quiet murmuring was the response. I ignored it and started walking, my voice growing more confident the closer I got to my destination.

"For many, it is our love for our fellow man that drives us to help others more challenged than we are. But *true* love, when it's found, is like no other force on this planet. We've all searched for that love. The kind that has you waking up first so you can watch the other sleep. The love that when you're sick, the other does everything in their power to make you better, with no expectation of return, other than your love."

Every eye was on me, and the tension in the room would need a chainsaw to cut it. I let my fingers trail across the linen table top beside me as I turned to the next row. I surprised the occupants at the next table as I picked up someone's water glass and took a sip. Then, raising the mic, I kept walking.

"Some of us are still looking. Some of us are lucky enough to have found this love. There are those unfortunate few who find it and lose it, through no fault of their own. And finally, there are those who find it, and, out of fear, throw it away." I paused. "For those wondering, numbers two and four describe me."

"Many of you knew Jeremy. I married him right out of college. People might have whispered the term 'trophy wife' about me. It wasn't untrue." I shrugged.

"Our marriage was not perfect. But we loved each other in our way. We each had our own wants and needs, and we supported each other. But our love was… comfortable. Safe. It matched the idea of what I thought was love. Recently, however, I found out that I was, oh, so blind as to what love *really* is."

I was now two rows of tables away from where Jake and Mark sat. I let my eyes wander through the audience, but I kept shooting quick glances at Mark. He was looking at me now. And he was *listening*.

"But love can also be fragile. It only takes a minor act, or a few words, to damage that love. Insecurities, jealousy, greed. Small things that can invade that love and, if left to grow, will sunder that love. You can put the pieces back together, but we know it's never the same. Little things are always missed. The sharing. The reaching for the other out of instinct. Most of all, trust."

I paused, gathering my breath, willing my heart to keep beating as I prepared to alter my world forever. Up to now, I could probably blame it on alcohol. These next words would dash that belief. Decision made, I resumed my trek.

"At our banquet last night, while talking to one of my friends, I said some stupid, stupid words when describing a wonderful man. I spoke those words out of fear and insecurity. They were *not* the same words that were in my heart, words I failed to express that very morning when I lay in his arms."

It seemed as if the entire audience was in sync and all took a breath or gasp at the same time. My heart was beating so hard I thought it explode out of my chest. Taking a deep breath, I focused on Mark and continued my walk.

"I let my fear of what others would think, and how they would judge me, overrule what my heart and my mind were telling me. I let my fear keep me from reaching out to grasp something amazing. Love."

By this time, I had made my way to the back of the room and was standing about four feet from Mark and Jake. Abby was standing off to the side, unshed tears in her eyes. She nodded at me to continue, blowing me a kiss. I owed her a big raise, assuming I still had a job.

I know I was crying only because I my cheeks were damp. My knuckles were white from gripping the microphone so hard. I gazed at the man I loved and hoped he could see that love in my eyes.

"Mark, would you please stand?"

He looked at me and then at the door and, for a moment, I thought he would flee. I let my heart drive my next words.

"Mark, my love. Please stand?"

There was another collective gasp behind me, which I ignored. My world, all that I cared about, was right in front of me.

His eyes snapped back to me and locked on like lasers. I didn't shy from his gaze, didn't flinch, just happy that he hadn't fled.

He slowly stood, his eyes still fixed on me, and I lost myself in those deep, caring eyes. I vaguely noticed Jake moving around the table, doing something. I found out later he'd spoken to the others at the table and had persuaded them all to move away, leaving Mark and me standing by ourselves.

"For those of you who don't know him, this is Mark Danlock. He's twenty-five years old, five-feet, eleven-inches tall, weighs about 200 lbs, has pecs for *days*, and is an *extraordinary* man. He is a farrier. That means he trims and cares for a horse's hooves. He has a secret weakness for rom-com movies and has a heart greater than the mountains. And for those of you who will focus on the math, yes, he is fifteen years younger than me."

I took a small step forward, gazing intently into those eyes. I again prayed he would see the truth and love in mine, and the regret I had for hurting him.

"He is also the man I am totally and completely in love with. I said earlier I had an idea of what love should be, but this man showed me how *so* uneducated I was. I resisted dating him. I threw every argument I could think of at him and he just laughed and told me they didn't matter."

I took another small step forward, close enough now to reach out and touch.

"And then I hurt him by belittling what he was to me. What he *meant* to me."

I couldn't help it. My voice cracked at that admission.

His words came out in a whisper. "Kathi, you don't—" but I held a hand up to stop him.

"Yes I do, love. Yes. I do."

I took a small, deep breath and focused on what I was seeing in those eyes. Love, not hate. So much love that I could drown in it. I pulled the strength I needed from that love.

"Mark, I am so, so sorry for what I said, for those hateful words." I glanced over at Jake and nodded towards him before returning my gaze to Mark's. "A wise man told me I couldn't unsay them. He was right, so I didn't try. But what I hope I've done tonight is to say some other words that will drown out the memory of those awful ones. You wanted me to break that last barrier, to acknowledge to others what you were." I waved around and the venue and all the faces staring at us. "For you, I have destroyed it."

I took a deep breath, letting it out in a ragged sigh. "Mark, I beg your forgiveness and ask for another chance to show you I am worthy of the love you offer. I never again want to feel the pain I felt last night when you left me. It almost killed me. I love you, Mark. Please. Forgive me."

My speech finished, I let my hand drop to my side, staring at him, trying to figure out what was going through his head. The mic slipped from my hand and landed on the floor with a loud thump, echoed through the speakers.

You could have heard a pin drop. I wasn't even sure people were breathing. Then a man's voice broke the silence, his words ringing throughout the room like a roar.

"In case you were wondering, Mark, this is the part where you kiss her," said Jake.

As laughter consumed the room, Mark stepped forward, took me in his arms, and his lips met mine. The world dissolved around me and all that existed was him. My whole body shuddered as I cried. I grabbed onto him like a life preserver, tightening my hold so he couldn't escape me.

As our lips parted, his hands came up, gently cupping my cheeks. I felt his thumbs wipe the tears away.

"Mark, I am so—" His finger on my lips stopped me from speaking.

"Forgiven," he said.

My body sagged as all the fear and tension drain away. I searched his face and only found truth and love. Then his lips were on mine again. The kiss started gently, but then became more passionate. I moaned, clutching him tighter, doing my best to become one with him. There was no mistaking the response we were having to the kiss.

It was Abby who embarrassed me next.

"Get a room, you two!" she yelled, having moved down to stand near Jake.

The crowd roared with laughter and cheers as we broke apart.

I looked up at Mark and let a slow, evil grin appear on my face.

Mark studied me. "Kathi?"

The last part of my plan came into play. A hope that at all would go well.

"Room 1273 is available for... use," I said, emphasizing the last word with a lust filled whisper. His eyes widened and filled with a hunger that caused the heat in me to roar like a blast furnace. I barely had time to gasp before he swept me off my feet and into his arms and headed for the doors. The room erupted in hoots, cheers, and clapping as I threw my arms around his neck.

I planted several small kisses on his jaw and licked his earlobe before taking it between my teeth and gently sucking on it as he pushed the doors open. I let the lobe go and whispered in his ear.

"I bought a box of thirty condoms. Think it will be enough?"

I heard a low growl come from him as the hall doors closed behind us, shutting off the cheers and applause.

People milling in the lobby stared and pointed as Mark marched us to the bank of elevators near the back wall. He dipped down and hit the up button without putting me on the ground. I laid my head against his shoulders, reveling in the feeling of love and comfort as he held me.

As we waited for the elevator, I turned his head to me and kissed him softly before snuggling my head into his shoulder. When the doors dinged and opened, he walked us into the elevator.

"I love you," I said, staring up at him.

He turned his head and met my gaze. "I know." His lips twitched as he stared at me.

Our laughter filled the elevator as the doors closed.

EPILOGUE

The tension in the waiting room was almost palatable. We gathered here today once Jake told us Julia's labor was progressing, but slowly. Mark and I were standing near a back wall. Jake and Julia's family and friends occupied all the chairs.

"I hope nothing's wrong," said Wilma, Julia's mom, wringing the handkerchief in her hands.

"I'm sure everything is just fine," Mary quickly assured her.

Mark slid his arm around my waist, and I leaned against him. I let my mind drift back to the trouble we had gone through to get to this point. Thankfully, Mark had forgiven my stupidity, and I had done my very best to show him he had not made a mistake.

It was amazing to me the outpouring I received from some of my society friends. A few made crude and disparaging comments, which made it easier to cut them from my life. Many were happy for me and I kept those relationships, which included all of my sorority sisters.

Mark and I agreed to take it slow, but that plan went out the window after a month. At his urging, I moved me and Simon into his place and spent more time in his bed, and other places, than at my house.

God, the stamina of youth. It was a good thing I was in shape or the sex would have killed me. One weekend, Mark had made it a personal goal to have sex in every room in the house. Some twice. I was sore for the next week, but oh *God, it* was so worth it. Mary peed herself laughing when I told her.

When I realized I hadn't been back to my home in almost five weeks, I put it on the market. Mark helped me go through all the items in the house. I saved some cherished memories of Jeremy, but let everything else go. It was yet another step along my path of moving on from the past.

That was yet another thing about Mark I loved. He didn't begrudge me my memories or talk of Jeremy. He simply accepted it as part of me when he gave me his love.

The Monday after the dinner, and my grand gesture, I beat Samuel to the punch and tendered my letter of resignation. I informed the board of directors I would sell my shares and sever all contact with the company. I thanked them for the support they had given me and Jeremy in that past, but it was time to close this chapter of my life.

An unfortunate, but not unexpected, outcome of me leaving was Abby. Samuel released her as well, probably out of spite. When I talked with her last week, she had a new job and a new man in her life. Seems she had taken her own advice and talked to Mario, in the mailroom. I refused to ask if the rumors were true.

My desire to sell my shares kicked off a small bidding war. I thought Samuel would have a coronary when I turned down his offer. He was frantic to gain full control of the company. Several members were just as determined to see him fail in his quest. It all worked out for me as it drove up the price of my shares. Samuel failing to gain the control that he wanted was just a small bonus.

We all looked up as Jake burst into the room. He slowly made eye contact with each of us, drawing out the suspense. It was Mary that finally caved.

"Jake, spill it, son. You're not so old I can't take a rein to your behind."

His face exploded into a goofy grin.

"5lbs, 12ozs, 19 inches. Mom and *daughter* are doing fine!" he crowed proudly.

"A girl!" shrieked Mary. We descended on him, congratulating him and asking about Julia all at once.

When the madness died, I asked the burning question on everyone's lips.

"What's her name?"

He grinned again and shook his head.

"Nope. No one hears the name until we both can tell you."

Jake spent the next hour updating us on the delivery while we waited for his uncle and Sarah to show up. We all beat him up when he mentioned using an ex-girlfriend's name to motivate Julia for the final push.

A few minutes after Sarah and Jake's uncle arrived, the nurse informed us Julia was awake and had just finished feeding the baby. Everyone stood to go back for the visit. I stepped forward and gave Jake's arm a squeeze.

"That's our cue to go. Give Julia our love and tell her I'll stop by in a week or two once she's up for visitors."

He nodded and shifted Sarah to his hip so we could hug. He stepped back, nodded at Mark, and then led his family back to see the newest Attwood.

I waited as the others left, several of them wishing us well and offering to see us later. I glanced longingly at the doors where Jake and his family had disappeared.

"Kathi?"

Looking up at Mark, I smiled and slid my arm around him.

"Just thinking, love. Wondering what it will be like."

He slid a hand over to rest on my belly and I dropped mine on top of his.

———

A few weeks prior, I thought I'd caught a stomach bug and had gone to see my doctor. Janice had asked me if there was any chance of me being pregnant. I had laughed hard.

"Janice, I'm forty and while I *am* having a ton of sex with my boyfriend, we're careful and use condoms. I also started birth control two weeks ago."

"Condoms *every* time? And I told you that there would be a small window after you start birth control that it would be ineffective."

"Well, there have been a couple times when we got caught up in the moment, but we took precautions then, if you know what I mean."

"When was your last period?"

"Well, the last one was about two weeks ago, but I only spotted. The one before that was spotty as well. I chalked it up to stress. I'm telling you, I'm not pregnant."

"Humor me and let's at least rule it out."

So I peed in the little cup. Twenty minutes later, she came back to her office, took a seat at her desk, and called up some information on her computer.

"So, I'm pretty sure this bug will run its course," Janice said, smirking.

"Good. What do you think, another couple of days before my stomach settles down?"

She finished working on her computer and turned back to me.

"The nausea will go away soon, but it will take slightly longer for the bug to finish running its course."

"How long?"

"It's only a guess, but I'd say about eight more months, give or take a few days," she said, before breaking out into a big grin.

I stared at her, my mouth hanging open and eyes fixed on her, like a clown with no makeup. She burst out laughing.

"I'm... are you sure? Janice, I'm forty years old. I can't be pregnant!" Disbelief vied for panic in my tone. "We used condoms! I started birth control!"

I swear she was enjoying my distress. "Well, condoms are not 100%. Maybe one of your 'precautions' wasn't as good as you think?" she said, her cheeriness as bright as my disbelief.

"But you are most definitely pregnant. You had your annual physical four months ago along with your peek-and-poke. You're healthy, you exercise, and take care of yourself. Hell, you're in better shape than most of my twenty-year-old patients. I'm going to write you a script for some prenatal vitamins, and I want you and... Mark, is it?" She trailed off, looking at me for confirmation.

I nodded, still in shock.

She continued. "Good, I want the two of you back next week and we can do some bloodwork and talk about any challenges you might face. Kathi, I can't find any reason to prevent you from carrying this baby to full term. We may have to monitor you more, but, again, not seeing any issues we can't handle. Congrats mommy!"

Mommy. I was going to be a mommy.

We wrapped up the visit and left. I know I drove back to Marks, but I had no memory of the drive.

Arriving home, I staggered into the house, dropping my purse on the table and flopping down on the couch. I stared at the TV on the wall, my mind going in twenty different directions. Simon curled up in my lap, laying his head against my stomach. He began purring as he lightly head-butted my belly. It was as if he already knew what was growing there and approved.

That was how Mark found me when he came in. He plopped down next to me, took one look at my face, and immediately took my hands in his.

"Kathi, what's wrong? Oh shit, your doctor's appointment was today. What's wrong?"

I turned my head slowly to look at him. His jaw was rigid and those deep eyes were filling with fear.

"Whatever it is, we'll get through it," he stated firmly.

"Do you mean that?" I asked. I knew he meant it, but I needed to hear the words.

"Of course I do. I love you, Kathi. Whatever it is, I'm there for you. What's wrong?"

I looked deep into those eyes and tried to say the words, but they stuck in my throat.

"Kathi, you're really starting to scare me. Talk to me, honey."

I gazed at him, seeing the worry and fear in his eyes. I let out a big breath and smiled.

"I'm pregnant."

For a few seconds, his face probably matched mine when I got the news. Then the ghost of a smile started. It slowly got bigger and bigger. He looked down and placed a hand gently on my stomach. I could feel it trembling as he looked back up at me, sporting the biggest shit-eating grin I'd ever seen.

"You're pregnant? We're going to have a *baby*? Are you sure?" I nodded at each question. He opened his mouth to speak, then closed it. His face began changing, losing some of its excitement. He studied my expression intently.

"Kathi, do you *want* to have our baby? Is it, um, safe for you?"

As he asked those two questions, I don't think I could have loved him more. His first thoughts were about me, even though he was excited about the news. *God, how did I get so lucky when I had been so stupid?*

Our baby. Two simple words. No hesitation, no making excuses. Just two simple words. I knew right then everything would be okay.

I dropped a hand to his, where it lay on my abdomen. I looked back at him and smiled.

"We're going to have a baby."

He nodded, the goofy grin back.

"I'm going to be a forty-one-year-old mother." *Oh shit.*

He squeezed my hand and then kissed me deeply. The tingle of that kiss lit up my toes and all points in between.

"No," he said. "You're going to be a mother. You're going to be a great mom."

I looked at him, worry crossing my face. "Do *you* want to be a father?"

"Hell yes, but only if you're the mother."

"I guess that's a good thing, since I'm never letting you go," I replied, squeezing his hand. He gazed at me, and I couldn't make out what I saw in his eyes.

"What?" I asked.

"Soooo, you know what that means, right?" he said, twitching his eyelids up.

"No, what?" I asked, confused.

He leaned in and kissed me again and I swear my nerves all fired at once, sending shocks throughout me as heat blossomed in my panties.

"We don't have to use those stupid condoms anymore," he said.

I stared at him as the grin came back. I rolled my eyes and swatted his chest. He laughed, and before I could blink, he stood, scooping me up in his arms.

I squealed as he started for the bedroom.

"Mark, what…" was all I got out before his lips were on me again. I groaned as he pulled back.

"We have condomless activities to take care of," he said. I laughed and pulled my arms tighter around him, kissing his neck and nibbling on his jaw.

We agreed kept the news to ourselves, waiting for the tests and confirmation. At the next appointment, another test confirmed my status. Janice had us led to a small exam room with an ultrasound.

"Let's find us a baby, shall we?" she asked.

Janice assisted me in changing into the blue paper gown and getting me up onto the table. The paper crinkled underneath me like a candy wrapper as I laid back. She elevated me so that I could see what was going on without compressing my stomach too much. Mark kept a solid grip on my hand.

"Sorry, this will be cold." She promptly squeezed out a gloop of something onto my stomach. I shivered as it landed on my skin. She hadn't been lying. It felt like ice cream had dropped on my belly.

She turned to the machine next to the table and moved it so we could see the small screen. Flipping some switches, she grabbed a small wand and pressed it to my belly, spreading the goop around. On the screen, a gray and white, grainy image appeared and whispery, raspy sounds came from some speakers.

As we watched, she moved the wand around my stomach, sliding it through the goop. All kinds of gurgles and squeals came from the speakers as the image on the screen blurred and moved.

As she moved towards the lower part of my stomach, the sound changed. It started softly, but grew louder. A steady *thrum thrum thrum thrum* began pounding from the speakers, and Mark's hand squeezed mine tighter. A small blob appeared on the screen.

"Well, hello young thing," said Janice. "Mark, Kathi, meet Baby."

The thrumming melted into my bones and heart. Mark leaned down, kissed the top of my head, then whispered in my ear. "God, I love you."

"Heartbeat sounds good, about 153 beats, right in the range. Let me get a measurement so we can confirm the gestation and due date."

We watched as she fiddled with the machine some more.

"Okay, good. Well, all looks good so we can…" she said as she moved the wand away and the thrumming got weaker. Then it got stronger again. "Well, well. What is this?"

She started moving the wand again, and the thrumming got louder. She hit some buttons, checked the screen, then looked back at us with that same grin from earlier, only this one was even bigger.

"Kathi, Mark, meet Baby number 2."

"Twins?" choked out Mark.

Janice nodded, working her wand again. I squeezed Mark's hand, and he looked down at me, his expression almost comical. I couldn't help but poke some fun at him.

"Don't look at me. This is your fault for taking advantage of me," I said, pointing at the screen.

For just a second, fear flashed across his face, and then he gave me a look that left no doubt in my mind what he was thinking. Good thing I wasn't hooked up to a heart monitor.

"When we get home, I'll be doing it again," he said. His voice was low, deep, and rumbly. God, I loved that rumble.

"Hey! Doctor in the room. I don't need to know about any advantage-taking or any of that stuff," said Janice, still staring at the screen.

We both laughed as she finished sweeping the wand across my

belly. After confirming there were no more surprises, she grabbed some paper towels and wiped the goop off my belly.

She sat back, looking between the two of us. "Looks like the count is two. You guys don't do things by half, do you?"

I looked up at Mark and all I saw was love in his eyes.

"You okay with two?" I asked.

He kissed me on the lips lightly and pulled back to look at me.

"Two, one, three, who cares? After all, it's just a number."

ABOUT THE AUTHOR

When he's not writing, or working his day job, Bob spends his time helping his wife take care of their three horses, four cats and the multitude of chores one finds around the farm. When there is free time left, he enjoys playing golf, video games, and DnD with his friends on the west coast, and watching their three kids grow up and explore life.

ALSO BY B.D. STOREY

<u>Standalone Novels</u>

Second Chances

<u>Bare Ridge Series</u>

When Love Comes Knocking

Love's More Than a Number - Coming Summer 2024

SNEAK PEAK

Read on for an excerpt from my debut standalone novel, *Second Chances*. If you enjoy small town, second chance romances about finding love after loss, with some spice, some suspense, and a lot of heart, you'll fall in love with Jacob and Josie.

Is it possible for two wounded
hearts to heal each other?

Second
Chances

B.D. STOREY

Prologue

Jacob

Mist from the early morning rain clung to the trees and mixed with
the light breeze to cool the sweat on my face as I walked up the small
trail.

Just past the halfway point to the glade, I stepped over the roots of
old Splitjaw. At some point in its past, the aged fir tree had been bent
over and broken, creating a neck-like structure where the shattered
ends split open, making the trunk look like the opened jaws of an alli-
gator. Kara, my fiancé, named it Splitjaw during our first hike in this
area.

I smiled, thinking back to that day and her silliness. She'd insisted
that Splitjaw needed to be fed. She had dug through her backpack and
pulled out some beef jerky, which she opened and stuck in its jagged
"mouth." Pleased with herself, she'd shouldered her pack and
continued with our trek.

Digging into one of the cargo pouches on my pants, I pulled out the strips of beef jerky I brought with me for this very moment. I unwrapped them and placed them into Splitjaw's mouth. Pocketing the wrapper, I patted the tree and proceeded on my way. Tradition satisfied.

It was close to noon when I stepped out of the trees and into the clearing. Sunlight bathed the meadow. The tall, waving grasses forming a sea of green, almost like a calm lake. The lone Oregon white oak dominated the center of the clearing, a soldier standing guard over

the meadow and its denizens. I had no idea how that acorn made it to this area, but I was happy that it had found a home here.

Its branches spread outward to provide shelter and shade to all those who gathered below them, perfect for the task I had given it.

I drew in a cleansing breath, shaking myself from my reverie, and continued walking until I stood under the oak's branches. I unshouldered my backpack and set it down against the tree before letting one hand rest gently on its trunk.

"Sorry I'm late. I was finishing up some drywall in one of the upstairs bedrooms and lost track of time."

I bent down, opened up the pack, and pulled out a collapsible rake. Unfolding it as I stood, I began clearing the detritus of small limbs and leaves from around the area.

"It took longer than I planned, but I got the flooring finished in the kitchen. I know we talked about that white checkered slate tile, but it was out of stock and the backorder was going to take too long. So, I ended up doing a grey, sixteen-inch tile that has four small black diamonds in the center. I think it looks fantastic against the backsplash."

I continued my rundown of my construction highlights as I kept raking.

Satisfied that no limbs or leaves remained, I collapsed the rake, stowed it back in the pack, and pulled out a small set of shears. I squatted down on one knee and began trimming the grass around the two small bronze markers. I worked in thoughtful silence, letting the metallic snip-snip of the trimmers soothe my mind and heart as I cleared back the grass and weeds that had grown since my last visit.

Once everything was pruned to my liking, I stowed the shears and retrieved a small rag and bottle of brass cleaner. Pouring a small bit of the solution onto my cloth, I began scrubbing the bird droppings off the markers.

With the bronze gleaming again, I stowed all of my tools and supplies and gazed down at the markers, telling myself I wouldn't cry even as the first tear worked its way down my cheek. Every time I thought I had cried myself out, I found that with these two, I never would.

Kara Berman
   Loving Wife

Karen Berman
   Beloved Daughter

"I love you both," I whispered, letting my fingers lightly brush the metal.

I stood up, grabbing my backpack and swinging it up and onto my back. I shrugged my shoulders a couple of times to seat the straps comfortably, then fastened the belly band, tugging on it to make sure it was tight. With a final, pained glance at the markers, I turned and headed east, passing quickly out of the meadow and into the trees beyond.

CHAPTER 1

Josie

I shook the small handheld GPS unit in an attempt to make it work.

"You've got to be freaking kidding me! I will smash you into a million pieces, you worthless hunk of plastic!"

The small, yellow electronic devil was obviously unimpressed with my threat and mocked me with its refusal to comment. Looking up at the sky, I almost asked the heavens, 'What next?' But I didn't want to tempt fate. Little did I realize at the time that the heavens could read minds, and fate could be a real bitch.

Sighing like a teenager being asked to do the dishes, I shoved the worthless plastic demon into my backpack and pulled out my trusty old compass. Flipping open the lid, I began turning in a small circle, talking to myself while the needle danced inside its glass case.

"Okay, let's see," I muttered to myself. "If that's north, then that way is west and towards the lake. If I can make it to the lake, I should be able to get to the marina and use their phone."

I nodded to myself, taking a deep, calming breath. This was good. Everything was going to be okay.

"I'm going to call Brianna Cranston and give her a piece of my mind. Wait, no. First, I'm going to get her to come pick me up and take me to my car, and while she's driving me to it, then I'm going to give her a piece of my mind. She'll be trapped then and can't escape my wrath. Nice plan, Josie. Less walking, more righteous satisfaction."

Brianna had been the one to talk me into this jaunt when I *should* have been helping Mom with the store. I knew that somewhere in those spreadsheets and invoices was the answer to our financial situation, something that would pull us up out of the hole we were spiraling into.

Apparently, I had been getting a tad bitchy with folks lately. Brianna cornered me in my small office Wednesday. Mom apparently let her slip back to harass me.

"Girl, you need to get away from the sheets of numbers and clear your head before you bite one of your worker's—or worse, Kaylin's head off," she told me, crossing her arms and skewering me with an icy glare.

I scrubbed my tired eyes, glancing up at her. "I don't have the time. We're losing money every day and if I don't figure out how to stop it, Mom and I are toast."

Brianna began lecturing me, using her finger like a conductor's baton. "Get your lazy butt out in the woods. You and your dad loved the woods and trails around here. Hell, you were a tomboy for most of your time here. Get out there, walk among the trees, and clear your mind. Maybe an acorn will fall on that head of yours and give you the idea you need!"

I had reluctantly agreed, more to get her to leave and to stop her nagging. And I had to admit … she had a point. I needed a break.

Putting my compass in the pocket of my shorts, I began walking in the right direction, only slightly limping, thanks to the blister on my heel. Normally, I'd have fixed it with some moleskin, but since I was in such a hurry to leave this morning, I neglected to pack my first aid kit.

My pack contained everything else I might need. Bear whistle, snacks, water, and dry socks. I even had a copy of *Cosmo* that I had filched from the beauty shop. Figured it could double as emergency toilet supplies should the need arise.

No GPS, no moleskin, a squishy blister on my heel, and still a long way from my car. The day was just a winner all the way around.

"Just you wait, Brianna, I've got two sweaty socks with your name written all over them!"

I chuckled evilly at the thought of taking off my boots in her car and launching an odoriferous attack. If I were lucky, she'd puke. Hey, if you can't make your best friend puke, why are they your bestie?

While I might have thought Brianna gagging on sweaty socks would be funny, what galled me the most was that she was right.

About an hour into the hike this morning, I realized I actually felt better. The rich smell of the trees and the sounds of nature slowly eroded my stress level, lowering it to what most folks considered normal. I was bordering on darn near relaxed. Even with the blister and the evil GPS unit, I was feeling better than I had in several weeks.

"Okay, Brianna, maybe no socks this time." Nodding to myself, I continued on down the trail.

After another thirty or so minutes of walking, I came to a ridgeline. Taking a moment, I glanced down into what appeared to be about a fifty-foot drop-off. It wasn't a straight drop, more of a steep downhill, something you might ski on if there were snow, and if you didn't mind rocks and trees at the end of your run. Unhooking my water bottle, I took a small sip as I drank in the panoramic view. I could just see the lake on the horizon. Clipping the water bottle back to my pack, I took a deep, refreshing breath.

"Finally, something is going my way."

I began walking along the edge, hoping to find a way down that looked less like a blue diamond run and more like a bunny slope. I enjoyed skiing, but the lack of skis and snow put a damper on shooshing down the ledge. With my luck today, I'd fall and break an ankle.

At that exact moment, the heavens showed me that they had been paying attention to my thoughts. Just as I walked near a patch of scrub brush, a small rabbit burst out of it right at my feet, moving as if it was late for something.

Like any red-blooded girl seeing something that looks like a mouse on steroids flying at her, I screamed and high-stepped away from the impending rodent mauling that I just knew was coming my way.

Unfortunately, in my adrenaline-fueled rush to escape, I forgot about the ridgeline I had been admiring. I screamed again as I toppled over the edge. I smashed flat on my side and began tumbling end over end as the loose rocks and dirt gave way. I saw ground, sky, ground and then felt a sharp burst of pain in my leg and a punch to my stomach.

I barely had time to think, "Ow … *shit,*" before blackness took me.

Keep reading *Second Chances* <u>here</u>

Made in the USA
Middletown, DE
10 September 2024

60119380R00156